Days to the Gallows

Days to the Gallows

A Novel of the Hartford Witch Panic

Katherine Spada Basto

This is a work of fiction. Names, characters, organizations, places, events and incidents are either products of the author's imagination or are used fictitiously.

Cover design and map by Corvid Design. (Map based on an original map of Colonial Hartford, dated 1640)

ISBN: 1536978043
ISBN 13: 9781536978049
Library of Congress Control Number: 2016913135
CreateSpace Independent Publishing Platform
North Charleston, South Carolina

In Memory of my Aunt Jean
who believed in this story

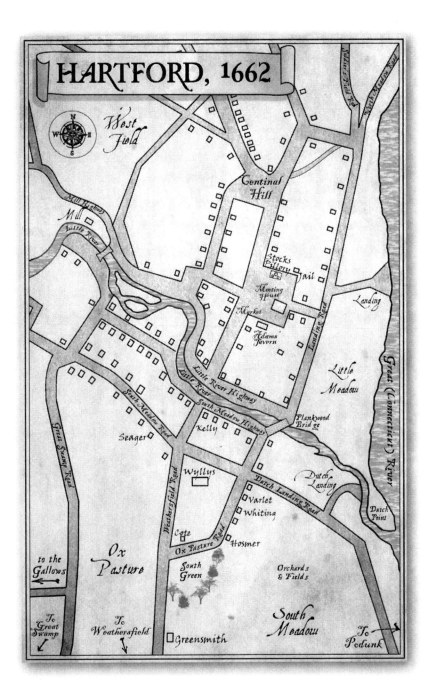

Chapter 1

January 1662

I watched Ann Cole slip out of her father's house under a full moon. I saw her from the loft window where I read nightly from my book of psalms. Poor girl, I worried for her. She was standing there next to the great oak still as ice, arms stretched to the sky, wearing her long white nightshift and a heavy woolen cloak. She held the remains of a thin, pine torch that glowed like a tiny star. Ann lifted her head and let the moon shine on her face.

The other town girls snicker out of her earshot and call her a mooncalf. Her senses seem addled, awhirl with fanciful notions. Ann is my friend and neighbor. 'Tis no wonder but she hasn't been right since she lost her mother to a fever a year ago. She complains about cooking and cleaning for her father and brothers.

Her mother doted on her being the only girl. When Ann would whine and stomp her foot, her mother indulged her. But Ann's mother was gone. Now she must sweep the fire embers, feed the chickens; her life is dull and she longs for a husband. I am patient and listen to her woes because I have my mother and sister still; my heart hurts for her loss. I also desire a husband of my own but my mouth will not speak of such hopes.

"Ann, we are but seventeen. There's time enough for marriage," I calmly remind her.

Sighing, I closed the psalm book and snuffed out the nub of the tallow candle. I trod down the loft stairs, careful not to wake my sleeping family. I needed to know what was ailing Ann and to remind her she mustn't be outdoors. The winter night held many dangers. Hadn't Reverend Stone announced to the congregation just last Sabbath week that wolves had been seen prowling close to town?

In the dim light of the fading hearth fire embers, I found my woolen winter cloak on its peg and wrapped it around me. Then I took a small tallow from the mantle and quickly touched it to a hot coal. Cupping my hands round the flame, I steadied myself and peered out the back door. There she was, staring into the moonlight.

Ann stared at everything and everyone. She would even run to the ox pasture to stare down the cows. Blinking contests she'd call them. If the cow she gazed at blinked before she did blink, she'd spin around laughing, dizzying herself only to flop down in the grass. But she would stare down townspeople as well, coming close to their faces. Then she'd pull away as if she'd seen a ghost. "My mother helps me to understand. She warns me of the evil folk destroying our godly town," Ann would whisper to me. She carried the memory of her mother like a heavy chain around her neck.

I closed the back door to my house. I did not want to disobey my parents, but I knew that Ann would be discovered, either by her father awakening or the night watchman making his rounds.

I crossed over the road and found myself standing close by her, watching her breath flow like cold smoke.

"Ann, what must thee be doing? Why are you out of doors now? Go inside your house," I whispered. Ann clutched my arm with a strong grip.

"Because I must stay out this night," she replied. "Something is amiss this full moon eve."

She gazed down the road leading to the ox pasture. "Look, can you see the light coming from the South Green? Here Hester, watch now."

Ann lifted her hand and pointed in the direction of the South Green. She seemed like a specter, a ghostly creature at one with the moon's pale light. But truly there was a bright light with small trails of smoke rising from the South Green. We always waited with anticipation for militia muster training days on the green where the young men practiced their drills and shot musket fire into the air. We'd never think to venture there at night. But Ann was right. Something was indeed amiss.

"Do not stop me Hester. I think I hear voices." She leaned toward the road. I pulled her back anyway. "Hasten, Ann, keep behind the tree. It is not safe to venture out on the road now. You must get back to your house."

Chilled, Ann and I huddled behind the oak and peered down the road leading to the green. The smoke billowed and I could smell burning wood. I wondered who could be on the South Green at this hour? Grasping Ann's arm, I pressed against the cold, tree bark.

A moonlit curl sprang free from Ann's nightcap. Ann hated that curl and was always trying to tuck it away.

"Do you hear voices?" she asked again.

I listened. Was that noise coming from the South Green? No, it was coming toward the green!

The distant voice grew louder now and neared our hiding place. Ann and I stood still, each holding onto the other for comfort and warmth.

"Take heed, Ann," I whispered. "If it is the night watchman, I will speak. Hold your tongue."

We moved not a muscle behind the great oak save to extinguish our flames.

The footsteps drew nigh. Ann and I clung together like twine and listened for any sounds. Soon, we heard a dim humming and the lilting laugh that I now recognized.

The voice belonged to our neighbor, the Dutchwoman Judith Varlet. Dutch Judy we called her in private. Judith's family had been banished from New Netherlands several years before because her father Caspar could not pay his debts.

The Varlets were trouble in Hartford. Caspar traded with the Indians and received hogsheads filled with tobacco from Virginia. Townspeople complained that these Dutch took our trade away and rumor was that Caspar had a liquor distillery near the crumbling Dutch fort. They claimed he supplied the Indians and some townsfolk with the strong waters that they called the "kill-devil."

Now Judith was keeping a pace toward the green and was soon to pass us, so we stayed tight against the tree.

Before I could grab her, Ann stepped forward full into the moonlight.

"Good evening, Mistress Varlet. You look radiant and are a vision in the moonlight. Where must you be going so late past my house?"

Judith halted and stared. From behind the tree, I watched her eyes blink wide open at the sight of Ann. Townspeople called them the North Sea eyes. Calm one moment and filled with storm the next. Tonight they looked like they were filled with blue-gray fury.

"Why it's Ann," she said. "Cannot sleep of the bright moon shine?"

Judith Varlet wore a hood to cover her raven locks. Silver embroidery shimmered down her cloak. A headdress gleamed under her hood. Specks of pink and blue cast sparks from her hair. Was Judith wearing jewels?

"I watch the moon and feel the need to wander," Ann said with certainty. "But what brings thee walking this evening, Mistress Varlet?"

Judith turned her back and pointed toward her house. She seemed to be hiding something under her black, woolen cloak. "Ah, my father is ill and I need the fresh air tonight. Mother and Sarah stay at home to tend him," she said in her Dutch accent.

"Your father Caspar, he is ailing?" Ann seemed concerned. Although Caspar was known to cause trouble, the townspeople respected him because he was once a very rich merchant in the Old Country.

"Yah," Judith continued, "I think he suffers from a heart broken. So far from home."

She began to speak in Dutch, fretting about like an angry hen. "Curse this town! What I would do to be in my old country or back in New Netherlands, away from here. Nothing but talk of sin, disobedience, and punishment." She balled her fist to the air and shook it hard. "Puritans! Pooh! May the Devil find the night watchman and the wicked Marshal of this town. I walk where I may and talk what I will." She stomped her boot to the icy ground.

"May I walk with thee, Mistress Varlet?" asked Ann. "The night air revives my spirit."

"Of course Ann, but I make haste to the South Green. Now. I must not be late. They wait for me."

Ann gasped. "You make haste to the green? B-but the Reverend Stone forbids it—to associate with the likes of such people. I have heard they have a merry meet on the green. Is it true? I must know."

I stepped out from my hiding place and tried to speak sense to Ann. "Ann, we must go now. It's time to return home."

Now Judith gasped. "Why Hester, to see the likes of you out this evening as well…You are a true friend to Ann, are you not?"

Cautiously, I nodded. There was no woman as beautiful or as dangerous in Hartford as Dutch Judy.

"No, Ann, they are not witches." Judith laughed with a high-pitched cackle that told me nothing would stop her from doing what she pleased this full moon eve.

She bent toward us and met Ann's round, brown eyes, "But they promise me tonight if I bring them a bottle of sack from my father's cellar, I will see my future husband in the fire." Judith smiled broadly now. "Do you believe this, Ann?" She tapped Ann's cheek with her gloved fingers but did not await an answer.

"Tonight is the Feast of St. Agnes, a tradition from England," Judith went on. "Ach, to find a husband to sail me away from this dreadful town. I will get married. There shall be no spinsterhood for me!"

Ann's mouth hung wide open.

"Why this is naught but superstition," I replied. "Reverend Stone said so, so it must be true."

"And 'tis only you and your family who are left of the Dutch in Hartford," Ann added. "Where will you find a husband round these parts?"

Judith laughed aloud. "Isn't that why I go? You are silly girls, Ann and Hester—for you need your own husbands soon. You must come with me. Come! We go together. Let us make amusement in this town of dreary Puritans."

"But we are godly maids," I blurted out.

Judith flashed a bright smile that held secrets. Her red lips and blue eyes glowed in flashing colors.

"So you say girls—so you say." She flung her cape tight around her and hurried onward.

We watched the hooded figure disappear down the moonlit road toward the South Green.

"Judith is a spectacle of adornment. How I envy her," Ann sighed. "'Tis a pity that God blessed her with beauty, but the Devil has made her a woman of fascination. I see the way the men all watch her down at Jeremy Adams's Tavern. With lust in their eyes, that's what I see."

"Ay, Ann, it is neither proper nor godly. It is—brazen!" I replied. I sensed that the presence of Mistress Varlet cloaked in her jewels had unsettled Ann. I shook her at the cloak sleeves and pleaded with her to return home.

Just when I thought she had come round to her senses, she grasped hold of my gloved hands and exclaimed, "Now Hester, I have an idea."

I frowned seeing Ann's eyes, as round as saucers and flickering like the stars above us. She stared back at me. Strengthening my resolve to see my friend to safety, I gripped her sleeve tighter.

"Ann, we need our sleep to prepare for the morrow. There will be chores to get done,"

Ann beheld me with glazed eyes. "I will make my way through the stand of elms and oaks that surround the green. No one will see me. The path round the trees is clear. I must see what transpires there or my thoughts shall not rest."

I sighed and looked to the bright heavens silent in prayer. No sound came from my house or Ann's. All was quiet.

"'Tis cold, Ann," I murmured.

But when I looked back, Ann was gone.

Chapter 2

$\mathcal{G}$rasping my cloak round my neck and treading with care, I ventured toward the stand of trees that grew thick round the South Green. Ice crystals had formed on the path. The cracking sound of my boots on the hard earth seemed loud as musket fire.

Ann was crouched by an elm tree overlooking the green. She seemed bewitched, eyes wide open, nostrils flaring, and cheeks a-flush. "How now, Ann?" I whispered. "So, you will walk to the green and espy on Mistress Varlet and the others?"

"Hester, you who love God so dearly, don't you think we should know?" Her breath came close to me now, frosty and cold.

I studied those eyes, awhirl with light. "Know what, Ann?"

"Why, what they may be doing this night and this hour on the South Green."

So we skulked like Indians in the woods, hiding behind trees and large rocks to keep full out of the bright moonlight. We finally rested behind a large boulder on the Green and watched the revelry.

A great earthen pot sat atop a small flame, and logs had been placed round the fire. Here some people sat while others stood.

Ann leaned toward me. "There be Rebecca and Nathaniel Greensmith. Imagine, a merry-making right across from their house. Who else do you see, Hester?"

I angled my head around the boulder and studied the eight or nine people gathered round the cauldron.

"I see Goodwife Seager, and she is smoking from a pipe. For shame! And there is Andrew Sanford the chimney sweep and his wife, Mary."

Judith stood close to James Wakely and Goody Seager. She poured liquid from a bottle into the earthen pot while another poured what looked like cream.

"James Wakely? Why, he's a God fearing man—or so they say," Ann said. "What brings him to the green this hour?"

I stared in shocked silence.

Ann nudged my arm. "Why, there be Goodwife Ayres and her rogue husband. Just last week he was in the stocks for stealing. I'd expect them to be out on a night such as this."

Rebecca Greensmith began to stir the pot with a wooden spoon and then dashed some spices into the brew. She bent down to retrieve a small basket full of eggs and began to crack them into the cauldron. A short, round figure, she seemed lost in her black cloak.

"What brew are they a-stirring, Hester?"

"I dunno, Ann. I'm not sure." I sniffed the night air. Scalded, burnt milk, sweet wine, cinnamon and nutmeg, that's what I thought I smelled.

Rebecca Greensmith, clearly the leader, called to the others. "The Feast of St. Agnes Eve is a night when maids and fair women may see their husbands in the fire. So we harken to make the sack posset for warmth and comfort. After the drink, we may begin divining, for Mistress Judith has joined us this full moon eve. But first we invoke the Lord of the Moon. Let us prepare for the Merry Meet."

"Let us make haste and prepare," I heard a man repeat. Someone in the circle was giving candles to each one in the group. In turn, each person lit the candle from the fire until all had their candles aflame.

Ann gasped. "Look what comes from the woods now!" She pointed as a two-legged creature, wearing antlers atop its head, slowly descended from a small slope. His face wore a strange mask. His arms and legs were covered with leather wrappings. *Who or what is this creature?*

Rebecca Greensmith cried, "Let us begin our full moon Merry Meet."

Holding their candles aloft, the group began to chant strange words as they welcomed the horned man into the circle. Someone held up an offering of a small cake as he walked about the center. Now the antlered man sang in a low and mirthful voice:

"When lads and lasses merry be
With possets and with banquets fine
I eat their cakes and drink their wine
And to make sport, I frolic and snort
And out the candles I do blow."
(Suddenly the candles went dark.)
The maids I kiss, they shriek,
Who's this?
I answer naught but ho, ho, ho."

The group began to chant ho, ho, ho as the horned man embraced and kissed each woman. Then he left the circle and strode into the blackness leading up the slope.

A murmur came from the group. I could not make out their words. They hovered over the cauldron, preparing the sack posset for the merrymaking. I thought a sip of this warm drink would aid my shivers. I breathed in the scent of the frothy brew.

But then it became quiet, still as the shadows that loomed around us. The whispers fell silent. What happened next I shall never forget. How they knew, I shall never know. Pairs of eyes stared in our direction, and then I heard the words of Goodman Ayres. "Ay, so it's Ann Cole and her friend, come to join us. 'Tis time to see her future husband. But alas, she runs and hides behind her rock." They all began to chuckle and chant, "ho, ho, ho" in low, steady voices.

"Come, Ann, come," I heard Judith say. Ann bolted from the safety of the rock and was suddenly standing amongst them. I could not and would not move a step; I was filled with terror.

The men backed into the darkness for a brief moment. The cloaked women gathered around Ann. "Tell us what you see, Ann," said Rebecca.

Ann stared deep into the flames as the women waited for her response. Did she truly see her future husband? Suddenly, she wailed, "'Tis true Mother. I see now." She covered her face with her hands, and then rushed back to the refuge of the rock.

We fumbled about and then dashed like deer, thrashing through the woods for our houses. We never looked behind. I ran the faster, when out of the corner of my eye I saw a pair of yellow eyes that blinked at me from the ice-blue shadows cast by the trees.

Chapter 3

On my return from the South Green, I slept naught. Night terrors plagued my dreams. I shivered with fear under my warm quilt. Visions of yellow eyes blinking and staring, dark figures around the fire, and the chant of ho, ho, ho kept me tossing the rest of the evening. Had anyone witnessed Ann and me running from the green? The revels I watched last night unnerved me. Distraught over Ann's spectacle, I found no peace in my bed.

I rose before the sun, before the morning bell woke the town. I lit the candles, raked up the dying embers, and placed kindle atop the coals. The morning fire crackled and hissed. I sat on a stool, hunched over the hearth, and ladled out leftover porridge for breakfast.

The barn rooster had not yet crowed up the light of day. I began my chores, sweeping out the corners of the family keeping room and tidying the table board.

"Hester, what brings thee up at such an early time of this morning? Has God called thee to prayer?"

My father came forth from the next room, hair tousled, carrying his musket with one hand and a mug of cider in the other. His voice bellowed like a bull. Soon the whole family would awaken. He was no longer Constable of Hartford, but that musket was never far from his side. "Just in case Indians attack or a wolf prowls the barn," he'd shout.

Father came from a long line of "Puritan Yeomen," farmers and soldiers who fought bravely in the English Civil War. When he was in a good mood, he'd tell us how his family participated in the beheading of King Charles I; that the dethroned King's head was displayed on a pike overlooking London Bridge. "Be proud of your Puritan heritage Hester. Never forget where you come from."

Father's family sailed to Massachusetts so they could have their religious freedom. But they separated from the church in Massachusetts and followed their leader, the Reverend Thomas Hooker, through the wilderness of Connecticut. My father helped found Hartford, and for this he was always proud.

But now he trained his blinking blue eyes on me. He was still half asleep and was awaiting my reply.

"I've been preparing for the day, Father. I'm memorizing Psalm Ninety for Lecture Day a fortnight from now." I quickly pulled my worn psalm book from my apron pocket and turned to a page. (Often I opened my psalm book to whatever chapter and verse God had prepared me to read. Some in Hartford might call it divination or prophecy. I called it blessed guidance.)

Father yawned and stretched out his arms. "Could thee recite a passage from memory for me?" He waited and watched me close the psalm book. The words came loose from my tongue. "For we are consumed by thine anger and by thy wrath are we troubled. Thou hast set our iniquities before thee, our secret sins in the light of thy Countenance."

"Ay, Hester—the anger of the Lord—'tis dreadful indeed. May we never be consumed by our secret sins. For God's wrath is far worse."

I shuddered and picked up the bellows to fan the fire.

"Now, that's my righteous girl. Remember, after break-fast you must scour and polish up the pewter, for we are expecting a guest in a few days time."

I paused and looked up. "Who would that be?"

Father opened his eyes wide now. "Marshal Jonathan Gilbert himself. Fancy the marshal paying us a visit. He must speak with me about certain matters. Gather my advice, so he says. Please Hester, all of our finest pewter must be rubbed to a shine."

Marshal Jonathan Gilbert. The name sent gooseflesh up my neck. What could the current Constable of Hartford wish to speak with father about? I dared not ask.

The marshal had fought in the Pequot War of 1636 with Captain John Mason, the "Indian Killer." Marshal Gilbert liked to boast of the plan they devised to burn the Indian village to the ground. He claimed he was the first to throw a flaming brand over the palisade walls. "Nothing left but charred remains and a few Indians for slaves."

He was never to be called "Constable" in Hartford; he must always be known as Marshal Gilbert. "I was Marshal in the war and Marshal I shall remain in Hartford." The marshal owned great tracks of land west and south of Hartford. Many of the warehouses down by the landing bore the marshal's seal. He was rewarded for his bravery, and most townspeople admired his outspoken, law-abiding ways.

Father ran fingers through his graying hair, trying to make it stick to his head. "After chores and midday meal, what are the plans for the day, Hester?"

I thought about Ann and the night before; I wished I could find time for sleep and prayer. "Ann and I will watch Betty Kelly while her mother rests from her ailments. We may walk along the Little River and then perhaps head to market ourselves."

Father nodded. "Of course—it is market day today. God has blessed us with this January thaw after such brutal cold; so the weather remains mild. Your mother will be down to market-square, no doubt trading her homespun for something far less useful." He frowned.

My mother was a master spinner. Her homespun was much sought after. For hours she'd sit at her loom, pumping the treadle and singing hymns. Although I have my mother's honey-colored hair, hazel eyes, and comely shape, I had naught of the spirit or the disposition for spinning.

For I had trouble keeping still. I needed to walk, run, amble, roam. I needed to be among the trees and God's creations, or by the banks of the Little River or watching the boats, canoes, and rafts traveling up and down the Great River. This brought me peace.

"Wanderlust," my father claimed. "Hester will settle down when she marries."

Reading and books also brought me peace and joy. Unlike Ann, I enjoyed learning. Many townspeople mentioned I should be the next head teacher of the Dame school, since I did enjoy teaching and working with children.

"Remember to be home for supper preparations at four of the clock. Your mother needs your help."

———

I scoured and rubbed the pewter plates with lemon until they gleamed like a looking glass. Then, I hurried across the road and waited for Ann. After a time she barreled out of the house.

"What of last night's mischief?" Ann asked, out of breath. "To see the likes of Goody Greensmith and Goody Ayres standing round the Devil's fire!" She paused. "I wonder if Dutch Judy beheld her future husband in the flames? Was it all but a dream, Hester?"

I shook my head. "Nay, it was real Ann, for my feet are much sore from the run back home. But tell me, what vision did you behold in the flames?"

Ann grabbed me by the shoulders and pulled me so close I could feel her breath on me. She started that staring, blank gaze again. "Mother revealed who I am to marry. 'Tis your brother, Stephen. Then we will truly be as sisters." She gave me a half raised grin that rose on one side of her face.

My brother Stephen worked as a blacksmith at the Forge. I knew he had little interest in Ann. But I could not hurt her feelings or dissuade her of this vision.

We walked the hard rutted road toward Betty's. Last evening it had glistened in moonlight. Today it was just the old dirt road, cracked with ice and hoof prints.

Ann and I both loved Betty. At eight years, she had little chestnut-colored curls that bounced up and down. Her turned-up nose was sprinkled with freckles, and her gray eyes shone with specks of blue and yellow. Betty giggled at everything and loved to ask questions. We'd whisper, "Where's the squirrel?" and she'd scamper about, stick her teeth out, and chatter as if she were gnawing on a kernel of corn. Her little hands would come together like paws. Betty's mother, sickly and frail, rarely made it to meeting on the Sabbath, but often enjoyed the activities of market day.

"'Tis a blessing to watch Betty, for it's good practice for when you have little ones of your own," my mother would say. "God knows how you help Goodwife Kelly."

Mother warned me each week, "Watch the little girl with good sense, Hester. After all, she's in your care,"

We trudged past the Varlet homestead. The apple orchards lay bare; black branches silhouetted against the frosted sky. My father's orchards and flax fields abutted the Varlet land that led to the Dutch Point.

The remnants of the old Dutch fort stood behind the orchard, its blackened chimney stack still standing. The foundation of yellow bricks was stained with soot and darkened by years of cannon and musket fire. The old stockade fence still surrounded the fort. Judy's father Caspar had a makeshift trading post down by the South Meadow, near the Fort, where he sold goods to the Indians.

All was silent around the Varlet homestead with the exception of a lone hog rutting in the front yard and a few geese fluttering about. Then Judy emerged and stood on the stoop, hands on her hips. Her black hair seemed to glint violet and gold in the bright sunlight.

"Nein, keep out—swine!" she shouted, waving her hands at the hog. The barnyard geese stretched up their wings and honking, followed Judith round the back of the house.

Ann and I continued toward Betty's house. We both noticed Rebecca Greensmith's daughters, Elsbeth and Sarah strolling down the other side of the road. Both had the same yellow hair, blue eyes and looked like twins. Only two years separated them. Seventeen and fifteen years of age, they huddled together like chickens. Their heads bobbed up and down as they walked.

"Ay, if it's not the mad maid, Ann Cole," said Elsbeth. "Her brains are addled."

Sarah chimed in. "She needs milk from her moon mother." Hands tucked in their woolen muffs, they cast us icy glances, then covered their mouths with their hand muffs and giggled under their breath.

Ann bit her lip and twisted her body round to face the Greensmith girls. She pointed with a straight finger across the road. "Ay and your mother is a *witch*!" She balled her fists to her belly and glared at her tormentors.

"You must be a witch to know a witch, Ann Cole," Elsbeth answered, sneering. "Thou should take heed."

Ann stood like a pillar of stone. "'Tis a pity you know not your own mother and what she is doing," she said. "'Tis not godly. So, take heed *yourself*, Elsbeth."

The Greensmith girls just laughed.

"I may no longer have a mother, but 'tis far worse to have a mother who is a witch!" Ann cried.

"What say you, Hester?" asked Elsbeth still snickering.

But Ann continued with an angry passion, her eyes flashing. "Leave Hester out of this. And heed what the Bible says about witchcraft, Elsbeth. 'Thou shalt not suffer a witch to *live*.'"

The girls flounced their shirts and cackled together. They continued past us on the road, turning up their noses high in the air.

We knocked on the oak door of Betty Kelly's house and waited. Tiny scurrying could be heard inside; then the peephole carved in the door popped open. A wide-open eye stared back at us.

"Hester, Ann—you are here at last!"

Betty came bounding out, little brown curls springing about her bonnet. She hugged me tight around the apron.

"A good morrow to you, little Miss Squirrel," I exclaimed.

"Squirrel nut, you mean," said Ann.

Betty started twittering and scampering about doing her finest imitations. Then she stopped and had a droopy look on her face. "Mother is sick today. But she says I can go with you. She always needs her rest—always." The little girl sighed, cast her eyes down for a moment, and brightened up again. She pulled something out from her apron pocket. "Look, mother gave me some shillings so I can buy something at market. I am a big girl now." She beamed with pride.

Betty squirmed between us, took our hands, and swung them gaily, happy to be free from her house.

Winter market at the Meeting Square was different than the summer. We'd look for dried goods to trade, warm cloth, and perhaps a fine piece of pewter. Townspeople milled about on the cobblestones, walking from the market to the trading post. The smell of meat cooking, fish, and pitch tar filled the air. Betty skipped around the square.

"Hester, Ann—guess what I did just see?" Betty's face was glowing.

"What did you see?" I asked.

"Why a man is tucked inside the nutcracker with a sign hanging from his neck. It has a B on it."

"Betty, you are learning your letters well, I see. But it's a pillory, not a nutcracker." I laughed because this was our name for the pillory, a device that kept criminals in a wooden hold round their necks, arms, and wrists.

"What does B stand for, Hester? Ann?" She gripped at her own little wrists as if she felt the pain.

Ann said, "It stands for blasphemy, Betty."

Betty looked puzzled and shook her head. "Blasphemy. I know not what it means."

"It means when you curse or swear, and that's the punishment when you say bad words. So take care with your words, little squirrel," I replied. Betty ran off again, satisfied to watch the man stuck in the pillory.

A woman cloaked in a black velvet cape, shawl, and a fine black pointed hat strolled by. "Good morrow to you, Hester, Ann." She nodded her head at us.

"A good morrow to you, Goodwife Ayres." I blushed with the knowledge Goodwife Ayres was on the South Green last evening. I could feel shudders from Ann's shoulders against mine.

Betty came running back, huffing and wheezing out of breath.

"Why, Betty, you are a bundle of life. What will you buy this day at market?" Goody Ayres asked. She peered down at the little girl.

"I'd like to buy a piece of lace—like the one you are wearing on your hem," Betty exclaimed.

I nudged Betty. Lace was *not* supposed to be worn in Hartford.

"Ah, child. I will bring you a piece of lace soon. I promise," Goody Ayres said. Her violet eyes twinkled as she patted Betty on the head.

Then Betty became serious. She stared up with intensity at the tall thin woman. "Is it true what you say, Goody Ayres? Is it true? The stories you tell?"

Goodwife Ayres bent over and lifted Betty's chin up. "True, child? I know not what you speak of."

Betty stiffened up straight. "Why," she stammered, "You said you met the Dark Man when you lived in England. You said you met him at the church gate and that he was handsome. Remember?"

Goody Ayres sighed and wrung her hands as if to wipe her self clean of such a comment. "Child, I know not of what you speak," she said. "Hush now."

But Betty would not be hushed. "You scared me about the Dark Man, Goody Ayres. I want to know if it's true. Remember you told me...."

Ann and I met each other's eyes and frowned.

"Told you, child? 'Tis no fit conversation. I told you naught." Goody Ayres spoke gravely.

"Remember you said that the dark man you met had hooves for feet. That means he's a devil." Betty started to squirm. "Is it true, Goody Ayres? For I know I've seen him in my dreams." She stamped her foot and began to mumble under her breath, *devils, devils, devils.* Then Betty shouted aloud, "I hate devils. And imps. They scare me." She rushed to Ann and grasped her around the apron. She wouldn't look at Goody Ayres anymore. *What is Betty speaking of?*

"Fanciful hogwash, child," Goody Ayres grimaced. "This is utter nonsense. I'll hear nothing more of the sort."

Holding on to Ann, Betty turned her face back to Goody Ayres. "But what of the other story you told me, of the little man who sets pranks on children who don't clean or do their chores? Is it true? You told me he'd pinch me—if I were naughty. I made sure my room was clean and I did my chores!" Betty was half crying and half whining.

"Never you mind, child," Goodwife Ayres said. "Hmmm, I wonder who else is filling thee with lies?" She watched Ann and me. Then she pointed her finger and shook it to our faces. She stomped off toward the river where her husband awaited her.

Betty stood forlorn as a dove. Then she bunched up her cheeks and began to cry. "I—I am—a wicked, horrid girl. Now I will never get a piece of lace from Goodwife Ayres. Or anything pretty ever again," she sobbed.

"Squirrel, you are never wicked," I told the distraught girl. "Let us go find a special present for your mother and forget such foolish talk."

I glanced at Ann. She had that look in her eyes. Again.

Ann stared at the Ayreses—two lone figures standing by the water's edge—and said not a word.

Chapter 4

A hard knock thudded four times on the door.

"Hester, get thee to the door and welcome our guest." Mother smoothed her ruffled skirts down, and stirred the frothy mutton stew hanging by a pothook over the fire. The table board was set with the family pewter ware. Bayberry candles glazed the windows.

I moved to the oaken block door and pushed the bolt aside.

"Good evening, Hester. I pray this night finds you hale and well."

Marshal Jonathan Gilbert stood before me, narrow black eyes glinting amid a broad forehead that bulged when he spoke. He lifted his beaver hat to me revealing a slight bald spot on his head. His stringy dark hair hung to his shoulders. His nose was sharp and pointed, like a heron's beak. His short grizzled beard came to a point on his chin. His long black coat and knee-high boots made him seem taller. Standing alongside the marshal was his black mastiff, Titus.

"Titus will guard the sanctuary of any place I enter. And he helps keep the calm. Titus, stay." The marshal flashed a grin that cut like pin pricks. The dog obediently stood like a sentry, his thick jowls dripping with drool. I was relieved the dog would remain outside during the marshal's visit.

The marshal limped, favoring his right leg; he had been injured in the Pequot War.

He stamped his dirtied footprints on the doorstep and spit to the side. "God, Titus and the militia." He lifted his musket to the air. "They be the saviors of our town." He grinned. A winter wind jarred wide the front door and I shivered.

"Please do come in, Marshal, for a winter chill is upon us," I said. "It is God's honor to have you as a guest at our table this evening."

"Indeed," said the marshal. "I look forward to breaking bread with such God-fearing folk as the Hosmer family."

We crossed the hall to the keeping room. My parents awaited him.

"Welcome, Marshal. How now this eve?" My father's cheeks flushed with heat as he bent forward and extended his right hand.

"Good evening Thomas, Goodwife Hosmer." The marshal nodded toward my mother. "I must say you are looking well."

Mother began to fuss by the hearth. "Please sit at the table board, Marshal. You have much to discuss, and supper is almost ready." She smiled with her warm, honey-colored eyes.

The marshal hung up his cloak and hat and stood admiring the table, now filled with pewter platters and trivets to hold the warm food.

"Please, Marshal, make sure you sit in the chair above the salt cellar, for you are a special guest in this home," said father.

"Ay, the stew smells just right for a winter's eve." The marshal sat eyeing each place at the table, then studied each corner of the room while my mother and I scurried about, making sure all was ready. Hannah, my older sister, was home for the night. She was married now but often stayed whilst her husband was away on business. The only family member missing was my brother Stephen. He often slept the night at the forge instructing James Ensign, his apprentice.

I pulled the brown bread from the bake oven and wrapped the warm loaf in a cloth.

"Hannah, bring over the pitcher of beer and fill our guest's tankard," my father ordered. "Then I shall say grace."

We all remained still, heads bowed and hands clasped together, as father began his lengthy prayers over the steaming food. I listened but could not help tapping my foot, for I was restless. I opened my eyes and peeked in the direction of the marshal. His eyes were fixed upon me. Quickly, I closed my eyes and resumed listening to my father's prayer of thanks.

We ate in silence. No sound but the wind. We savored the stew and bread between sips of beer. After supper, I cleared the table and prepared to serve the apple nut cake my mother and I baked earlier that afternoon.

My father and the marshal began to discuss what crops they'd be planting come spring, the price of seeds and when the flax fields out back would be ready for tilling. Then the conversation shifted to another subject.

"That Varlet man is causing me trouble again, Thomas," the marshal said. "Seems he's determined to control the warehouse down by the river. And he's still receiving tobacco from Virginia and English linen. What I wouldn't do to remove Caspar and his family back to New Netherlands. The man is a nuisance. His daughter, Judith, not much better." He shoved cake into his mouth.

"What? Taking business from you again, Marshal?" my father mumbled between bites of apple cake, shaking his head.

"Ay," said the marshal. "Seems he thinks he and his family can do whatever they choose. His liquor still is against our laws." Marshal Gilbert paused and looked round the room. "I have no choice but to fine the man for his indiscretions. He's supplying both the natives and our townsfolk with the kill-devil, causing nothing but drunkenness and disorder." He coughed and stretched out his legs, leaning his hands on the table.

I got up and began to clear the pewter dishes from the table board.

"Leave be, Hester," my father said. "The marshal and I have some discussing to do. Best if you go to the loft for a time and read your psalm book." I excused myself and made my way up the stairs. I opened the door to the loft then closed it. I remained on the stairs so I could listen.

"So, Thomas, the main reason I am here is that a witness has come forward. One Robert Stern. Seems he was out walking the night about a week back. Claims he needed to go abroad in the night air to clear his head. Claims he was walking the bounds of the South Green and says he witnessed a merry making. Have you information, since you live but a short distance?"

I crouched low so I could hear my father.

"I know little of any activities on the green," he answered. "Especially at night. This is news indeed."

I shuddered and remained still, trying to calm my breath.

Then I heard Hannah. "Souls as black as night they have, given over to the devil himself."

"Hush now, Hannah," mother chided. "The Lord hears all."

The marshal continued. "Seems Goodman Stern saw a small fire and several folk stirring a pot. He recognized Judith Varlet and Rebecca Greensmith. Of the others, he could not be sure."

"Well, what of it, Marshal?" I heard my father reply. "Seems these people care not for the laws of our land. We know 'tis not right to revel in Satan's ways."

"Ay, they be reveling in Satan's ways is right. They may be witches, practicing the Devil's mischief and the black arts. After my query, I will report my findings to Captain Mason."

"Captain Mason? Is he inquiring?" asked father.

"Why yes, so he is," said the marshal. "Now that Governor Winthrop has gone to England to receive the charter, Captain Mason remains in charge. He can do what he deems right, when it comes to the nuisance of natives and witches."

The wind had picked up and whipped round the house now. Tree branches tapped against the diamond- paned windows. Gusts blew strong, and I held tight to the banister leading to the loft. Suddenly, the house quivered, and a loud noise quaked it to and fro. I ran down the stairs in a panic.

"What is happening, father?" I asked. "I'm frightened."

"'Tis only an ill winter wind, Hester."

The wind grew fiercer and made whistling sounds. Mother was fretting with the dishes when a gust blew down the chimney and filled the room with a cold stream of air. The bayberry candles went out, the hearth-fire sputtered out little sparks, then burned with low flames. The keeping room a few minutes before had been light and warm. Now all was dark with the exception of the waning fire, bowed down from the gusts.

"Throw some kindling on the fire, Hester. It needs some wood," commanded my father, who always knew what to do in times of distress.

The marshal approached me as I fed the fire with kindling.

"Know you of any merrymakings on the South Green, Hester?"

My father came to join us around the fire. "Ay, have you seen anything from the loft window where you read at night?"

I stared into the fire.

"Nay, I have seen nothing from my window. I have seen no mischief or merrymaking on the South Green." I could not look into their eyes.

A high-pitched howl joined the eerie winds. Whether it was a wolf or the dog Titus, I could not be sure. I heard loud clucking sounds and the lowing of a cow coming from the barn. Was something out there disturbing the animals?

The marshal arose and grabbed for his musket, hat, and cloak. "If there be a wolf out there, rest assured I will kill the creature. The scourge! Neither wind nor storm shall stop me." He briefly shook my father's hand. "I thank thee for the meal and for your time. We shall speak later, Thomas. Good night."

The marshal limped out the door into the blustery evening, mumbling about the wolf. A few minutes later I heard a shot and then silence. I knew a new wolf's head would hang on the meeting-house door come Sabbath Day. Townspeople were paid five shillings for the bounty of a wolf's head. I shook with cold and fear. Marshal Gilbert meant business. Especially when it came to the matter of wolves—and witches.

Chapter 5

March 1662

"There shall not be found among you, any one that maketh his son or his daughter to pass through the fire or useth divination or be an observer of an enchanter or a witch, Amen."

A chorus of amens echoed in the meetinghouse.

The Reverend Stone closed the Bible and slammed it against the pulpit. He held his palm on the book. "Ponder these words from Deuteronomy, chapter eighteen verse ten, during the noon break. We shall talk more of this at the hour of two prompt. God keep you."

I sat with Ann, Betty, and the other girls in the back of the meetinghouse, waiting for the service to end. My mother and sister Hannah joined with the other women sitting opposite the men. I had a clear view of the congregation and craned my neck to watch the townspeople removing for the break. I noticed Goody Ayres and Goody Seager sitting and whispering together. The tithing man holding his feathered tickle stick approached the pulpit and turned over the hourglass. The noon break had begun.

I told my mother I would walk Betty home for the noon break. The child was always tired from the effort to stay still for the lengthy sermon—as was I.

Ann returned home to tend to her father and brothers; we arranged to meet back at the meetinghouse for the afternoon sermon. I grabbed Betty's hand and turned round. A freshly killed wolf's head was nailed to the meetinghouse door. It was soaked in dried blood with its teeth bared in a death grimace.

While the congregation milled about the meetinghouse or headed to Jeremy Adams's Tavern, we kept on the path to Betty's house. Heedless of Betty's chatter, I mulled over Reverend Stone's sermon and the remnants of the Bible quote, *"or to be an observer of an enchanter or a witch."* Had Ann and I observed enchanters and witches that night on the South Green?

The day splashed with bright sunlight. Snowdrops and crocuses popped their white and violet heads toward the strengthening sun. The snow was starting to melt in Hartford and soon the annual flooding of the meadows would begin.

I heard the shuffling sound of light boot steps from behind us on the path. Betty stopped and turned about. The child quivered and her eyes popped open. "Why Goody Ayres. A happy Sabbath to you," she exclaimed.

"Good Sabbath." Goody Ayres wore a dull violet skirt and a dark brown bodice. She even had bits of lace around her bonnet, with a pointed leather hat atop her head. Silk ribbons twined round her cloak. "The winter is finally leaving us. For this I am grateful," she said.

Betty gazed up at the tall thin woman transfixed; for Goody Ayres did indeed possess colorful clothes and was not afraid to wear bits of silk and lace.

Betty's gray eyes opened wide and seemed to plead with Goody Ayres. "Goody Ayres—I was naughty and wicked to bring up the Dark Man—the one that Reverend Stone spoke of at meeting," she said in a tremulous voice. "Won't you please walk with us and share the noon meal at my house before afternoon services? Then we shall return together." I felt taken aback. Was Betty feeling ashamed for speaking to Goody Ayres so boldly at market so many weeks ago?

Goody Ayres smiled at Betty. "Ay, child, I'd be walking that way. They shan't miss me at the tavern for too long."

Betty grasped Goodwife Ayres's hand. "Does this mean I will get a pretty piece of lace now?" she asked. "For my bonnet, hem, and corn dolly?"

Goody Ayres sighed. "Ay, Betty, but of course." She lifted her hands to tilt her hat straight ways. "You do remind me of the little girl I once called daughter so many years ago." We tried to keep pace with Goody Ayres's long strides as she continued speaking. "But, alas, my dear Alice is gone now, buried for several years."

Betty gasped. "But how? How did she die?"

I ran forward and tapped Goody Ayres on the arm. "'Tis a subject best not spoken to a little girl," I said quietly. "She does not understand and 'tis too upsetting for her."

Goody Ayres brushed her brown hair from her face and pushed back her hat. Then she glared at me. As if I must mind my business.

"How did your daughter die?" Betty again asked. The rosy hue on her cheeks was gone. She seemed small and tired, her mouth turned downward. I grabbed Betty's tiny hand and squeezed it.

"Betty, it is the nooning time, and you must get your rest. Let us go to your house. Your family awaits us. Remember, we must return to the meetinghouse by two."

Betty's house was dark on this spring day. The shutters were half closed, and blankets hung over the windows, letting in scant light. *Betty's mother is sick again*, I thought. We stood on the doorstep, waiting for someone to answer. Finally, Betty's father opened the door and greeted us with a broad smile. Then his eyebrows rose in puzzlement as he spotted Goodwife Ayres.

"Betty, I see you have brought home guests for the noon break," he said. "We refuse no one our Sabbath day meal. We have naught but a meat broth cooking over the hearth. But God in His generous mercy blesses us."

Goody Ayres mumbled a thanks under her breath and pushed her way toward the boiling kettle. Finding two wooden bowls in the cupboard and two spoons, she ladled some broth into the bowls. No candles were lit this day. Only the hearth-fire sent shadows dancing across the walls.

Goody Ayres walked to the settle where Betty sat swinging her legs back and forth. She handed the young girl the bowl of broth. Betty grasped the bowl with her tiny hands as Goody Ayres placed the spoon inside the bowl. "Here child, have some warm broth."

"Will there be any broth for you, Hester?" Goody Ayres asked, now sitting at the table to sip from her own bowl.

I pulled a small brown loaf of bread and a piece of cheese wrapped in cloth from my apron pocket. "No, I am fine," I replied. "Would you care for some bread, Betty?" I watched the child stare with hungry eyes at the bread. Her face was as pale white and violet as the March crocuses that bloomed out in the yard.

"Of course she shall have some bread." Goody Ayres stood up and reached out a bony hand. I broke the end off and gave the crust to Goody Ayres. Betty's father entered the room, carrying with him two mugs of cider and a noggin filled with drink for Betty.

"Here's your cider, Betty. Now tell me what the Reverend Stone preached all morning at meeting. Did you learn something that you can teach me?" His eyes had a dim twinkle in them.

Betty sipped the apple cider from the noggin and then drank the steaming meat broth.

"Oww! This broth is too hot," she wailed. "My tongue burns!" She set the bowl down on the settle and began to squirm, jerking her legs like a frog. Her gray eyes watered and she slumped on the settle, seeming to ready herself for a nap. But then she pointed at Goody Ayres, who had taken her knitting needles and yarn out of a black bag.

"Why *must* you torment me so, Goodwife Ayres? I know how you try to prick me with your pins and needles. Stop!" She let out a howl, and her curls bobbed round her cap.

She hopped up and rushed toward the fire, then lay back down across the settle. Clenching her tiny frame she grabbed at her belly, sweat pouring from her forehead.

Goodman Kelly pulled the trundle bed out for Betty to lie upon. Then he lifted up his daughter and carefully placed her down. "Betty, get your rest on the bed. Your mother sleeps in the back room and must not be disturbed. Why must you say this about Goodwife Ayres? Clearly, the broth scalded your throat."

Goodwife Ayres laid aside her knitting needles on the settle and bent down toward the little girl. The thick smell of her lily perfume filled the smoky room. "Come now, child, I mean you no harm," she said smiling. "I am a friend."

Betty continued to clutch at her stomach. I knew not how to help her myself. She tossed about and made grunting noises. "Where is my corn dolly? I want my dolly!" I quickly retrieved her doll, which dangled from the settle and cuddled it next to her.

The meetinghouse bell began to chime. It was time to return for afternoon services.

"Goodwife Ayres, you must go now. My household needs peace," Goodman Kelly said. "Both my wife and now Betty are ill." He looked into the fire flames, lost in thought for a moment.

"I want Hester to stay with me—please!" Betty begged.

I nodded. "Of course I'll stay with you, Betty. How could I leave my little squirrel ailing so?"

Goodwife Ayres stood and began to make for the door, grabbing her knitting and shoving it back into the black bag.

"I thank thee for your kind hospitality, Goodman Kelly. God bless and keep you well."

———

"She pinches me! Goody Ayres chokes me!"

I held Betty's sweating hand and washed her damp face with a cloth.

"Hush, Betty 'tis but a nightmare. Your belly is sore from the hot broth. Rest now."

"But she grabs me *still*, Hester. She sets the furnace on me and squeezes my bones. Father, make her stop!"

What possesses Betty to say such things?

Goodman Kelly came over to the bed and observed Betty. Then he glanced at me with a pained look on his face. He reached down to grasp his daughter's little hand. Then he rushed back to the kitchen and returned with some crushed white powder on a wooden spoon. He mixed it in with the left over liquid in the noggin.

"Here is some angelica powder, Betty. 'Tis good for the blood and keeps the evil spirits away. Take this and drink now," he said.

Betty sat up and opened her mouth, gulping the liquid down her throat. Her face twisted up in a grimace as she swallowed the mixture.

"But Father, you must believe that Goodwife Ayres tries to hurt me. Keep me safe, Father. Hester, please keep me safe." Betty bolted upright and threw her thin arms around my neck. "Never let me go, Hester. Promise?" I hugged her tiny body tight to me.

"Hush, Betty, you'll wake your mother in the back room," said Goodman Kelly.

Betty began to quiver and sob softly to herself, half asleep and mumbling about Goody Ayres. The powder seemed to be working.

I sang to her, quiet hymns I knew were her favorites. Her breathing grew deep and seemed to calm with my voice. Before long, Betty was asleep.

—

I heard footsteps climbing to the doorstep. A brisk series of urgent knocks sounded against the door. *Who can this be?*

Goodman Kelly answered the door while Betty slept. I listened.

"We heard dear Betty was ailing and we wanted to make sure she's better." It was a woman's voice.

"She sleeps peacefully now. Hester is here keeping a watch over her," said Goodman Kelly.

Into the front hall stepped Goody Ayres, Rebecca Greensmith, and Elizabeth Seager.

"We felt it was our duty after meeting to make sure little Betty was feeling better," said Goodwife Ayres, face all a-flush. She moved closer to gaze upon the sleeping girl. Then Goody Seager and Goody Greensmith gathered around to watch Betty. They bobbed up and down chattering and reassuring themselves all was well.

"She breathes easy enough," said Goody Seager. "She'll be well in no time."

Betty began to stir, then sat straight up and opened her eyes. She turned with a ghostly eye that found Goodwife Ayres sitting in a corner near the hearth, knitting.

"Why do you torment me so, Goody Ayres? Why must you prick me?"

Goody Greensmith said sternly, "Child, speak not against Goodwife Ayres, for she comes in love."

Betty began licking her lips and mouthing the word drink. I rose to get Betty some liquid to ease her thirst.

Goody Ayres moved over to sit on the stool next to Betty.

"Why say these things about me, child? Speak not such lies and hold your tongue," she murmured.

Betty drank the cider but seemed no better. She continued to accuse Goody Ayres and demanded her father call the marshal.

"Lay still, child. Why speak such?' Her father frowned in confusion.

Then Goody Ayres leaned close to Betty's ear and I heard her whisper, "If you stay quiet, I'll bring you a piece of lace tomorrow."

Betty watched the woman and with a weakened voice said, "Do you promise…to bring me some lace?"

Goodman Kelly nodded. "Yes, tomorrow you can come round with lace for Betty. She'll be better tomorrow, God willing. It's best if you take your leave now."

"She will be well again—I hope," said Goody Ayres sighing. "I will bring you a special piece of lace tomorrow, Betty." She paused and in a dramatic tone announced, "Tomorrow, Betty."

Chapter 6

*T*here would be no lace or tomorrow for Betty. According to my father, Goodman Kelly reported that Betty died the next morning, just after midnight, begging her father for water and pleading for him to get his ax to chop Goody Ayres's head off, "because she will kill me!" Rumors already flew around town like angry bees. What spell had Goodwife Ayres cast on poor Betty?

My heart was torn apart by the news of Betty's death. Ann crossed the road that bright morning and found me out in the barn tending the chickens. She ran into my arms and collapsed.

"She's gone. Our little squirrel is no more. And she died accusing Goody Ayres of trying to kill her." Ann shook her head and took in a deep breath. "Rest assured, the hand of the Devil is upon Hartford. You know full well I am correct, Hester."

We both sobbed in each other's arms. "Betty will go to heaven to meet the Lord, but the others…" She spoke harshly. "They shall meet their punishments."

My mother baked a mourning cake that Ann and I carried up the road to the grieving family.

"Hear ye, hear ye, a call to assemble at Meetinghouse Square. Townspeople all. Hear ye, hear ye, Marshal Gilbert has an announcement."

The town crier, Mr. Stanton, marched his way down the road past our house, shaking his little brass bell, stomping his boots, and huffing out of breath. His black cape ruffled in the wind. I watched the little man out the window.

"An announcement will be made in thirty minutes time." The meetinghouse bell began to solemnly ring—*dong, dong, dong.*

I dreaded the thought of listening to the authorities with a heart so heavy. Though the day was bright, even the spring sunshine could not cover the dark cast I felt around me and around Hartford.

"What does this mean, Father, this announcement?" I asked as my father fetched his musket, hat and cloak.

"I know not, Hester. I know 'tis not good. With the death of little Betty, suspicions abound. I will see you and your mother at Meetinghouse Square."

A crowd had gathered in the square. Marshal Gilbert limped up to the newly erected wooden platform near the stocks, pillory, and whipping post. Six other men and Goodman Kelly followed the marshal and stood behind him. Then an older man hunched over, wearing spectacles and walking with a cane, hobbled up to the platform and joined the men.

Marshal Gilbert cleared his throat and began scanning all the faces in the audience.

"We are here to present to you the findings of little Elizabeth Kelly's untimely death. She has been gone from us but days now." The marshal paused, wiped his brow, and took a deep breath. He started to pace from one end of the platform to the other.

"The good men standing behind me represent the jury who witnessed the autopsy of Betty's body." The crowd remained silent.

I gasped. *Autopsy?* I scoured the crowd looking for Ann. Goody Ayres stood beside her husband and Goody Seager. Rebecca Greensmith and her family watched the proceedings near the stocks. Where was Ann?

The marshal continued. "Goodwife Ayres, please come forward and take thy place on the platform."

Goody Ayres, head held high, made her way up the wooden steps and stood glaring at the marshal. Facing one another, they reminded me of a pair of black birds.

"Goodwife Ayres, know this is not a trial but an inquest. Do you admit to viewing the dead body of Betty Kelly in front of these six jury members upon my request and the request of our acting governor, Captain John Mason?"

"Ay," said Goody Ayres.

"Do you admit that when you were asked to pull up the dead child's sleeves, a bruise, in fact a purplish mark, lay fresh on her arm?"

"Ay," she said. "I know not how that bruised mark came to be. I have naught to do with bruises and marks."

"But the little girl accused you of pinching her before her violent death. What say you to this charge, Goodwife Ayres?"

Goody Ayres hung her head low and said nothing.

"It's a sign—of witchcraft!" a woman shrieked.

"Lord, protect us from evil," I heard another woman cry.

Goody Ayres looked up and cast a squinted glance around the crowd. "I know naught of such doings," she said loudly. "I never pinched or harmed the child. I am innocent."

The crowd began to murmur, one to the other. I noticed Ann, standing with her father and brothers, fixing Goody Ayres with a look of black rage. Judith Varlet and her father Caspar were present watching the proceedings.

"Would you deny, upon witnessing the deceased child's body, that a red mark appeared on her cheek, the same cheek you touched moments before the large mark revealed itself?" the marshal asked.

Goody Ayres stood tall again, but her thin body began to sway as if she was close to a faint.

"Ay, Marshal Gilbert, but I had naught to do with the mark on the child's cheek. I loved Betty like she was my own."

Goody Ayres began to weep.

"Silence, woman," the marshal thundered. "That is enough. You are not here as an object to be pitied. We must think on poor, dead Betty."

The Revered Stone came forth, wearing his teacher's cap and long black gown. He carried his Bible and a roll of parchment paper. He joined the men and Goody Ayres on the platform.

"Friends, townspeople. We pray and mourn for the death of dear Betty, a child taken too soon from us," he called out.

Upon hearing his words, tears spilled from my eyes. I grasped my mother's arm and leaned against her shoulder for strength.

"Remember this law," the Reverend Stone continued, "If a sick person dies and accuses one on his or her deathbed, such a one accused..." He stopped and pointed at Goody Ayres, "Of bewitchment, these are strong grounds of suspicion for witchcraft. Therefore, a strict examination is necessary for a conviction. Please, Magistrate Wyllys, step forward."

The aged magistrate, dressed in a black gown, hobbled up to the platform.

Where is this all leading?

The Magistrate began to speak. "We have suspicions of Goodwife Ayres, and rest assured we will have her examined for signs of witchcraft and causing Betty's death in a preternatural way."

Preternatural?

So the marshal, the jury, the magistrate, Goodman Kelly, the doctor, and Reverend Stone all suspected Betty had died an unnatural death, bewitched by Goody Ayres. Had she made an unholy pact with the Devil and thus caused my little squirrel's demise? I shuddered at the thought.

The marshal's forehead bulged. "Guards, militiamen. I need at least two men now."

Two militiamen stepped forth with muskets against their shoulders. They approached the platform.

"Seize this woman and remove her to the jail immediately, per my order and the order of Captain John Mason, Acting Governor of our colony." The marshal grinned, looking well pleased. He limped about the platform, wiping his brow, and then pointed out toward the crowd, finding Goodman Ayres.

"Take her husband as well. Anyone consorting with a known sorceress must be examined for witchery."

The crowd erupted with a series of huzzahs and cheers. "God bless the marshal and all the pious people of Hartford. The Lord will save us," someone yelled.

"God save us from this murdering witch. Take her away," I heard the old scold Goody Migat holler.

Someone began pelting Goody Ayres with rocks.

"Stop," demanded the marshal. "A strict examination of the Ayreses for witchcraft will be conducted." He paused and looked the crowd over again. "They shall endure the water test. When the weather warms in a fortnight or so, I shall post the time and location on the meetinghouse door. All may attend as we continue our examination of possible witchcraft, punishable by death. In the meantime, the Ayres will remain in jail."

A drum beat echoed loud and steady. The two militiamen began dragging the Ayreses to a jail close to Meetinghouse Square. It was nothing more than a rotted dugout cellar covered by wooden planks. Townspeople began to spit and throw rocks at the couple.

I suddenly felt ill, and a wave of nausea made me dizzy. Sweat beaded my forehead. I watched Ann pick up stones to throw at the Ayreses.

The marshal spoke his final words and wagged a finger at the fevered crowd.

"We shall never forget what Betty suffered, and how the Kelly family mourns the loss of their only child; she who was healthy one minute—and dead the next."

Chapter 7

I walked the road to Jeremy Adams's Tavern, carrying a basket of linens and cinnamon biscuits. The linens and sweets
were intended for Goodwife Adams in exchange for some freshly
dipped candles, honey, and preserves for my mother.

Passing the Wyllys mansion on the hill overlooking Ann's
house, I noticed the apple and cherry trees were bright with white
and pink blossoms. The house gleamed white and stately in the
sun. On the other side of the road, the Varlet homestead's apple orchards were also abloom. But the brightness of this spring
morning could not lift my despair over Betty's death.

I thought it must be nearing the time for Sam Flagg, the peddler and his twenty-two year old son Tom, to come down from
Springfield for a visit. They'd often travel to Boston by way of the
Bay Path. But always they'd return to Springfield and then head
south to Hartford, following the old Indian trails. Many a time
they'd arrive with their horse-drawn cart filled with goods, but
often they'd raft down the Great River and dock along the rivulet
close to the Landing.

Tom and I had grown up together in Hartford. But several years ago, Tom's grandmother, Granny Flagg died, so Tom and his father took wing and moved to Springfield. The remnants of Granny Flagg's house stood near the Little River. Tom and I would walk to the flood-battered cottage and recall happier times.

I never knew when or how they'd arrive. Sometimes, I'd mill about the tavern, listening for the tinkling of the wagon bells, the clopping hoofs of Scarlet, their Narragansett Pacer, and the brass horn announcing their presence. I would know then that they'd come out from the trails to travel directly to Jeremy Adams's Tavern.

"How could you do the trip, Tom? The perils of the journey, 'tis fraught with dangers," I'd say. Tom would then tell me stories of Indian ambushes, getting lost in storms, and how he and his father fended prowlers off with musket, knives, and wit. The weather was their best friend and worst enemy. "If it's not the weather, it's the wolves. Still, life on the road suits me," he always said with a wink.

Although I loved his tales of adventure, it caused me anguish to think of Tom and his father in the harsh elements. I prayed for them daily and thought of Tom on the road each night. Luckily for the Flaggs, they had more friends than foes along the Bay Path and the Indian trails.

Jeremy Adams always gave Sam and his son a warm welcome at the tavern's hearth. He provided Tom and his father bed and board, in exchange for a mound of spoons, knives, or pewter plates. Often they'd knock on doors to sell needles, pins, and buttons to the goodwives in need of household items. Sam, a tinker by trade, repaired pewter plate-ware for the townspeople.

One never knew what items they might carry in their leather saddlebags. They often had news from London. Sometimes they'd have pamphlets and papers of interest to barter with folks.

I ambled by the tavern in the hope Tom would be about. Several months had passed since I'd last seen him. I needed to talk with him about Betty and the witchcraft rumors spreading in Hartford.

As usual, many people gathered around the tavern for the midday break.

"Watching for Tom, are you now?" My brother Stephen's eyes twinkled like sharp stars. He stood on the porch that wrapped around the tavern and drank from a frothy mug. Then he leaned over the railing, stretched his leg on a post, and grinned at me.

I glared at Stephen and tossed my head. "Of course not. I'm carrying fresh linens to Goodwife Adams as a favor for mother." I felt heat on my neck and noticed how my skirt swung about from side to side. I could not keep still.

"You're blushing, Hester."

"You are impudent. Of course I am not." The heat from my neck spread to my cheeks. "I'd only welcome some news from England, that's all. I'd like to know what Governor Winthrop may be saying to the King right now."

Stephen's expression turned grim. "Ay, tidings from Boston and London Town are in order. With Governor Winthrop gone to England to negotiate the Charter, I wonder if he shall ever return."

He drank down his ale with blackened hands from hours in the forge. "The custom laws from England drain our colony every day," he added wiping his mouth on his sleeve. "It helps not that Marshal Gilbert argues with the Dutchman, Caspar Varlet, who pays no duties on his goods. And that daughter of his, Judy, is vain and thinks herself too good for us."

I longed for Governor Winthrop's return, because nothing had felt right in Hartford in the weeks since Betty's death. The Ayreses still languished in jail, and the water test was days away.

I sighed. "Ay, but I do miss Governor Winthrop and pray for his speedy return from England."

Stephen smiled. His eyes skimmed the group of townspeople sharing midday news then lifted his head toward the horse stables out back.

"Oh, not that you are interested in such matters, but Tom and his father pulled in on the wagon but a few minutes ago. Mayhap I will get my piece of news from England and another pewter mug for my collection." He lifted his tankard and drank down the last drop of ale. "Time for me to return to the forge."

I propped the basket of linens on my hip. "Tom and Sam are here in Hartford? Now?"

Stephen's eyes held a merry glint as he raised his tankard to me. "Go bring the homespun to Goody Adams and look back in the stables. And for my service, sister, I'll take one of those sweet-smelling cinnamon biscuits." Before I could protest, he leaped over the rail and grabbed one straight out of the basket.

———

The tavern brimmed with gossip. A hog sizzled on a spit over the hearth flames and Mr. Adams was serving up many a pint of ale, toddies, and flips. I pushed my way to the back of the tavern and found Goody Adams slicing up some fresh cheese and bread.

"Why child, you look out of breath and your face is flushed red." She glanced at the basket and gathered up the linens and then the biscuits with her plump fingers.

"God bless your mother, Hester. And you are a good girl. Here are the candles and the other goodies." She stuffed the wrapped candles and pots of honey and jam into the empty basket and handed me a slice of bread. "Here you are, dear. You need sustenance for the walk home. God bless thee and please thank your mother."

I left the tavern by the back door and made my way to the stables. Through the open doors, I saw the tall, muscled figure with thick brown curls, white linen shirt, deerskin breeches and tattered hat currying a horse. It was Tom tending to Scarlet after the long ride from Springfield.

"Tom, you are here at last!" I dropped my basket and I ran to him. Startled, he looked up and wiped his sweating forehead.

"Hester, 'tis good to see you after all this time. 'Tis been a long journey."

I wanted to cuddle up in Tom's muscled arms to make the pain go away. I halted, watching him smiling and wondering what to say next.

"Did you bring me anything from your travels? I've been waiting all these months." I swayed closer, feeling Scarlet's breath and petting her head. Then I laughed, "You smell like Scarlet, Tom," I said.

"Ay, and I prefer it that way." He took off his hat and ruffled his thick, dark hair. "Scarlet is used to me and I her." He chuckled and gave me a short embrace. "Yes, I know I must wash soon. Otherwise, Pa and I will be banished from Hartford proper."

He paused. "Of course I brought thee a present. I could not forget." He narrowed his eyes and lifted up my chin. "Why so sad, Hester?" His dark brown eyes met my own, serious and still.

"Have you not heard?" I exclaimed. "Betty Kelly is dead and accused Goody Ayres on her deathbed of pinching and bewitching her. The marshal has ordered the Ayreses to remain in jail on suspicion of witchcraft. They must endure the water test, and it is but days away." I waved my hands as I spoke—I had so much to tell Tom. "And then Ann and I..." But I stopped short of sharing with him the details of that full-moon night. "I cannot bear to think of what Betty suffered and that this bewitchment could happen in Hartford. The Ayreses and others, they may be witches."

Tom rested a foot against the wagon and chewed on a piece of straw.

"We did hear rumors of a witch scare happening in Hartford. Even the gossips in Springfield are speaking of a witch panic. I didn't believe it. And I knew not of Betty's demise. Truly, I am sorry Betty suffered." His eyes met mine. "I am sorry you suffer here as well, Hester. You always have had a sensitive soul."

He shook his head and began rustling around the leather bags strewn in the wagon until he poked his head into a pouch.

"So, I do have a few gifts for thee. I bartered them from a captain himself come off a ship in Boston." He handed me a little bundle wrapped in twine.

"Is that so, Tom? What is it?" I could not contain my curiosity.

"Slip it into thy apron pocket and let not a soul find it."

"You cannot tell me what you brought me?" I asked in my sweetest voice.

Tom smiled and his teeth shone white. "We'll find time for a walk in the meadows soon. The floodwaters are receding somewhat, and I'll be trading with the natives down that way the next fortnight. In the meantime, I must get Scarlet fed, find Pa and then get myself fed." He paused. "Cleaned up as well, from what some of my friends tell me."

We both smiled. I had something to look forward to. Then Tom's face fell.

From somewhere behind me I heard shuffling footsteps.

"Idling, Hester? With the peddler's son, I see."

A dark shadow cast itself over the stable. I turned around. There was Marshal Gilbert glaring down at me. Then his gaze turned straight toward Tom and back to me again.

"Hester Hosmer, idleness is a punishable crime. Three hours in the stocks if I am not mistaken."

The marshal pulled a copy of the *Blue Laws, The Code of 1650* from his waistcoat pocket. He began to leaf through the book, his pointed nose between the covers. I found Tom's eyes and gave him a reassuring look. Tom took his hat off and nervously scratched his head. He started to speak in my defense, but I gave him a stern look and raised a finger to my lips.

"As you know, Marshal," I said, "a pewter plate did fall during that windblown night you supped with us weeks past. The plate fell straight off the cupboard and broke."

Tom rubbed his neck.

"Yes, Hester—hmm—please continue," said the marshal, poring through the book, I assumed, to find the correct punishment for idlers.

"The plate cracked, and we need Tom and his father to fix it readily." I blew a deep breath out. "So, Marshal Gilbert, idling I am not."

Tom cocked his head to the side, pushed his hat back, and raised an eyebrow.

The marshal slammed the book shut. "I'll allow for this indiscretion this one time—for the sake of the pewter," he grumbled.

I picked up the basket, pulled it to my chest, and pressed it against the bundle in my apron pocket. My gift from Tom was safe.

The marshal then addressed Tom. "It's good to see you again, boy." He limped over and patted him on the shoulder. "Where's your father?"

Tom pointed to the tavern behind us. "Pa needed a good pint and a washing up. You'll find him inside, Marshal."

"Do you happen to have brought a fresh set of needles, pins, and buttons, Tom? I am in sore need."

"Ay, Marshal. Pa and I never forget an important man such as you. Of course we have what you need." Tom's smile flashed at the crane-like marshal. His smile had the power to calm a snake.

The marshal harrumphed, mollified. "I've come for other reasons today besides noting idleness in young maids," he said rustling some papers in his pocket. "I will be posting this notice on the meetinghouse door. Share the news. Tomorrow is the water test for the suspected witches, and all townspeople will congregate down by the Little River for noon."

Chapter 8

*T*he day dawned cloudy and a cool gray mist hovered in the air. The night before, I hid the flat bundle from Tom in my mattress, nestled between the goose-down feathers and sweet herbs. But before I stuffed it under my mattress, I had to see what Tom had gifted me from his journeys. Just knowing he was in Hartford brought me some relief and distraction from the witchcraft gossip spreading around the town.

Carefully, I pulled out the bundle tied in leather cords and held it to the candlelight. It felt as if it contained several small thin items, like printings of a sort. I was eager to see what treasures Tom had bartered from the sailor in Boston. Just for me.

I sat at the table, loosened the knots and tore open the paper. Inside were two small, cloth-bound books no more than ten or twenty pages each. One held poems, the other ballads. A third printing was a flat, square booklet with black and white designs. This was something I had never seen before. I began leafing through the pages.

It was an almanac for the Year of our Lord, 1662, published in London. Each month had the planting phases and the moon's quarters. Black and white moon faces grinned up from the pages.

Quotes from poets such as Dryden and Spencer, along with home remedies filled the ornate page borders. I realized I could use the almanac to mark the passing of days and note the events transpiring in Hartford.

Then I noticed a bit of paper that appeared to be a bookmark nestled onto the August page. This proved to be a folded note. Holding it close to the light, I recognized Tom's handwriting in black ink.

Dear Hester,

Here is a small gift for you. To thee I give the reminder of time on paper now, for time is passing. I hope for more time together in the future. I hope you like the almanac. You will find the Master poet in one book. Read Sonnet 116; I read this and thought of you. And the other, some ballads from the peasant folk to cheer your spirit during the bleak hours. My father and I will go abroad, back to Boston come mid-June. I will watch for you in town before we must leave again. With much fondness,

Tom

I found the book of sonnets and quickly leafed through the pages until I came upon Sonnet 116. I read the first stanzas,

'Let me not to the marriage of true minds
Admit impediments. Love isn't love which alters when
In alteration finds or bends with the remover to remove
O No! It is an ever-fixed mark
That looks on tempests and is never shaken
It is the star to every wandering bark.'

Tom *was* like the north star to me—strong, steady, never changing. Did we have a true marriage of the minds?

But today was the water test. The Little River's waters had finally dropped to acceptable levels; so the authorities could throw the Ayreses in—to see if they floated—or sank. The ducking stool was reserved for scolds and tattlers. But in the case of suspected witchery, they would use the ropes.

"Hester, churn the butter out in the barn, feed the chickens, and collect the morning eggs," my mother reminded me. She was sitting at her loom, carding wool. I had already filled the water buckets, kindled the fire, and swept the keeping room.

I removed round the back door and began to walk toward the barn, shooing hungry chickens away from my skirt. I turned around and saw Ann, heavy-hipped and cap askew, ambling across the road.

"Hester, did you know that Tom is here in Hartford?" Ann was out of breath. She came close to my face. "I saw him yesterday down at the tavern."

I shrugged as if it mattered not. Ann's eyes opened wide. I made my way round to the coop and began to collect the eggs.

"After I spoke with Tom, I ran by the meetinghouse door and saw the notice posted by the marshal. Today is the day. They will finally prove that the Ayreses are witches." Ann had a half smile on her face. "What think you? Will they float?"

"I know not," I said as I carefully lifted a new egg and set it in my basket. "What thinks you?"

"I don't think—I know—that the Ayreses be witches. Why, Goody Ayres bewitched little Betty, our squirrel, who has gone to her grave. Dead as dust she is, and the Ayreses are to blame." She paused. "You remember my father was a juror who witnessed Betty's autopsy?" Ann continued watching me collect the eggs. "He told me she did indeed have bruise marks on her arm."

I silently continued on with my morning chores.

"When the meeting bell peals afore noon, I shall meet you on the road. We shall find a spot on the Little River banks, a spot that affords the best view. What say you, Hester?"

I sighed. "Of course we shall go. I will meet you when the meeting bell rings."

———

The meeting bell rang close to the noon hour. Townspeople began to gather on the knoll by the Little River. The swirling eddies that posed dangers during the flood season had calmed; the wind was naught and the waters stirred only by dragonfly touches and light ripples from hungry fish.

Ann and I joined with the others on the hill. Surrounded by rushes and weeds, it sloped down to the river's bend and provided an ideal overlook for the water test. Several onlookers gathered on the other side of the river. I noticed Tom and his father watching the proceeding from across the riverbank as well. Many people stood on the plank-wood crossing bridge that led to the meeting-house. Guards with pikes protected each side of the river to keep peace and calm. A raft was moored to a tree trunk. A tangle of rope awaited the prisoners.

A wagon cart ambled up the path, hauling the Ayreses. Marshal Gilbert stood atop the knoll. The Reverend Stone, Reverend Whiting, and several magistrates stood alongside him.

The crowd began to murmur, restless for the spectacle to begin.

"Good people of Hartford, as part of our thorough examination for the crime of witchcraft, the accused will endure the water test," the marshal shouted. "We will make note if the accused float or sink. Rest assured, if they float, they be buoyed by the powers of Satan. If they sink, it proves they be no witches."

The marshal waved a hand. "Guards, prepare the accused for the water test now."

Two militiamen approached the wagon and helped the Ayreses off to the ground.

"Mark my word but they be witches," a woman said. "They'll float like logs, floating like all witches do."

"Then we'll hang 'em on Gallows Hill," a man replied, then cursed and spat.

Goodwife Ayres was stripped down to her smock, her thin, knobby legs exposed. Goodman Ayres's shirt was removed, so he wore but his breeches. Their hair was uncombed, their faces haggard and their clothing soiled from spending weeks in the dugout jail.

"Tie the rope round the left thumb. Next, tie it to the right big toe," ordered the marshal.

With fumbling hands, the guard began to cross-bind Goody Ayres.

"Right. Now, tie the right thumb to the left big toe. Once that is complete, tie the accused around the middle with the rope."

The guards then proceeded to do the same to Goodman Ayres, who looked ashen. Greasy strands of hair hung over his face. His eyes had dark rings around them.

The marshal beckoned for the rafts-man to take his appointed place. "Rafts-man, ready? You are witness to testify whether the accused do sink or float. Rest assured if they float, they be witches."

The crowd fell silent now. Goody Ayres curled over like a ball of yarn and hid her face.

"For shame," screamed Goody Migat. "Afraid to show your face for bewitching an innocent, little girl to her death."

The guards carried the Ayreses to the knoll all knotted up in ropes. Marshal Gilbert held the ends of the ropes tied to the Ayreses's stomachs.

"Before we commence the water test, Reverend Stone will bless and pray with us."

Reverend Stone bowed his head and the spectators lowered their heads. After the prayer, the marshal began: "Rafts-man, prepare your position. You may use your raft pole to prod the prisoners if need be. Take your post."

The man loosened the raft and stuck his thick, oak pole deep into the water to steer the craft close to the hill.

"We are ready. Let the water test begin," announced Marshal Gilbert.

I glanced over at Ann, whose mouth gaped open, her eyes wide as plates. The crowd stayed still but a moment—until the Ayres were hoisted up and thrown into the calm, cold water by guards. A loud chorus of huzzahs erupted. The water test had officially begun.

Goody Ayres gasped for breath, her head bobbing up and down.

"Why, you see she's floating. This can only mean she's a witch," said Goody Migat to Goody Garret.

Goody Ayres turned onto her back and indeed appeared to be floating.

"Witch!" Ann suddenly screamed out.

Goodman Ayres fared no better. He floated to the surface and struggled in the ropes, lifting up his head for air.

"Witches, both of them!" shouted Goody Migat, lifting a gnarled finger to the air. "The hangman awaits them. They float."

Like a contagion, the crowd began to chant, "Huzzah, they float. They be witches."

Marshal Gilbert stepped up and raised his hands.

"Man on the raft. What say you?"

We all regarded the man holding the pole balancing on the raft.

"I say, Marshal, the accused do float."

"Indeed," said the marshal. "It is as I presumed."

The marshal pulled at the ropes attached to the Ayreses and dragged them to shore. The ropes were untangled from the pair who looked like drowned cats soaked from head to toe. Goody Ayres coughed and grabbed at her throat, gasping for air. Goodman Ayres stood dripping. No one even gave them a cloth to dry off. The guards dragged them back into the hay wagon, and they were carted off to await their fate.

Marshal Gilbert's crooked figure loomed on the hill. "The water test is over and it's time to return to your chores. The Ayreses shall be jailed until further notice. We have our proof of witchery."

A man stepped forward from the crowd. He was covered in sweat and wiped his stained hands on his work apron as he approached the Marshal.

All eyes were on him: George Givens, the tanner.

"Ay, Marshal, thou kept the Ayreses afloat by keeping the rope taut. Otherwise they'd be sure to sink." The tanner paused. "Like a big rock."

The marshal peered down at the portly tanner from his position on the knoll.

"Goodman Givens, I think that perhaps thou would like to try the water test?" The marshal's black eyes flashed like a serpent's and his forehead bulged. "Right now."

Goodman Givens had no choice. "I'll try," he said and shrugged his shoulders

The marshal had Goodman Givens thus tied with ropes and thrown into the river. Ann and I stayed to watch as the rafts-man came close again to view the water test.

The tanner immediately sank to the bottom of the river, and there he stayed. Townspeople began to demand he be pulled up before he drowned.

"Pull him up now," ordered the marshal, still holding the ropes. "It's clear this man is no witch. He sank and almost drowned. Dropped to the bottom—like a big rock."

Marshal Gilbert laughed and leaned over the gagging George Givens. "Let this be a lesson to those who doubt," shouted the marshal. "The Ayreses floated and the tanner sank. No more needs to be done to prove our point. You can all return to your homes now."

———

The meetinghouse bell rang out sometime in the night. Three rings and then one ring. This was the warning bell. Something or someone was afoot. The alarm sounded loud and urgent. I jolted from my sleep and then sat up to listen. I could hear footsteps running up the road. I heard my father bellowing to my mother. I listened to horses' hooves pounding on the road.

"Escape!" I heard someone shout. "The prisoners have escaped!"

I swung my feet onto the loft's warm floorboards and tiptoed to the window. Several men on horseback were riding toward the meetinghouse with dogs at their heels. Who had helped the Ayreses escape? Would they be found and captured?

Chapter 9

————————————

Soon after the Ayreses's escape, my mother approached me one late morning. I was working on my chores. I still had not found the right time or opportunity to read the entire bundle from Tom that lay under my mattress. My mother seemed to busy me all the time with work.

"I spoke with Reverend Whiting yesterday after meeting," she said. "He asked if you and Ann would watch little William and Sybil for an hour or two. He needs to meet with Reverend Haynes in his study for a time. Mrs. Whiting will be out ministering to the neighbors. He has spoken to Ann's father as well."

I shrugged my shoulders. I did not have a choice, so I finished my cleaning and sweeping, then readied myself. Of the Whitings' two young children, Sybil, the oldest was eight—the same age as Betty. William was only four. The Whitings had lost a daughter a few years before to a fever. Sybil and Betty had been close friends, sharing and playing with corn dollies, learning to read from their hornbooks and singing hymns.

It pained me to care for the children while we still mourned Betty. Her round eyes, chipper voice and freckled face still haunted me. Often I would awaken from sleep to hear her voice cry out, "Goody Ayres pinches me. She chokes me. She will kill me!" What tales of the Dark Man had Goody Ayres shared with the impressionable girl? I knew naught. What of the little man who pinched her—if she didn't do her chores? Why tell Betty these stories? My heart broke to witness the other young children in Hartford. The memory of Betty was very much alive in my mind.

Reluctantly, I walked over to Ann's house and knocked on the door. After a time, Ann's brother John, whose leg was maimed from an accident years ago, offered me entry. He was a kind and gentle man who had a sweet but sad smile. Ann always told me John was the man I would marry.

He brushed his dark hair from his eyes. "Good morrow, Hester. How do?"

"Well as to be expected, John. And you?"

"As best as possible. I have my good and bad days with this leg. All depends on the weather now, don't it?" He gave me a wide smile and lightly took my shoulder to lead me into the house. "Come in. Ann's almost ready."

I entered the keeping room where a fire raged in the hearth. Shadows swayed around the room, light and dark shapes bowing as if they danced together. The smell of fresh baked bread filled the room, making my stomach grumble. Yet there was a lingering feeling of loss, loneliness, and pain that floated within those shadows.

At last Ann stomped down the stairs. "You could wake the dead with those heavy steps," John muttered.

"Better that than your hobbling about this house," said Ann, looking for her shawl. "There's leftover corn pudding and fresh bread to eat. Tell Father I'll be home after noon."

Ann found her shawl and wrapped it around her shoulders. "So, we must watch the Whiting children today. Imagine the Reverend Whiting requesting us to care for them. What an honor!"

I nodded. "I wouldn't mind, but for thinking of Betty."

"Oh, never mind that now, Hester." Ann sighed. "Just being in the presence of Reverend Whiting is a blessing. There's naught a godly or more handsome man I know in this town—with the exception of your brother." She grabbed my arm. "I espouse to find a man like the Reverend Whiting. Young, handsome, and a man of God who has charm, intelligence, and grace."

"Ay, so the Reverend Whiting has charmed thee, Ann?" John was standing at the doorway listening.

"Ay, he hath more charm in his little finger than thee could ever have, brother." Ann laughed as we took our leave.

———

The Whitings lived up the road between my house and the Varlet homestead. Like my father's land, acres of apple and cherry trees spread far behind the house. Like us, they had a barn, several outbuildings with chickens, geese, cows, some sheep and a horse.

Reverend Whiting's father, William, was a founder of Hartford and a well-established merchant. He, like Marshal Gilbert and rival Caspar Varlet, owned warehouses at the landing. Reverend Whiting had graduated from Harvard with a degree in divinity and ministry. The Reverend Stone was preparing both Reverend Whiting and Reverend Haynes to replace him. Reverend Stone was aged and would retire soon. It was rumored that Reverend

Whiting would take the role of teacher and leader for our community. He was known as a kind man who saw things differently than Reverend Stone. He was young and vibrant, whereas Reverend Stone was old and battered.

Who in Hartford had not heard of the time Reverend Stone gave the prayer and blessing to Captain John Mason's fleet that fateful day in 1636, when the Pequot Fort burned to the ground? Reverend Stone had received a message from God giving clear instructions of where, when, and how to destroy the Indian village. This included the fateful decision to throw the burning brand over the palisade walls.

Captain Mason, Marshal Gilbert, and others followed "God's decree" and the war was won. "God spoketh the truth through Reverend Stone. A true man of God," my father would always say. "If it weren't for him, our land would be overrun by the natives."

But times were changing, and many people such as Ann and I desired the Reverend Whiting as our teacher and pastor. We thought Reverend Stone's ideas old and outworn. But we respected our leader and knew one day Reverend Whiting would take his place.

We climbed up the small hill to the Whiting stoop, and Mrs. Whiting opened the door. "Thank goodness you are here, girls. Sybil and William are waiting for you. My husband is meeting with Reverend Haynes in his study."

She checked the basket she carried to make certain she had everything for her neighborhood visits. "There's fresh cheese, warm bread and freshly churned butter inside for you. I'll be home by late afternoon." Mrs. Whiting fluttered by us, leaving the door open.

The Whiting house always felt warm and inviting. The keeping room was strewn with a hobbyhorse, dollies, and knickknacks. Blue and white Dutch tiles from the elder Whiting's travels surrounded the hearth-fire. And Mrs. Whiting clearly loved the color yellow. Yellow porcelain vases from China, yellow rugs and candles brightened the mood of the room.

What I loved most was the Reverend Whiting's study. A small room aside the keeping room, the burnished wood walls were covered from top to bottom with books. Reverend Whiting had studied Latin, Greek, and was familiar with the classics. A set of diamond-paned windows looked out into the back garden.

Reverend Whiting sat behind his massive desk. "Girls, what a blessing to see you."

Ann's face turned a bright red. She always seemed flushed when she was around Reverend Whiting. She fawned over him just as she did with the children. "'Tis always a blessing to see you, Reverend." I nodded my head in agreement.

Reverend Whiting stood up. " Let me call for the children. They will be excited to see you both."

Reverend Haynes sat in the study, poring over a stack of papers. He looked to be a few years older than Reverend Whiting. His thinning, blonde hair brushed across his forehead and he smiled up at us.

Sybil soon bounded in, while chubby William teetered, fell forward, and struggled to get himself up. He had not had his breeching ceremony yet and still wore a child's gown.

Ann scooped him up in her arms and showered him with kisses. Sybil buried her face in my apron and gave me a wide hug with her tiny arms. "What will we do today whilst Father is at work?" She gazed up at me with wide blue eyes and then looked to Ann.

"We shall practice your letters on your hornbook while William rides his hobbyhorse. Mayhap we will tell some stories as well," suggested Ann.

I heard Reverend Whiting murmur something to Reverend Haynes and then he turned to face us. "If you are in need of anything, Hester and Ann, please let me know," he said. He escorted us to the keeping room, leaving the study door slightly open.

"We will be fine, Reverend, rest assured," Ann said. "If you hear us naught, mayhap we will be out in the garden or orchards."

"Perhaps we should start with your hornbook lesson," I told Sybil. "'Tis time to witness your progress."

"Then I can recite my lesson for Father. Just like he recites his lessons to all of us on meeting day. He'll be Hartford's teacher soon." She jumped up and down, her movements as quick as her mind.

"Of course," I said lovingly as I patted her head. We all removed to the settle near the fire. We found Sybil's hornbook hanging on a peg while William raised his arms to Ann. "Lift, lift," he requested. Ann set him atop his little horse. "Riding stick," he demanded. He laughed, his black curls bobbing as he galloped on his pretend horse.

Sybil stood and pointed to the first letter. "A, Adam, B, boy, C, cat." She stopped, blew out a long breath of air, and sat down on the settle.

"What's wrong, Sybil? Your letter reading is perfect today," I said. Sybil stared into the fire and shook her head.

"I just want to know, I want to know how my friend Betty died. I cannot stop thinking of her." She burst into a torrent of tears.

I grabbed the little girl's limp wrist. "Why, Betty had a fever. That's how she died," I reassured her.

"But will I also get pinched by the dark man or a witch and die as well—because I'm bad?"

My heart melted for Sybil. At that age, it was hard to fathom death. Ann came round the settle and put a hand upon Sybil's shaking shoulders. "Betty was never a bad girl, and neither are you. The only bad people are those who tell lies and want to make mischief."

Sybil looked up at Ann, blinked, and wiped her tears. She worshipped and adored Ann like no other. "Like Goodwife Ayres, you mean? The witch who escaped?"

"Ay, and rest assured she or her dark man will not hurt you. God and your own father watch you, each day and night."

"What of the dark man? I like not the thought of mischief and devils. They scare me." Sybil shuddered and then dropped her voice. "I've seen him in the woods out back. He wanted Betty. The dark man used Goody Ayres, and now Betty my friend is dead. And now he wants me."

She hurled her hornbook across the room. William, sensing something was amiss, began to scream.

The Reverend Whiting appeared at his study door. "Is everything all right here?" he asked. Ann snatched up the hornbook and hung it back on the peg. "Sybil still pains for the loss of Betty. She cannot make sense of her friend's death."

"Ay," Reverend Whiting replied, brushing his light, brown hair. "Who can make sense of God's mysterious ways?"

"Mayhap I should take Sybil for a walk to the orchards?" Ann asked.

"I see no problem with a walk out back," said Reverend Whiting.

Ann glanced over at me. "Hester, would you watch William while I see to Sybil?"

"Of course," I replied. "I'd be happy to watch him"

A smile came upon Sybil's face. She grabbed Ann's hand and they walked out back to the yard.

Now it was quiet. William's eyes were becoming droopy so I tucked him into his trundle bed. He was ready for a nap but still demanded his noggin filled with milk.

I made my way to the kitchen, where a fresh pail of milk sat by the door. Filling William's cup, I made certain not to spill a drop. Quietly, I returned to the keeping room and gave the sleepy boy his milk.

The door to Reverend Whiting's study was still ajar. I paused, unable to resist the temptation to listen to the discussion.

"But the Greensmith woman is a lewd, ignorant disturbance to this town—and her husband is a known thief," Reverend Whiting was saying. "I plan on penning a letter to the Reverend Increase Mather pertaining to the problems these people are causing to our godly congregation."

"Do you think it prudent, John, to seek help from Boston?" asked Reverend Haynes "Can you not see we have the means to handle this here in Hartford?"

There was a long silence. "Then what must we do? Betty Kelly is dead. The Ayres have escaped. Each night my daughter asks me if she is safe. She is filled with ungodly terror. I like this naught. If anything happens to my Sybil…."

"Marshal Gilbert has a mind to rid this town of bewitchment. Let him take care of the lot of them."

"But perhaps Increase Mather and his son Cotton need to come to Hartford to test the likes of them for witchery?" said Reverend Whiting. "The water test was conducted. What of witches' teats and familiars? We know not what they have or do."

I remembered the story of the Lancaster witches that Granny Flagg had told Tom and me years before. In England, any mole or unusual growth could be considered a witch's teat. Familiars such as cats, birds, or other creatures might suckle them for nourishment.

"And John," the Reverend Haynes continued, "We are patiently gathering evidence against these people. Rebecca Greensmith has been arrested once for lewd behavior. Her husband Nathaniel arrested for thievery. How these two bought the land across from South Green, I know naught."

I heard the shuffling of papers. "Perhaps the devil does have his hand in Hartford," said Reverend Whiting. "To think these people may have merry meets amongst the godly? It's wickedness. I don't know if I told you, but just last week old Mrs. Migat sought my counsel about that Goody Seager. Imagine, she told me that she met Goody Seager down by the Little River. There, according to Mrs. Migat, Goody Seager told her, 'God is naught. God is naught.'"

A fist pounded the desk. "Let us pray together for God's wisdom and mercy upon this town."

"Mercy?" Reverend Haynes asked. "These people deserve no mercy. Remember the Bible says, 'Justice and vengeance is mine, saith the Lord.'"

"Ay, so we wait, watch, and try to keep peace in Hartford. The Reverend Stone will know what to do. He's had experience with the evils of witchcraft before."

"We'll soon know what to do with the devils amongst us. The signs will be made clear," the Reverend Haynes replied. "I tire of this travail."

"Ay, it's in God's and Marshal Gilbert's hands; to them we must trust."

When I returned to the keeping room, William was fast asleep. Even after Ann and Sybil scampered back into the house, Will lay quiet and his breathing was calm.

"Guess what game we were playing, Hester?" Sybil skipped around me in a circle.

"What game?" I asked.

"Ann made it up. Shhh." She stood on tiptoes and whispered in my ear.

"Oh forsooth, Sybil!" Ann laughed.

Sybil cupped her hand around my ear. "It's called the marriage game. It's what we wish for. Ann told me when she was ready, she would marry a man just like my father, the Reverend Whiting—or maybe your brother." She covered her mouth and giggled.

"Oh?" I looked askance at Ann. "Is that right? And what of your prospects, Sybil?"

"Why, when I grow up, I shall marry a man like Reverend Haynes. He'll protect me from all witches and devils." Sybil smiled brightly. "But don't tell, Hester. Promise?"

"Promise, Sybil." I also realized I would not and could not tell a living soul what I had overheard this day in the Reverend Whiting's study.

Chapter 10

"*H*ester, make certain you eat not," called my mother. "Remember, today is a fast day for the congregation. Not a morsel of food in you until we break the fast this afternoon."

Last Sabbath, a day of fasting and humiliation was decreed by the Reverend Stone. After Betty's untimely death and the escape of the Ayreses, he told the congregation that we must fast and pray for forgiveness. This was a time of sorrow.

The fast was to be held at Magistrate Wyllys's mansion. All churchgoers must be in attendance.

—

The meeting bell clanged right before noon. I watched from my window as townspeople gathered to make their way up the hill to the Wyllys mansion. I decided to walk alone. Grabbing my black shawl and psalm book, I proceeded past the row of elms and oaks that partially shaded the pathway. The stone path leading to the Wyllys mansion was already lined with people awaiting entrance to the grandest house in Hartford.

I spotted Ann waddling along toward the front of the crowd. She turned around and upon seeing me, lumbered toward me, out of breath.

"Hester let us pray together during the fast." She grabbed for my hand. "The Reverend Stone says we must humble ourselves to set things right in Hartford. This fast will relieve us of the bewitchment in this town."

"I will see you inside. First, I must greet the Wyllys family."

Ann returned to her place in line. The crowd was solemn; most people dressed in black. Many had their heads bowed low, a Bible in their hands.

The white door with its brass lion-head knocker stood wide open. Upon greeting the magistrate and his wife, I entered the hallway that led to the great room of the mansion.

The massive hearth-fire, surrounded by blue and white Dutch tiles, was ablaze. Thick logs burned on the brass andirons. Carved wood paneling and checkered wainscoting lined the walls. Candles flickered in silver sconces. Stools and chairs had been placed around the room. A grand table board with a Bible on it stood in the center. Magistrate Wyllys fluttered around the table, and placed the hourglass upon it. Finally, he took his seat in the high back chair at the table's head.

I saw my family come through the door, followed by the Reverend Whiting, Reverend Haynes, and the Reverend Stone who was hunched over and using a cane. Someone spoke up that Marshal Gilbert was out riding in pursuit of the Ayreses. Rumor had it they were hiding close to the Rhode Island border.

When everyone was seated, Reverend Stone stood up and raised his arms to the congregation.

"Welcome. We thank God for the generosity of Magistrate Wyllys, who out of kindness has let us have use of his home for our fast day. We are filled with sorrow and pain over the loss of Betty

Kelly, a young girl who was bewitched unto death. Let us bow our heads in prayer."

I heard a cry and glanced at Betty's father and mother sobbing near the fire. Ann had removed a handkerchief and was dabbing her eyes. Feeling distraught, all I could do was study the floor-boards and hope the fast was over soon.

The Reverend Stone continued. "The accused have escaped. But let it be known, no one can escape the wrath of God." He pounded a gnarled fist against the table.

"If there be those who dabble in the Devil's ways, and those that have familiarity with Satan, they shall be found out. We will not abide heathens in Hartford. Neither shall we abide witches. For this we pray."

We all bowed our heads in silence.

Suddenly, there came a loud rap at the door. Mrs. Wyllys silently arose to answer the knocking. Who would arrive so late for the fast? She opened the door with a quiet grace.

In stormed the acting Governor, Captain John Mason, the hero of the Pequot War. He was flanked by two militiamen. Just a few years back, he and Magistrate Wyllys had been sent to Saybrook to examine a couple on account of witchcraft. They were both found guilty.

Wearing thigh-high leather boots, Captain Mason stomped over to the table board and stood surveying the room. A red feath-er sprang from the side of a wide-brimmed hat. His long, graying hair hung to his shoulders. His saber glinted from the scabbard he had hitched to his hip. He held his musket close to his side. A small but deep scar was etched along one of his cheeks. His piercing eyes continued to bear down on the crowd.

Reverend Stone's face became red and flustered. "Welcome, Captain Mason. We are honored for your presence at today's fast.

We pray for God's intervention that our town will be cleansed of the scourge of witchcraft." He coughed and mumbled a few words under his breath.

Captain Mason continued to turn round and stare at every person. He seemed to be doing a roll call, noting who was present and who was not. His black eyes found mine, and I quickly looked down at the sanded floorboards once again.

"Thank you, Reverend Stone," the captain said at last. "It is an honor to be amongst good, God-fearing folk. I will take my place amongst the people." He removed his hat and then glanced about for a seat in the crowded room.

Magistrate Wyllys rose and gestured. "Please, Governor, Your Honor, Captain Mason, kindly take my chair at the table," he offered. "I shall sit on the settle near the fire." Captain Mason nodded and proceeded to the high backed chair while the magistrate moved to the settle.

The praying began in earnest. The Reverend Stone droned on with sermons in between the prayers. My stomach began to rumble. All I could think of was the fresh bread and broth that would be served after the fast was broken.

The fast continued for three hours. I noticed many people slumped over their stools, eyes shut. The tithing man came round to wake them up, poking them with his tickle stick. No one was allowed to sleep. Children became restless, tugging at their mothers' sleeves, whining for some food.

I watched Ann sitting on a stool near me, eyes closed and mumbling some prayers. All was quiet. Suddenly she stood up.

"What is it, girl?" Captain Mason asked.

Ann clutched her stomach and bent over to the floor. She looked to be sick. Her cheeks were a pale white. She held her breath for a time. The three reverends rushed to Ann's side, asking if she needed to be removed for some air. I watched in alarm, wondering what was wrong with her.

Ann's father, sitting near the door, arose to aid his daughter as well.

"Wait!" shouted Captain Mason. "Let the girl be. The ministers will attend to her."

Ann still clenched her stomach and raised her heavy body.

All eyes were now upon Ann Cole. She stood stiff as a fencepost. Then it began. Ann swallowed, made a choking noise, started to shake and stared unblinking at what, I knew not. I wanted to leap up and take hold of my friend, but she was in the ministers' care.

Ann began mumbling in a voice I was unfamiliar with, low and guttural, like she was a-growling. The congregation waited on her words.

"They make mischief on me," she shrieked. "They wish to spoil me, to spoil my chances of marriage. They are my ruin—our ruin." The congregation let out a collective gasp.

Captain Mason strode toward the Reverend Whiting. "Minister, write what this young maid says. Write it all down for the record and leave nothing out."

Reverend Whiting was given a piece of parchment paper, ink, and quill. Then he began to record Ann's ravings.

Ann fell onto the floor with a thud, her body jerking with tremors. It was difficult to understand everything she said. Everyone pushed back in order to give her room and to gape at her. Reverend Stone peered down on Ann, now afflicted with twitches and spasms. Her guttural tones with growls and strange words continued. "Why, it sounds as if she speaks in Dutch," he said.

He and Captain Mason helped Ann to her feet. "She knows not the Dutch tongue. A spirit confounds her thinking," continued Reverend Stone, shaking his head.

"Who's causing your ruin, Ann?" asked Captain Mason. "Now is the time to tell," he ordered. "Speak."

Ann brought her hands to her forehead and covered her eyes. "Uhhh," she moaned. "Mother, help me!" She lifted her head and raised her arms to the ceiling. Everyone in the room waited in silence, to see what Ann would do next.

Ann then became still as night. She really did look like an addled mooncalf, all white and huddled in her rumpled skirt, shawl, and cap. The fire crackled and townspeople began to whisper. I started wiggling in my seat and remembered that night on the green. *Is Ann possessed again...like that full moon eve in January? What is she doing?*

Suddenly Ann grabbed at her throat and began cawing. The guttural croaks that sounded like a blackbird got louder.

"Rebecca Greensmith, she be the one," Ann spat out. "And her husband, Nathaniel."

Captain Mason came closer to Ann now.

"Your neighbors next door, Ann?" the Acting Governor asked. He looked around the room. "Where are they now?"

"We know not, Captain Mason," said Reverend Whiting. "They are no members of the church." Reverend Whiting scribbled the names down furiously.

"Who else?" Captain Mason marched round the four corners of the great room, his hand on his saber.

"Mary Sanford. And the Dutch woman, Judith Varlet. Goodwife Seager and James Wakely. These people wreak mischief on my soul." Ann crumpled to the floor in a heap of her linens again.

"On my *soul!*" she wailed again and again, pounding her hand to the floor.

A woman stood up from the circle of people crowding the room. Goodwife Elizabeth Seager, the only one of the accused was present at the fast, and her face was pinched and red.

"Why, this is nothing but hodgepodge, Captain Mason. The girl speaks lies. Perhaps *she* is afflicted by the Devil himself."

"Quiet, Goodwife Seager. We have asked naught of your opinion. It's best to remain silent." He paused and narrowed his eyes. "For your own sake, woman."

Ann, still lying prone on the floor, began to shake, tremble, and cry.

"They laugh at me—and tell me to run to my rock. They pinch girls in the nighttime. They dance and make merry." Ann began to sob. "They seek to spoil my good name. They afflict me and bring pain. And unto Betty—they cursed and poisoned her to death!"

Captain Mason scowled and turned to Reverend Stone.

"How doth she know this?" he asked.

The Reverend Stone shook his head. His brow wrinkled and he grimaced at Ann.

"I know not, but I think the Devil confounds her speech."

Captain Mason continued to pace. "We shall find out, rest assured, the cause of such a fit," he proclaimed

She runs to her rock.

The memory of that cold, full moon night months ago came back to my mind. Rebecca Greensmith chanting words round the fire. Judith Varlet with the bottle of sack, divining and wishing to know her future husband by staring into the flames. Elizabeth Seager passing round the candles and joining in the merrymaking. The horned man and the odd song that ended with a "ho, ho, ho."

I could think on this no more. My head was hurting, pounding with heavy beats. I stood up and watched Ann shaking on the floor.

"Ann, no!" I screamed. The white walls around the room began to spin. "No!"

My head pounded, stabbing with sharp pains. My legs felt light and my knees wobbled. The beamed ceiling looked about to fall on me. I tried to grab onto a stool, but it was too late. I felt myself drop hard to the floor.

Then, there was nothing but darkness.

Chapter 11

*I*t was nightfall when I woke alone in the loft. *How long have I been in my bed?* A single tallow candle burned in a sconce by the window. The flickering flame sent dancing shadows across the walls. The dried herbs hanging from the rafters rustled like raven feathers. The window, slightly ajar, allowed a May breeze to help wake me.

I was soaked in a cold sweat, my hair matted to the pillow. I reached to push some tangled strands from my face. My skin felt cool under the quilt. I took a deep breath. One thing I did know— my fever had broken.

I tiptoed to the stool by the window. The floorboards creaked and groaned. Leaning out the window, I inhaled breaths of air. Several candles were alight over at Ann's house. What had befallen Ann at the Wyllys Mansion—after I fainted?

I heard footsteps on the stairs to the loft, then a light rap. "Come in," I said with all my strength.

My mother gently nudged the door open. She carried a tray with a trencher steaming with what smelled like beef broth along with a brown roll and a mug of cider.

"God be praised." My mother watched me with care. "But what a sight you are, tangled hair and all skin and bones." She scurried to the table and placed the food in front of me. "Doctor Rossitier told us it would take a few days for you to revive. The fit you suffered through child…." She moved toward the basin of water in the corner. "Don't forget to wash yourself, Hester. You've been through a trial and you reek of illness."

"What happened to me, Mother? What happened to Ann?" I asked, picking up the spoon to sip the hot broth. "I can recall but little."

"Why, you suffered a fever." She looked into my eyes and felt my forehead. "You seem to have sweated this out. And you've been ranting in your sleep, Hester. 'Tis been a fitful time for you." My mother put her hand on my shoulder. "Eat now."

I paused and met her gaze. "But what of Ann? What else did she say in her rant?" I needed to know.

"Remember Hester," my mother spoke softly. "You had not eaten and we know how much sympathy you have for Ann. You were concerned for your friend. That's why you fainted."

My mother's brow furrowed and she placed her arm around my shoulder. She combed her fingers through my matted hair and kissed the top of my head.

"We shall talk in the morrow. Take your sustenance and read your nightly psalms. God chose to save you." She wiped her forehead with her apron, rubbed her hands together and moved toward the door.

"Mother, what of Ann—?"

But my mother closed the door and was gone.

—

I remembered the bundle that Tom had given me several days ago. I made my way to the bed. My back ached from tossing and twisting; I was bruised from the under-bed ropes holding the mattress in place. Even the soft down had not prevented the painful rope burns on my back. Still, I felt nourished from the broth and bread. I reached in between ropes and the mattress. Yes, the packet was still there.

Carefully, I pulled out the bundle again and held it to the candlelight. I wanted to leaf through the collection of ballads. Someone had taken time to bind the ballads together. The book had a faded blue cover with a woodcut design branded on the front. Its dark grooves etched out a market scene in the country with a milkmaid and a cow.

I perused several more woodcuts and the list of many old ballads from England. One of them caught my eye, and I immediately turned to the page. The title of the ballad was "The Mad, Merry Pranks of Robin Goodfellow." It had a date of 1628 with no author's name recorded. I began to read the ballad.

Then I came to a stanza that gave me pause. Where had I heard this before? I read and reread the lines.

When lads and lasses merry be/with sack possets and banquets fine
Unseen of all company/I eat their cakes and sip their wine'
And to make sport/I pout and snort
And out the candles I do blow

The maids I kiss/They shriek, "Who's this?"
I answer naught but ho, ho, ho!

Then I remembered.

This was the ballad that Rebecca Greensmith and the others had recited around the fire that winter's night. The sack posset, the candles, the cakes. Who was this Robin Goodfellow?

I continued to read the stanzas in the ballad and another made me stop and wonder.

When house or hearth doth dirty lie
I pinch the maid there black and blue
And from the bed, the bed clothes I pull off
And lay them naked to view
Twixt sleep and wake
I do them take
And on the key-cold floor them throw
If out they cry, then forth I fly
And loudly laugh I,
Ho, ho, ho!

I stared at the woodcut next to the ballad. In the center was a man with horns and cloven feet. Around him people danced in a circle. He had a candle burning atop his head and held torches in each hand. *Is Robin Goodfellow another name for the Devil?*

I shut the book and could read no more. I hid the ballads with the other books, for no one must find them. I would talk to Tom about this Robin Goodfellow; perhaps he knew of him? I had to find out.

Chapter 12

The sound of horses approached the house. I watched out the open door as the Horse Battalion trotted by, heading to the South Green, led by Captain John Mason on his black steed, alongside Marshal Gilbert. The Captain shouted loud orders to the long line of militiamen. Horns blared and a steady drumbeat announced that training day, otherwise known as Muster Day, was soon to begin.

Muster days and Election Day were holidays for townspeople. Muster days happened six times a year, the autumn training day being the grandest of all. Today was the late, spring muster, and townspeople were preparing for the competitions and then the feast afterwards. Chores were excused for the day.

Food was a favorite part of Muster Day. Tents set up with pies, cakes, bread and butter, fresh ham; all were for barter and sale. Jeremy Adams promised free rum and mead at the tavern for the artillery and horse competition winners.

I loved admiring the embroidery and needlework that the goodwives of Hartford worked on throughout the long winter. I especially enjoyed watching the young men display their talents as militiamen. How handsome and brave they were!

"Hester, are you ready?" my mother asked. She pulled the training cake from the bake oven. The smell of gingerbread mingled with cinnamon spice filled the room.

"Ay." I straightened my freshly washed bonnet and lavender-scented clothes, and tucked strands of curled hair into my cap. Walking past the pewter-ware, I glanced into a shiny surface to see my face, pale as the spring sunshine. I pinched my cheeks, hoping for a brighter bloom.

"You look lovely in your violet shawl, Hester. 'Tis becoming with the yellow of your hair and hazel eyes. But 'tis vain to stare at yourself so close."

My brother Stephen had stepped into the room, dashing in his brown leather jerkin and dark blue doublet. He wore his militia jacket, breeches, and leather boots. I noticed his musket was polished and ready to be fired. It gleamed in the thin sunlight.

Stephen grabbed for his hat. "Watch for me on the green." He paused and sniffed. "Ah, the smell of Mother's training cake." He smiled over at her. "Your training cake will win the top prize today, Mother. And I will win first prize in the drills." He puffed his chest out and patted his stomach.

Before Mother could reply, Stephen was out the door to join the procession. I listened to the drumbeat and the clanging of bells.

"Mother, may I follow the parade to the South Green as well?" I asked as I headed to the door.

"Be careful, Hester," my mother said, wrapping the cooled cake in a cloth. "Trouble has been following you of late. I shall see you on the green."

"Given my chance, I would make a mischief on the marshal. Ann Cole too."

I heard the Dutch accent, turned around, and saw Judith Varlet, Mary Sanford, Goody Seager and Rebecca Greensmith milling around an oak tree near one of the tents. I noticed they were glaring at Marshal Gilbert. eyeing him with dark, mean stares.

"Make a noise," prayed the Reverend Stone. "That the noise of thine enemies be quelled, be they amongst us or near us. Let them hear us and let them be afraid." Gunshots rang out in unison. Standards were raised and salutes fired off into the air. The roll call was taken as each man answered "Ay" when his name was announced.

Marshal Gilbert, appointed Master of Troops of the Horses, began conducting the military drills with precision. Back and forth the horses trotted, as Judith and the others glowered with rage. Inventory of gunpowder and ammunition was counted. Shots fired in the air again and again. Swordplay began. Several pairs of men demonstrated their moves and thrusts.

Bunches of townspeople gathered around now to watch the displays on the Green. I turned around again to glance back at the old oak. Judith was still sitting there. She raised her arm up this time and pointed a long finger at me. *What did this mean?*

———

I searched the South Green for Ann. Usually she attended Muster Day, flitting about the militiamen and batting her eyes at them. I expected her to be watching the young men perform their drills and then eating her favorite food, muster cake.

Ann's father, a cooper by trade, was giving a barrel- making demonstration near the blacksmith's tent. He was pounding and stretching staves and hoops to hold a hogshead barrel in place. Several young boys began rolling discarded hoops onto the dirt path with sticks; they wanted to see who could keep them up the longest before they fell to the ground.

"Goodman Cole, I'm looking for Ann. Is she about?" I asked him.

Ann's father set his mallet on the grass and wiped his forehead. He looked up at me from his stool and blocked the bright sunlight with his hands over his eyes. He seemed happy to see me.

"Hello, Hester. Ann is still not well. She's taken to her bed."

"Oh, I'm sorry to hear this," I replied. My head started to feel light.

"If you care to visit her up at the house, I'm sure she'd welcome your company." His face was ruddy and filled with lines, his eyes red and strained. "Go on up and say hello." He gave me a tender smile. "God knows you girls have been through your trials lately."

I nodded and looked to the ground. As if he were reading my thoughts, he said, "Yes, I'll tell your mother where you are when I see her on the Green. Don't fret about it."

———

"Ann, you are pale."

Ann lay in her bed motionless, but the blue quilt covering her rose up and down with an evenness of breath. I waited for her response. Nothing. But then she opened one eye and it glared sharp and strong upon me. She shut it and moved her head to the side.

I shook her by the shoulders. She turned her head and opened her eyes.

"I dreamt of her again, Hester," she said calmly.

I brushed my skirt to the side and sat down by the bed. "Who, Ann?" I asked.

"My mother, of course. She appears in my visions and dreams." Ann breathed a heavy sigh. "She has told me about these people. That's how I know."

"What people, Ann?"

Ann's eyebrows arched and she began blinking her eyes. "Of all people, Hester, you should know."

I paused. "You mean the likes of Rebecca Greensmith, Judy Varlet, Goody Seager, and the others?"

Ann rubbed her eyes, stretched, and pulled back the blue quilt cover. "Ay, Hester, you saw it for yourself, the night on South Green."

"Will you be going to Muster Day? It's your favorite holiday."

Ann shook her head. "Mother would never permit me to go." She rose from the bed. "At least not in my present state. Besides, these witches want to ruin my chances for marriage. Mother told me that again—in a dream last night." She reached for her skirt and cap and began dressing.

"Perhaps," I said, "our neighbors wanted naught but to frolic with Robin Goodfellow and sing his ballad from the Old Country. Perhaps they are papists or pagans who believe in the old ways." I paused and stared straight at her. "What say you to this?"

"Robin Goodfellow?" Ann asked. "Who is this Robin? I know not Robin." She pulled on her cap and tucked in her curls. "Where did you hear this name? Is this Robin the Devil himself then?"

Fumbling with my hands, I stated that many people might think that this Robin Goodfellow was indeed the Devil.

"Where did you come across Robin Goodfellow?"

I felt my face flush. "Why Tom gifted me with some books. One is a book of ballads. One of the ballads is about this Robin."

Ann wrinkled her nose and a frown appeared on her lips.

"Tom? You mean the peddler's son? So, he's sweet on you, Hester, is that it? Are you sweet on him? Does this mean you are courting?"

Ann walked to the window facing the South Green. A robin alighted on a tree branch and his head bobbed up and down.

"He's not one of us. His father is a peddler." She spun around to glare at me. "Your father would never approve, Hester. Those books he gave you—they are nothing but lies."

Was she jealous of my friendship with Tom? I knew then that I had shared with Ann far too much. In her mind, the Devil was in Hartford, and those who had merry meetings on the South Green were witches.

I wished Ann a speedy recovery and left her house.

Chapter 13

By the time I left Ann's house, people were making their way to the tavern. Clouds had settled low in the sky, and a thin mist filled the air. A chill came upon me as I pulled my shawl tight around my shoulders. Listening to the bang of drums and dim laughter from the green, I smelled roasted meat and smoke from wood fires. Muster Day was almost over.

Hoo-Hoo Whooo! The sound, like the cry of an owl or a dove, came from somewhere over the hill near the Varlet's house. I pulled back my cap to tuck my hair in and straightened out my skirts. *Hoo-Hoo!*

Tom appeared from behind a gnarled oak tree on the hill. He stepped out from the mist. I could see he wore his black coat and a thin, faded blue shirt underneath. His black, wide-brimmed hat hung over his eyes. Dark curls dangled round his shoulders.

He lifted his hat as if to wish me a good afternoon and pushed it back on his head. He motioned his hand out toward me. Then he vanished behind the tree, disappearing from sight. *Is my mind playing tricks on me?*

I glanced both ways up and down the road. Several militiamen, chests puffed like barrels, boasted about their Muster medals. I cast my eyes downward and quickly walked up the hill. Reverend Whiting, Reverend Haynes, and Reverend Stone stood like three crows, huddled in the middle of the moving crowd.

"Ay, that Judith Varlet was cursing our good marshal again today," I heard the Reverend Stone say. "Imagine, on God's Muster Day. She truly is the devil's strumpet." Reverends Whiting and Haynes nodded their heads in bowed consent.

"No good will come of this," murmured Reverend Whiting. "And to think I live next door to this brazen woman."

So, Dutch Judy freely ranted about her hatred for the marshal, far more than I was privy to hear on the South Green. Everyone in Hartford knew the Varlets hated the marshal. Most knew that the marshal hated the Varlets even more—for his warehouse was at stake down by the Great River. Lifting my skirts, I pushed past the Whiting family and other small groups of townspeople finished with Muster Day.

———

Tom appeared from behind the tree. He grinned at me and took a bow. "M'lady, a greeting to you this fine afternoon. It looks to be a promising evening as well." He smiled. "But it all depends, doesn't it?" He cocked his head and hat toward me and winked.

"Depends on what?" I asked, breathless from the climb up the hill.

"Whether you'd join me this fine evening."

I gaped at him open-mouthed. "You mean to Jeremy Adams' Tavern for a meal? With the rest of the townspeople?" I paused. "My father will surely be there."

"Then I shall talk to him at the tavern about my intention to walk with you to the South Meadows." He let out a low chuckle. "But of course not, Hester. I'm inviting you for a walk down to the meadows. I have some trading to do with the Indians before Pa and I take leave in a few days' time."

I could see the small sack bulging with candlestick holders and perhaps some pewter-ware he had left near the tree.

"Besides, it's a perfect time to walk and talk with you." Tom stopped suddenly. "Why didn't I see you down at Muster Day? Pa and I made a few trades and even earned a few pine shillings down on the green. We'll take the money these days."

"You were looking for me?" My cheeks warmed as I smoothed down my collar and skirt. I straightened up and looked him square in the eyes. "I was visiting Ann, who was ailing in her bed. But I was down at the green for many minutes before my visit."

"Well, were you looking for me?" he said.

I put my hands on my hips. "Are you trying to court me, Tom?" I boldly asked.

"You could say that." Laughing, he reached out the crook of his arm to me. "Well, what say you?"

I tucked my arm around his.

"Ay, a walk will refresh my spirit," I said.

We followed the path behind the Varlet homestead. Caspar was in the garden, smoking his pipe in one hand and holding a spyglass in the other. He sat on a wooden bench near the laurel bushes, looking out toward the Great River's bend.

A felled log served as the perfect place for us to watch the activity along the Great River. A few ships sailed this late afternoon, departing from the warehouses and headed south, steering clear of the Dutchman's Island, a sand bar that often left boats stranded. Natives paddled canoes about in wide circles in search of fish. The

South Meadows had a few Indian huts scattered about; thin smoke curled from the rounded wigwams.

I'm curious about something," Tom said as he sat beside me. "What say you about Ann and her witchcraft ravings? I heard about her fits at the Wyllys mansion." He looked concerned. "I heard thee had a fainting spell also."

"I had naught to eat and dizzied myself."

"Know you about these dangerous accusations?

I looked down at my hands. "Ay, I was at the fast when Ann accused the Greensmiths, Judith Varlet, and Goody Seager of being witches. 'Tis all true. I was shocked to see my friend carrying on in such a manner."

"Are you well now?"

"I am better. The likes of witches in this town—something seems amiss."

The sun appeared for a brief moment, bursting through the clouds. Its light painted streaks of shadows on the oak trees. And then it was gone again.

I tried to change the subject. "Many thanks for the gifts, Tom. I love them all."

He drew closer to me. "Did you read the *Sonnets* by Shakespeare? What of the ballads?"

I told him I cherished all the gifts and his note. Tom knew I loved books and that they brought me joy and a connection to other lands. Now I had a question for him. I could not restrain myself.

"But who is this Robin Goodfellow? I read his ballad. Have you heard of him? Is he—a devil?"

Tom paused, grinned, and slapped his leg hard. He seemed to find my questions amusing.

"Why, he's a part of English folklore and folktales. You didn't know that cheeky Robin would pinch the maidens if they didn't clean their room and place fresh clothing out for the morrow? Granny Flagg told me the tales of Robin years ago. She told me that young maids would leave milk out for him, and in return he'd do their spinning. Why would you think him the Devil, Hester?" He shook his head. "A fanciful hobgoblin, that is all."

I sat in the quiet of the late afternoon regarding blades of grass. "I know not. I have a feeling of dread."

"And what of you? Know thee the devil?" He moved his arm close to me.

"I know not any devil, lest of course 'tis you."

He smiled and put his arm around me. "Ay, what would the devil want with me Hester? Or you? I believe in no such Devil. I am but a peddler's son getting on in the world. Since Granny and Ma died, Pa and I have traveled the trails and survived." His eyes took in the sights of the river. "But..." he paused, "I have plans. Someday, I shall have my own warehouse overlooking Boston Harbor, a warehouse filled with books and other goods. Books will no longer be for the highborn and ministers only."

I smiled. "I'm neither highborn nor a minister's daughter. But I can certainly read and I love to read. Dame school taught me that."

"And they taught you well. This makes me care all the deeper for you. I admire a maid who can think for herself."

I felt the sun begin to warm my back.

Tom leaned closer. "So what are your plans?"

I studied my shoes and watched ants scurry round the dirt.

"Plans? I know not. I think my family and the townspeople want me to be Mistress of the Dame School. But my life is in the hands of the Lord."

"Are you happy here?"

"I know nothing else. I believe I am as happy as I can be for one who will be eighteen soon. I know no other life."

"'Tis true what you say. But there are other worlds out there—I would know. In fact, Pa and I will be felling trees this summer to help clear the Bay Path. It will make for easier trips in the future."

"What do I know about the world, Tom?" Then I muttered under my breath, " I'm sure you have a comely maid in Boston waiting for you."

"So that's what you think," Tom burst out. "Think what you may, but I have ideas and we shall see."

A loud bell began to clang from Meetinghouse Square. Now what was happening?

We stood up and watched people running toward Meetinghouse Square.

Tom yelled out, "What news have we?" to a passerby.

"There's news of the charter. A letter has arrived, and the talk is that Governor Winthrop has secured a charter for the Connecticut Colony."

"Has the Governor returned?" I asked with hope in my heart. I knew when Governor Winthrop did come home he would straighten out the problems plaguing our town.

"No sign of the governor. Rumor has it he'll be home next spring."

I sighed. So, until then, Captain John Mason would continue to be our governor and Marshal Gilbert would remain in charge.

Tom and I began to walk toward the square.

"I wish you didn't have to leave," I told him.

Tom halted and took my hand. His long, thin fingers curled around mine. "When I return, before Autumn Muster, do I have your permission to speak with your father?"

"Speak to my father?"

"Ay, that I may receive his permission to formally court you," he said boldly.

The bell continued to clang—or was it my heart?

Chapter 14

June 1662

Weeks passed and now it was almost summer. Tom and his father left soon after the announcement of the charter. I wondered about what he said. Would he return before the Autumn Muster as he promised?

Connecticut now had its own charter. We no longer had to abide England's laws so stringently, and New Haven was now officially a part of the colony.

This was all well and good. But I saw no difference in the daily life of Hartford. Our good Governor Winthrop would not return to us until the spring of next year. He was traveling about the Continent dining with royalty. Until then, Captain John Mason would remain our Acting Governor.

———

The sun beat down hot and dry. I had aired out some bedclothes and was sweeping dust from the corners around the hearth. Father came out from the kitchen mumbling to himself.

"What troubles thee, Father? Did thou not sleep well?" I sensed his ill humor for I knew my father's moods well.

"Is there enough porridge left for my breakfast?" he demanded. "Where's the fresh bread your mother baked yesterday?" He stormed around banging his feet on the floorboards.

"Father, I am clearing up dust and ashes. Please sit down." I scurried to the hearth and ladled him some porridge, then cut a slice of bread warming in the side oven.

"Where's your mother?" he asked.

"She's out back washing. I'll help her after my chores are done inside. 'Tis a fine drying day for laundry."

Father ripped off a chunk of bread and stuffed it into his mouth.

"Tell your mother I'd like to speak with her." I paused to watch his face. "Now."

I ran out the back door and smelled the pungent odor of lye bubbling from the washing tub. I called for mother to come into the house.

"Can this not wait, Hester?" she said. "I am busy with laundry."

"Father must see you now, Mother. Something is troubling him this morning."

She wiped her brow and her hands on the apron. We walked together through the back door.

Father beckoned Mother to the table board.

"Sit down, Frances. I have news that I am much troubled by. It seems that the marshal has a new witness of late, claiming that the Greensmiths, Judith Varlet and certain others are still holding what they call a witches' Sabbath. The witness says that they met full moon last behind the Varlet homestead near the orchard. How this could be, I know not."

My breath seemed to stop. I awaited his next words.

"No, Thomas, it can't be," my mother said. "The night watchman has been walking the roads all spring. All's been quiet. So I have thought."

My father slammed his fist on the table. "Quiet, wife!" We remained silent while my father continued. "So you've thought—so we have thought," he murmured. "Regardless, Frances, mark my words." He leaned toward her. "It will be days to the gallows, I say. Days to the gallows."

He swallowed his bread and washed it down with several gulps from his tankard.

"I have a bad feeling over all this, wife."

"But what can we do, Thomas? All we can do is pray," mother said.

I approached my father and stood by his side.

"What mean you—days to the gallows, Father?" I whispered.

He turned and looked me right in the eyes. "Hester, it's just what I say. The marshal is hard bent to serve justice. Those in our town—those heathen who practice witchcraft—the marshal is demanding justice. God will not allow witchcraft in Hartford. Sinners must pay." He paused for a moment and exhaled a long breath. "Perhaps with their lives."

I could not speak as father smacked his lips together. "A hanging or two might be in order," he added. "But my heart is torn asunder by this news. These strangers and their ilk ought to take leave of our godly town. Before it's too late."

He began to eat his porridge, then brandished his spoon in the air. "And mind to your own business, Hester. We need no trouble to come knocking on our doorstep."

—

We need no trouble to come knocking on our doorstep. What could Father possibly mean?

I finished my chores and left out the front door. Ann was in her front yard clearing weeds from her garden. Daisies and lilies clustered around the Cole house. I walked across the road and greeted my friend.

"How now, Ann?" I asked. "'Tis a hot day to be tending to your garden."

Ann stood up and pushed her cap back, shaking off the dirt on her apron.

"I am fine, Hester. Just fine." She had a scowl on her face. "Have you heard from Tom yet?"

"What?"

"You know, Tom the peddler's son. He and his father haven't been seen in some time." She began to yank some stray weeds. Sweat dripped from her forehead. "You know you could do much better, of course. He's probably in Boston, spending time with a merchant's daughter." She laughed under her breath. "I thought a Reverend's son would be more to your liking. Or James Ensign. We all know he's keen on you." She began to mutter under her breath.

I stood there, feeling hurt and upset. "What business is this to you? I thought we were friends and you are cruel in your words and tone." I shook my head. "'Tis wrong, Ann, what you do and say."

"Hester, I have not forgotten Betty. I shall never forget Betty." She paused and then tossed weeds into the bucket beside her. "But you seem to have forgotten Betty because you are love-struck. You know as well as I—that Betty was bewitched by that she-devil Ayres. You know as well as I that they bewitched poor Betty until she lay dead. With bruises from being pinched by Goodwife Ayres and the Devil himself."

She stood up, brushed her skirts down and clamped her hands on her wide hips.

"Good riddance to Goodwife Ayres and her thieving husband. She was one of Satan's whores. And the rest of these folks? Why they are nothing but tools that the Devil uses to do mischief. You would know. You were there that night."

I gasped and stood up straight, trying to make myself seem larger. "There that night? Yes. On account of your strange rants and speaking about your mother on the full moon. Can't you see, Ann?" I clenched my fists and held my breath.

"See what?" Ann smirked, looking across the road, and then toward the Varlet homestead. She turned and watched me. Her eyes were sharp as thorns. "I have seen enough and know plenty more, Hester. You forget too much because that peddler's son has filled your mind and your heart with nonsense."

I faced her down. "I've heard enough. I thought we were friends. It's obvious you are jealous of my friendship with Tom. So there."

I swung my skirts around and prepared to cross back toward my house. My mother was waiting for me to bring some laundry down to the Little River to rinse. But before this, I pulled my Book of Psalms from my pocket and opened it for guidance. Psalm 94 verse 16 was there in front of me. "Who will rise up with me against the wicked?"

I closed the book and shook my head. I knew not who the wicked were and who was innocent anymore.

"Make sure you stay on the right side of the road, Hester," Ann called to me. "And the right side of the law. I know I am." She laughed aloud and continued to mumble to herself.

—

I took up the heavy basket of soapy laundry and headed toward the Little River. Elder was in blossom and weeping willows hung over the steep banks. Their yellow-green reflections brightened up the waters. They also brightened my mood this hot June afternoon.

I crossed the plank-bridge, and followed the path that descended to the river. I began rinsing the potash and lye from the clothes, removed my shoes, and lifted my skirt to cool off my feet.

Then I heard that singsong, lilting voice. It was Judith Varlet with her sisters, Maria and Sarah. Maria, a few years older than Judith, was also a dark haired beauty. She had already been married twice. Her first husband, Johannes, had been killed in 1655 in an Indian massacre when the family lived in New Netherlands.

Maria was left a widow with a small baby, also named Judith. Little Judith was learning both English and Dutch.

Sarah, the Varlet's youngest daughter was just a few years younger than myself. She had been with Maria the day of the Indian massacre. She suffered serious head wounds from an attempted scalping. Now, the side of her head was dented and her forehead stretched up to her skull, so she never seemed to look at you straight on. One of her eyes wandered. Sarah always wore brightly colored scarves under her cap to hide the scars.

"Why, if it isn't Hester." Judith had separated from her sisters.

I continued rinsing out clothing in the cool running water. "Why Mistress Varlet. You startled me."

"Really? Tell me, Hester, do you think me still a witch? Like your silly friend Ann believes?"

I shook my head. "I know not. I am tending to my own business, and that's washing clothes."

Judith came closer to me, her dark blue eyes staring me up and down. "And I am doing the same. But I am no witch, Hester. That I do know."

I shrugged. "Ay, then why would you mingle with the likes of Goody Greensmith?"

Dutch Judy became very quiet. "Why? Why not? I tire of this town, the laws, the rules, so much drudgery. I crave life and I wish to return to New Netherlands, but alas, I must remain with my family here. These were the orders from Governor Stuyvesant. When we were banished."

"But you went to the green so you could see your future husband's face in the fire." I continued dunking the clothes in and out of the river.

"So I did, but he's certainly not in Hartford. And if I indulged in divination, this in my mind does not make me a witch." Judith laughed aloud and shook her head.

I agreed, but I felt confused. "Why did you point at me on Muster Day? Down on the green?"

"I pointed toward you because you saw me on the green that eve, now didn't you? You, not just your friend Ann, may think we are all witches."

Maria and Sarah began to call Judy. The baby was crying and they needed her help. Judith started to walk toward her sisters but turned around again.

"Remember, Hester, I am not a witch."

Can this be true, I thought?

Chapter 15

$\mathcal{T}$he next day, after my chores were finished, I decided to take an early morning rove. I walked to the forge. Perhaps a word with my brother Stephen or James would set my mood right. I made sure to sneak some biscuits from the cupboard. The sun shed thin piercing rays that burned bright and seemed to announce that today would be hot and dry. After all, it was mid-June; summer would soon be upon us.

I heard the bang of hammers, the clack of tongs, and the hiss of bellows firing up the hearth. James and my brother worked all morning when it was this hot so they could take an afternoon rest. Then they'd work late into the night.

Peeping my head around the open stalls, I shouted a good morrow over the din. Both James and Stephen wore their blacksmith aprons and had their heads down pounding the anvil with their hammers.

"Hester, a good morrow to you." Stephen wiped his brow. "What have you brought us this morn?"

James lifted up his head. I removed the biscuits from my pocket. "Here you are, something for your break-fast. Can you take a rest now?"

I heard some tittering coming from a corner of the forge. The two Greensmith girls, Elsbeth and Sarah sat on stools.

"I'm surprised to see you here in this smoky forge so early," I said.

"James is fixing some tools for our stepfather," said Sarah. "We like to watch the blacksmiths at work." I understood. James with his brawny muscles and my brother's wit, charm, and handsome ways would intrigue any maid in Hartford.

Elsbeth spoke now. "We needed to get clear of our house for a time. There is grim news."

"Grim news? What be that?" A sinking heaviness entered my stomach.

James brushed off soot and coal from his apron and shook his head. "There is nothing I have to say—nothing, but that I am disgusted. 'Tis not right, I say."

"What happened James? Stephen?" I asked.

"Go see for yourself, Hester. Up on Gallows Hill. Your friend Ann was here earlier, sweet talking your brother and giving us the news," James said with disgust in his voice. "'Tis not safe to speak of it here. One never knows who be listening."

I ran out of the forge, headed down the road past the South Green and beyond the Ox Pasture. Climbing the steep slope to the rocky ridge that overlooked vast stretches of land to the west, I searched about for a sign. There was none with the exception of the black birds who roosted in the trees each night on the ridge. They circled around the branches, cawing and croaking with loud determination.

When I arrived at the twisted elm tree, the first thing I saw were the shoes, dangling like puppet strings. My eyes turned slowly upward to see the twisted legs, the skirt and bodice and then the full body swinging, half shrouded in the morning shadows. The blackbirds aroused from their nests, flew in fierce circles around the tree—as if they guarded the body. I approached the body hanging by the noose. The head drooped down from the tightened rope. The hands folded together in a tight knot. My stomach heaved.

I came closer and recognized the grimaced face to be Mary Sanford. Pretty Mary who, with her husband Andrew, attended that winter merry meet. Mary Sanford, friend of the Ayreses and Goody Seager. A sign was pinned on her neckerchief—Hanged As A Witch.

Father was right. It was but days to the gallows.

When I was a child, my father shared with me stories of the first witches in Connecticut. In 1647, after the Reverend Hooker had died of a fever, Alyce Young of Windsor was hanged as a witch. She was the first person in the colonies to be hanged for witchcraft. More hangings followed over the years. But I never thought I'd see this for myself.

Standing on Gallows Hill, I felt stuck to the ground. *How could this be happening?*

Then I heard a low growl behind me. There was Titus, the marshal's dog. He approached the lifeless body, circled the tree, sniffed and placed himself like a guardian under the corpse.

"Get away from there, Hester. You've seen what you need to see." Marshal Gilbert limped up the hill. "Now, get home!" Titus began to tug on the dead woman's legs, trying to yank the body down. "Stop that Titus! You guard this body." The dog whimpered and returned to his stance.

I turned and fled down the hill until I came to the Ox Pasture.

Ann was amongst the cows playing her silly game, spinning and laughing aloud. I opened the gate, shooed away the curious bovines and ran to her.

"Ann, I just came from Gallows Hill. Did you know Mary Sanford was hanged?"

Ann rushed to me and placed her hands on my shoulders shaking me. "I won Hester. I won, don't you see?" she shouted. Then she pointed to the Greensmith house. "And someday I shall live in that house with my husband. And own all twenty acres of their land. What thinks you of that?" She brought her face close to mine so I could feel her breath. She smelled like fresh grass and cow.

"You won? A blinking contest with a cow?" I shook my head and tried to keep my composure.

"Ay. I watched, waited and used my powers and the stupid cow blinked first. Ha! I won. I won!" She spun her large frame around and around until she flopped down to the grass.

"So, you won Ann. Who are the losers? Just a cow or two?"

Ann laughed in a torrent of hysterics. *What is so humorous?* Then she frowned. "I care not for the losers, Hester. Mayhap you are one of them. All I care about is that I am winning. The righteous shall win!"

I ran back home and barged through the door out of breath. My father sat near the hearth watching the flames. "Why was no one aware of the hanging, father?" I asked him. "You told me hangings in Hartford were a spectacle attended by the townspeople."

Father remained silent and would not look at me. "Why did no one hear about Mary Sanford?" I asked again.

Finally, father answered my question. "This is what the authorities deemed proper. It is God's Will and Providence that this should happen so." Father paused then he shook a finger at me. "'Tis not proper for a godly maid such as thyself to ask such questions. Trust God, trust Marshal Gilbert, and the Reverend Stone. They follow God's precepts."

"But father, what did Mary Sanford do that was any worse than the likes of Rebecca Greensmith, Judith Varlet, and Goody Seager?" I shook my head. "I understand this naught a bit."

"Ay, daughter, it is not for you to understand. God, as you know, works in mysterious ways. It was His Will that sent Mary to the gallows."

"But what of her husband Andrew?" I asked. I remembered that Andrew, along with Mary was on the South Green the night of the Merry Meet.

"Mary Sanford was found guilty and hanged for the crime of witchcraft by the authorities. Her husband Andrew was acquitted of all charges," father said. He sighed and continued, "Andrew is no longer in Hartford. He has removed to the safety of Milford, his hometown down by the seashore."

"Because Captain Mason and Marshal Gilbert have deemed it such?" I shouted.

"Hester, this is a message to the others to take heed. Now, that is all." When my father said, "that is all", it meant our discussion on a matter had ended. But many more questions lingered in my mind. Mayhap the authorities *were* sending a message to the others. Beware for you might be next.

Why Mary? Yes, she had been dancing on the South Green that winter night. Yes, she and her husband made mischief with the likes of Rebecca Greensmith. But Mary's husband Andrew was safe in Milford, while Mary's lifeless body swung on the hanging tree at Gallows Hill.

I bounded up the stairs to the loft, retrieved the Almanac and recorded on the date under June 13th, "Mary Sanford hanged as a witch."

Chapter 16

———————————————

August 1662

*A*nn was right about one thing. I hadn't heard from Tom. My eighteenth birthday had come and gone with no word from him. I recorded each passing day he was gone in the almanac. It had been months now since I'd seen him.

Ann had another fit last week. This time she raved at meeting during Reverend Stone's sermon. In front of the congregation, she railed against the witches, screeching out the names of the Greensmiths, Judith Varlet, and Goody Seager—again. Even young girls like Sybil Whiting were sore afflicted; screaming, crying out and imitating Ann's every move.

I sat in my family pew, watching in silent horror as my friend, or one who once was my friend, fell to the floor and writhed in fits of torment.

The Reverend Stone decreed another Fast Day at the Wyllys Mansion in two days time.

—

On the appointed day, my mother removed to the fast early morning to help Mrs. Wyllys set up the great room. I complained to my father that I had too many chores to finish. And I had my woman's monthly; not eating all day would make me weak. I needed my strength for work and I could pray myself. Somehow, I was allowed to remain at home with my father, who rarely attended the Fasts or Days of Thanksgiving. He seemed convinced I needed my rest.

The morning sweeping was almost complete when there came a knock on the door.

"Get the door Hester," my father commanded.

I scurried to the door and opened it. There stood Goody Seager's daughter, Eliza, with a cloth-covered dish in her hands. Eliza was but a few years younger than me. Her large eyes, the color of a robin's egg looked up at me. Her turned up nose was twitching. She had thick, auburn hair just like her mother.

"A good morrow to you, Eliza. What brings you here?"

Eliza's lips quivered before she spoke. "My mother would like your family to receive this gift." I looked down at the cloth-covered dish.

"Thank you, Eliza." I sniffed. "This smells good. What is it?" I spoke politely because the Seagers were our neighbors. Although townspeople might call Goody Seager a witch, her husband, older than her by many years, was a well-respected man. Goody Seager's father, John Moody, was a founder of Hartford. When he died, he left her some money, making her a woman of means.

"It's a dish of freshly cooked parsnips. Please accept our gift."

I heard my father's heavy footsteps approaching the door. He stood behind me, staring down the frightened girl.

"What is this now?" he asked. "What have we here? Why aren't you at the Fast?"

"Mother insisted I do this errand. I have brought some freshly cooked parsnips. It's a gift for your family, and mother requested I bring it to you." Her slight body trembled. She stretched up on her toes and lifted the dish forward.

"Hmm now," spoke Father, "What can this mean?" He bent forward and removed the cloth. "Eh, a mess of parsnips I see." He paused. "We will not and cannot accept a gift from your mother, a woman accused of witchery. What will people think?" He began to drum his fingers against the door. "Next, they'll be accusing my good wife of consorting with the Devil. Indeed not. 'Tis not right. Take your parsnips and return home at once."

I watched the bloom pale from Eliza's face. I turned around. "Father, this is a gift. It smells goodly enough," I said, embarrassed by my father's gruff behavior. Eliza's body seemed to shake, even shiver in the hot breezes.

"Silence, daughter," my father shouted. "Would you have this godly town think us conspiring with people accused of witchcraft? We will have nothing of the likes in this house. Be gone now and remove this food from my doorstep!" Father clenched his fists. He had become the constable he was years ago, mean and stubborn.

Father stepped back inside, glared at me and pointed in the direction of the keeping room. I apologized to Eliza and she returned home with the uneaten food.

The house stayed quiet. I continued to sweep the keeping room floor. I did not want to cause more distress for my father. Thoughts of the fast up at the Wyllys Mansion stirred through my mind. I knew that Ann would be there. *What is she claiming now?* I would hear from mother about the fast later, though I was unsure if I really wanted to know.

Then I heard a loud, determined rapping on the door. Again. Who could this be now?

Father, aroused, shouted, "No, Hester, I shall get the door this time." Mumbling about such vile interruptions, he walked to the door and released the bolt lock. I stood aback in the hall.

"Richard, a good morrow to you," I heard father say in a respectable tone of voice. "What can I do for thee?"

The man standing at the doorstep was no other than Richard Seager, Goody Seager's husband. He was about three score in age, his hair streaked gray. His eyes had dark blooms around them, his face swollen. He had with him the plate of parsnips.

"A good day to you, Thomas. I'd like to know why you have not accepted my wife's gift of these parsnips. Our Eliza is now in a state, wailing and crying." The distraught man paused. "For shame, Thomas, to refuse a wholesome gift!"

Father glowered at the older man. "Ay, I certainly did refuse this gift. There's no shame in this." I watched father lift his pointing finger. "See here Richard. I know for a fact at the fast months back, Ann Cole, a godly maid and our neighbor, cried out at the Wyllys house that your wife was a witch." He stopped and waited for a reply, then continued. "And on God's honor, she'll cry out *again* that Elizabeth is a witch. Mark my words, Richard."

I froze, unable to fathom what I had just heard.

"But Thomas, you know I'm a God fearing man," said Goodman Seager. "I would naught have a witch as the mother of my children. Surely, I might know."

Father did not budge an inch. I thought back to when I was a young child and father was Constable of Hartford. It made me shiver.

Father continued. "Accepting a plate of parsnips from an accused witch may be used against my pious wife. It could be used against my pious daughter as well!"

Goodman Seager stammered. "B-but you know Elizabeth claims Ann's ravings are nothing but hodgepodge! Nothing but foolish talk from a young girl." He shook his head wildly.

"Hodgepodge? Foolishness? I think not, Richard!" Father took in a deep breath. "We cannot and will not accept anything from your family, Richard. Good day."

With these last words, Father slammed the door hard and loudly threw the bolt.

—

Soon after this, I heard the bell by the Great River's landing begin to ring. I wondered what was astir by the river docks. The air, thick with humidity, felt like a heavy woolen blanket wrapped around me. The hot noon sun blazed; its rays shot through the window like forged knives. Nary a breeze blew through the open windows of the house.

My morning chores were finished. I noticed that father was in the front hall tying up his bootlaces.

"Father, may I walk to the Great River for a time? My head is faint with the heat." I wiped the sweat from my forehead. Father frowned at me.

"Mayhap you should attend the Fast up on the hill, Hester. You've had nary a bite this morning. Mayhap you could pray with the others."

I crossed into the kitchen and found a freshly picked peach and dropped it into my pocket. Then I cut a piece of cheese from the cheese board.

"Father, I will be fine. I'll also pick some wildflowers and sunflower heads to brighten the table board."

"That sounds well enough, Hester. This place needs some brightening."

Father set his hat on his head. "I'll be round back weeding the garden and threshing the flax. Make sure you are home for late afternoon."

Chapter 17

The ringing of the Landing Bell usually did mean one thing—a ship had arrived to Hartford.

I kept to the road past the Wyllys mansion. No one was about that I could see. Most townspeople were inside praying at the Fast. I felt relieved to be away from the madness. I could not bear to witness any more of Ann's fits.

I crossed the plank-wood bridge atop the Little River and watched the waters swirling towards the Great River. Asters, goldenrod, mullein, and tansy dotted the steep banks with a palate of color. The great willows overlooking the Little River hung heavy, their bows and branches casting dappled reflections on the water's surface. Granny Flagg's battered house stood silent. It had dried out after the spring floods. Stray rafts were tied to tree trunks so they would not drift afar.

Following the road from the Little River, I ambled past the Little Meadows, now covered with clover and dandelions. In the far distance, near the Dutch Point, I could see the outlines of several red and white painted canoes paddled by the natives. A half- hidden sloop was docked near the mouth of the river.

The sand and dirt path led toward the Great River. How thrilled I was to see a ship had dropped anchor near the landing. Several men on rafts and small boats paddled out to the ship. Clearly, it was too large to dock near the rivulet. Crates and hogsheads filled with goods unknown were lined up, ready to be unloaded onto the rafts and boats. I stood entranced by the blur of activity.

"Hester how is it for thee today?"

I turned and saw James Ensign, the apprentice blacksmith. What a relief to know I wasn't the only one not attending the Fast. Tall and rangy, with thick black hair, James's muscles were taut from working the anvil every day. His skin was like tanned leather, smooth and burnished. His blue eyes twinkled at me.

"I am well as to be expected," I told him. "Getting some fresh river air. Mayhap a breeze on such a hot afternoon might help."

"Indeed," replied James. "I am taking my noon break by the water. You are not attending the fast today?" He pulled an apple from his pocket and took a crunching bite.

"Nay," I said and moved to an old tree stump nearby to sit upon. I found the thick slice of cheese in my pocket and began eating it in bits. James sat down besides me.

"Would you care for some cheese, James?" I broke off a piece for him, and he extended his hand.

In between bites he muttered, "No fast for you—or me today."

"I've cleaned the whole morning long, and I told my father I was faint from the heat. 'Tis all true," I replied.

James nodded in agreement.

I pointed out toward the ship. "Where do you think this ship hails from?" I asked. It looked like a merchant ship with its sturdy masts and heavily laden cargo.

"I know not. But I'm as curious as you. I needed a rest from the blacksmith's shop. In this hot weather, the forge feels even more like an inferno."

James sat eating his apple and gazing across the water. I sat on the stump wishing a breeze would cool the air.

Soon men began to embark from the rafts to unload the goods onto the sandy shore. They hoisted barrels on their shoulders and headed toward the row of warehouses on the north side of the landing.

I espied a strange man, one I had never seen around Hartford. He seemed lost and was headed in our direction.

"Good day," he greeted and lifted up his cap. His bright eyes glinted in the sun. "I wonder if you could point me in the direction of Jeremy Adams' Tavern. I'm in need of strong drink."

The stranger had a thick sack slung round his shoulders. His saggy breeches were torn and his black boots caked with mud and water. He smelt like bilge. His sun-bleached golden hair was parted on the side and tied back. He wore a red scarf around his neck and donned a blue sailor's cap. He looked only a few years older than James.

"Certainly, sir," I said. "We can show you where the tavern is in town."

James eyed the stranger with interest and stood up. "What brings you to Hartford?" he asked.

"I am here to do some trading," the stranger explained. "But I was paid some extra shillings to deliver something." He paused and looked around. "Would either of you know where a certain Hester Hosmer might reside?"

My cheeks felt hot and a-flush. I caught my breath. "I am Hester Hosmer," I said.

The stranger then asked me, "Do you have proof that thou art truly Hester Hosmer?"

"Ay, I can avow that this is indeed Hester Hosmer," James replied. He turned to me and seemed concerned, almost protective. "What of this, Hester? Do you recognize this man?"

I shook my head.

"Where do you hail from, stranger?" James asked.

"I hail from Boston these days. From a lowly sailor and peddler to a rich merchant I shall become." He puffed up his thin frame and tapped his foot with confidence. Then, he reached into his sack and began to fumble for something. "Once my service is complete, I'll spend my shillings at the tavern with little care. Hold up…" He lifted a crumpled, water-stained envelope from his sack.

"Here you be, Miss Hester. 'Tis fate and luck that brought me right to the person I need to see in Hartford." He smiled. "Now, if you would be so kind to show me the way to the tavern, I'd be much obliged."

Blushing with both surprise and pleasure, I slipped the letter in my apron pocket. "Thank you kindly," I added.

"What is your name, stranger?" James asked.

"I am Nathaniel Osgood. Friends call me Nat for short."

"It's a pleasure, Nat. I am James Ensign, soon to be a fully apprenticed blacksmith here in Hartford. If you care for company, I will show you to the tavern." James leaned toward me. "Were you expecting a letter?"

I smiled and shook my head. "I know not. Perhaps it's a letter from my cousin in Boston."

Nat let out a laugh. Then he seemed to take notice of the serious look I was giving him.

"So is it true the rumors that be circulating round Boston these days about Hartford?"

"What rumors?" James and I asked at the same time.

"They say that there be witches here, and many people are escaping from these parts." He gestured toward the activity about the landing. "A witch hanging in Boston is indeed a spectacle. I try to stay far away from the gallows, but business is often good after a hanging, you see."

"We've had but one hanging and few people were present. I know not what is happening here," I said. I could say no more to a man who had just arrived to Hartford.

Nat accompanied James back up the Landing Road toward the tavern. James turned back and shouted, "I hope to see you down by the landing again, Hester." I stuck my hand inside my pocket. The letter was there.

———

I must have dozed in the hot sun for some minutes, for when I opened my eyes the sun was behind me, sinking in the west. My shadow on the dirt path loomed longer and larger. I turned about.

There stood Marshal Gilbert, beaky nose pointed down at me. His black eyes narrowed and his forehead bulged. As was his custom, he had his musket. A thick canvas bag rested near him on the ground. Titus had rushed to the water's edge and was nipping at the heels of some of the warehouse workers.

"Idling again, Hester? And on a Fast Day?" The marshal glared down at my half-eaten cheese. I quickly dug into my pocket, slid out my Psalm Book, covered the cheese with it and began to read. I tried to keep my eyes on the page.

"I am not idling, Marshal. Father told me I need not attend the fast today on account of the heat. I am not well. I read my psalms for peace and understanding."

Marshal Gilbert limped around the stump so he now stood afore me. I closed my book and waited.

"Is this right? While your pious mother and pious friend Ann pray that our town remains as such, pious and free from the devil's scourges?" He stared hard into my face, his black eyes squinting in the sun. "Are you so different that you feel a need to remove yourself?" He paused. "From us, the godly ones?" The lines in his forehead looked like old ruts in the road.

"No disrespect intended, Marshal, may I ask why *you* are not attending the fast today?"

He pointed a long, bony finger at me. "So, you want to know, do you? Well, I'll show you, if you must know."

I really did not want to know; neither did I care.

He hobbled back around and gathered up the knapsack. "Here's what I've been doing this afternoon." He stretched his hand deep into the sack and yanked from the bag a freshly killed wolf's head. A gash ran across its neck. The blood had been staunched with cloth stuffed into its neck and throat. Its sooty fur still bristled and stuck straight up. Though its black and yellow eyes had dulled and glazed over, it looked like a devil come straight up from hell.

"Do you see this, Hester?" The marshal swung his trophy inches from my face. It smelled of death. I could barely look at it. "This beast will never harm another creature again. It is dead. Dead!" He lifted the wolf head into the air as if to show the entire town.

"Never forget, Hester. I am a soldier first and foremost. Never forget I have scalped and massacred many a red man in the Indian Wars. Never forget, dead men and women can't speak. And dead wolves cannot prowl or steal our food." A grim smile creased his face.

"This beast can harm no more."

Perhaps, I thought, *but what of the Marshal?*

Chapter 18

*H*eavy dark clouds had gathered overhead. I watched the marshal limp toward his riverside warehouse. "Time to show off my bounty to the boys," he chuckled before he left me. "Rest assured, you will see this creature nailed to the meeting-house door. He's soon to join the others." The rain began to pelt down in a fury. I had tarried by the landing for too long.

"Hester, you are late!" My father stamped his boots on the floor as if he was putting out a fire. My mother sat quietly spinning by the hearth.

"How was the fast, Mother?" I asked, trying to slow my breath. Soaked from the rainstorm, I moved near the fire to warm myself. Thunderous booms and cracks from the sky rattled the house. Rain drummed on the roof.

"Hester, take off thy apron and hang your wet clothes on the drying peg," mother said gently.

I stood shivering while father wagged his finger toward me. His hands were raw and swollen from threshing the flax.

"Where were you, Hester? We thought you might have run off," he said.

"I was down by the landing watching for ships. And reading my psalms."

"And did you see anyone down at the landing, while most of the town was standing the Fast?"

I paused, thinking how I would answer my father's question. "I saw Marshal Gilbert who had with him a freshly killed wolf's head." I watched the flames in the hearth spit out little sparks.

"Good. Another one for the meetinghouse," father said, drumming his fingers on the table board.

I watched mother content at her spinning.

"Well, what of the Fast, Mother?" I asked again still shivering. "Was Ann present?"

"Ay," mother exclaimed, never looking up from her work. "She spoke again in those Dutch tones, that guttural tongue that sounds like the Varlets do when they speak fast." Mother stopped spinning. "But to me and the others, they sounded like words from the mouth of Satan himself." She rested her hands in her lap. "The names of Elizabeth Seager, Judith Varlet, and the Greensmiths were on her tongue again. She still claims they are witches who serve the Devil."

"Do the townspeople believe her?" I asked.

Mother gave me a stern look. "Of course they believe her, Hester. We all do. Why? Don't you believe your friend?" Mother's wheel began again; it started to spin faster and faster, her foot pumping the treadle. More yarn could now unravel from the distaff onto the wheel.

"She's a godly girl that Ann. Her mother would be so proud," my mother said.

———

Father told mother about the mess of parsnips Goody Seager's daughter offered us while mother was at the Fast. Although it was impolite to reject a gift, mother exclaimed it was indeed the right thing to do. We would accept nothing from one suspected of being a witch.

I stood by the fire until my clothes were almost dry. I refused to hang my apron or anything else on the drying pegs. I asked my mother and father if I might be excused to change my clothes. Rushing up the loft stairs, I knew I had but a few moments of precious time to read the letter. My parents expected me to help with supper preparations.

I found some dry clothes and removed my damp apron, but not before extracting my Psalm book and the wrinkled letter.

I opened the letter and recognized the scratchy handwriting.

My Dear Hester,

Forgive the delay of this letter. I pray this arrives safe and that all is well and at peace with you and your family. The summer brought with it hard and trying times. Father suffered through a terrible grippe but praise God, he recovered fully. Thrice, I journeyed to Boston alone for the purpose of trading wares. What sights to behold in Boston, Hester. I know you would love the salt air, the busy harbor and all the colorful fineries you so deserve. Truly, Boston seems a world away from Hartford and Springfield. And the books Hester. They have warehouses in Boston just for books alone!

A few times I tarried along the harbor-side, lined with merchants and captains' houses in rows. I have moments when my mind wanders and I think mayhap someday you would like to visit Boston, mayhap even live there. When I am in Boston my mind wanders back to you and then I see your honey-colored eyes and hair and think how happy you'd be here.

But alas, I digress. I return to Springfield come the morrow. And I have heard word around Boston that Hartford is under a witch panic. Is this but a rumor? Could it be your friend Ann at her ravings again?

I dare not write anymore on the subject lest this letter finds itself "lost" in the hands of another. But for now, I have some fine news. Father has consented to an autumn journey to Hartford. He's in hardier spirits and better health now.

We hope to arrive around the time of autumn muster day. Perhaps I will also have time to speak with your father about my intentions. I hope you are enjoying the *Sonnets* of Shakespeare. I'd be interested to hear what you thought of the ballads.

Until the next time, I pray God keeps you safe and well. Wish me Godspeed on my journey. I hope and pray that Nat meets with success in Hartford. He is a dear friend and you can trust him. We are already talking about buying a warehouse at Boston Harbor.

Your obedient servant,

T

p.s. Father and I may load up the rafts and travel down-river depending on the rains. Father needs to trade with the Podunk Indians so we will stop along the east side of the river first. Watch for me and listen for my call!

I folded the letter and tucked it inside my psalm book. My heart raced aflutter. Tom was coming for a visit soon. It could not be soon enough.

Chapter 19

"*I* am not a witch!" she screeched.

It was market day and Goody Seager stood locked in the pillory. Her head stuck firm between the wooden beams. Both her hands were clamped and held fast in two small, round holds on either side of her head.

A crowd had gathered around to watch the spectacle of Goody Seager on display. I thought of little Betty and how we'd tease her about getting put in the "nutcracker" if she was disobedient. But with little Betty dead in her grave, the joke no longer seemed humorous.

Elizabeth Seager had been accused of adultery with James Wakely. I recalled that winter's night months before on the South Green. I had seen the two of them huddled together round the fire in a tight embrace.

While Goody Seager was being punished and humiliated for adultery, Mrs. Migat and the other town gossips made sure to let their opinions be known. After all, it was market day and towns-people reveled in the idea of a spectacle at Meetinghouse Square.

"Of course she's a witch!" I heard Mrs. Migat shout. "As well as a cheating harlot!" A few boys pelted clods of dirt at Goody Seager's face.

"How do we know you are not a witch?" I heard Goodman Sterne say. He poked his finger toward her. "Why should we believe you at all? The Devil is known to be a liar." The crowd began to chant, "Liar, liar, liar."

Goody Seager raised her trapped head to look forward at the gathering crowd. James Wakely sat in the stocks next to her; his arms and legs clamped in the wooden shackles. Had they—both married to another—committed adultery and fornication together?

"How do I know I am *not* a witch?" Goody Seager shouted, trying to hold her head up. "I know I am no witch because the Devil came to me and told me I was no witch!" She hung her head low now. Her cap had fallen off, and her auburn hair was loose. She was a beautiful woman, but she looked a sore sight in that pillory. I dropped my basket of homespun and reached for my Psalm book. I opened to Psalm 107, verse 12. "Therefore he brought down their heart with labor-they fell down and there was none to help." What could I do to help? I shook my head, for my soul could no longer comprehend the need for such humiliation and cruelty.

I turned from the spectacle of Goody Seager. The scent of early apples, grapes, and late summer fruits led me to the fruit stall near the Varlets' orchards. I picked a few apples from a barrel and gave the fruit seller a shilling. I dropped one into my apron pocket for later and took a bite from another.

The smell of roasting mutton, burnt chestnuts, and corn popping on small fires sent whiffs of mingled scents into the air. A stray dog bounded back and forth, thrusting his nose into the different food tents searching for scraps. Summer cattle were up for sale. A restless horse pawed his hoof to the ground so I gave him a piece of my apple.

Someone bumped into my shoulder, and I turned to see who it was.

"If it's not Hester herself. We missed you at the Fast. Where were *you?*"

Before me was Ann, along with Sybil Whiting. My mother told me that Sybil had fainted alongside Ann at the recent Fast. Sybil further complained to her father that the Greensmiths, Goody Seager, and Dutch Judy were all witches. Why, she had seen them flying over the house in the middle of night!

It was obvious Sybil worshipped Ann. The young girl gazed at Ann as if she were the Lord himself.

"How do, Ann. Sybil." I took another bite of my apple, hoping they would go away.

"Where were you?" Ann asked again. "Most everyone else was there."

I knew Ann was just being curious and I knew she really didn't care. She was disappointed because I had missed her recent ravings.

"I was ailing myself, Ann. I had my monthly, so I spent the afternoon in prayer down by the landing."

Ann tittered. "Waiting for the right ship to come in? Guess your ship hasn't arrived yet. Or has it?" She seemed to enjoy the jest. "Or maybe you are awaiting the right raft to float down the Great River just for you. Is that it, Hester? Come now, tell all." She began batting her eyelashes close to my face. She laughed shrilly, clearly pleased with herself. Sybil, copying Ann, chuckled as well.

"Methinks you are waiting on your beau, Tom. Ha!" She continued as if to judge me. "And I thought you were godly, Hester."

"And I thought you were godly, Hester," piped in Sybil.

Now my lips tightened and my head pounded with anger. "Remember Ann, what the Bible says, 'Judge not lest ye be judged.'"

Little Sybil seemed concerned now. "Are you a witch—like all the others?"

I leaned down and patted her head. "Of course not. I am a godly maid, just like Ann."

We stood by the fruit stall for several minutes making light conversation. I was ready to take my leave of Ann and Sybil, for I had errands to finish and the homespun must be delivered to Goody Adams up at the tavern. But then, of a sudden, Meetinghouse Square became very quiet.

"How dare you call my father a drunkard!" The thick accent echoed about the square. It was Dutch Judy. She was dressed in a satin skirt of violet, and her black tresses were wrapped high on her head.

"I would say her North Sea eyes are stormy today," Ann mused. We watched as Dutch Judy stuck her finger in the face of the tanner's son, Samuel.

"Ay, he is a Dutch drunkard," said Sam. "He takes our business and drinks up the proceeds—with money that's supposed to be ours."

Then we saw and heard it. A loud, resounding smack silenced the market square. Dutch Judy had hit Samuel Givens right across the face! She clenched her fists as he grabbed his cheek. It bloomed up swollen with a red welt on it.

Sarah Varlet ran up to her sister and tugged at her silk sleeves. "Stop this now, Judy. Stop. Father will have none of this."

"None of this? I will have none of this." Judy seemed to be spitting out her words. "Look at my friend there—in the pillory. What of her?" She pointed to Goody Seager. "What people do this?"

Marshal Gilbert, who had been selling his wares at the market, came hobbling over. His black eyes had a mean glint in them. But his mouth was turned upward in a slight grin.

"What? Slap a young man like this for naught? Most likely he speaks the truth, Judith Varlet. Control thy temper and outbursts at once."

Now Dutch Judy stamped her foot hard. "I will not control my temper. If one speaks ill against my dear father, I shall speak. No one shall stop me. Now. Or ever." She began to speak in a torrent of Dutch words that reminded me of Ann's rave. Sweat poured from her forehead and dripped into her eyes.

The marshal spoke with Sarah now. He waved toward the Varlet homestead. "Take your sister home until we know what to do with her. There she shall remain. Hysterics are not allowed in Hartford. Tell your father that she has breached the peace and is under house arrest for disorderly conduct. That is all for now."

Sarah escorted Judy home, dragging her by the elbows. Ann smiled at me with satisfaction. "She'll get what she deserves," she said. "Mark my words. We shall see who wins."

Chapter 20

The morning after market day, I was scraping the breakfast trenchers in the kitchen when I heard a commotion up the road: women screaming, men yelling, and dogs barking.

I scurried out the back door, shooing hungry chickens from under my skirts. The noise was coming from the Varlet homestead. Ann was outside watching the turmoil from the front of her house. I ran right by her. I had to see what was happening.

The road was filled with people clamoring for news and pushing for a better view. A lone, gray dappled mare hitched to a wagon waited in silence. Goody Seager, head hung low, slumped in the back of the wagon. She held fast to a bundle that looked like bedding.

All was in confusion. The Whiting family stood on their stoop, staring up the road.

"Come inside now, Sybil. 'Tis not a sight for young eyes," I heard Goodwife Whiting say.

"But why Mother, why?" Little Sybil's eyes were round as plums.

"Because God works in mysterious ways. We know naught of His strange workings, child. Now hush and get inside."

Sybil obeyed her mother, but turned her head in the direction of the Varlets to take one last look.

I found James Ensign in the crowd. "What is happening, James?" I asked out of breath.

"They are arresting Judy along with Elizabeth Seager." His eyes met mine. "Not just for disorderly conduct or adultery. But for witchcraft. Rumor has it, this could be the first of many arrests." He sighed, kicked at the ground and shook his head.

I thanked James and made my way closer to the Varlet stoop. Sarah Varlet, still in her nightshift, kerchief on to cover her scalped, hairless head came screeching from the house.

"No!" she wailed. "You cannot take my sister." She placed both her hands on her head as if she were ready to pull her kerchief off. Was Sarah reliving that nightmare years ago, when she and sister, Maria were captured by the Indians in New Netherlands?

Marshal Gilbert now appeared from the crowd and stepped up to address the people. But first he raised his musket into the air and fired a shot.

"Get back into the house, Sarah Varlet, lest you are next." He muttered something to the three ministers standing near him.

And then the bound prisoner appeared at the door, thrashing about like a wild cat. A guard gripped each arm. An iron manacle hung around her neck. Judith squirmed and spat in one of the guards' faces. I shuddered.

"How dare you? I am no witch. I disturb no one. Only those who blaspheme my father!" She clenched her fists and tried to scratch at her captors. Her eyes, I thought, were as stormy as the wildest North Sea tempest. Those eyes seemed to spit out blazing sparks today.

The rest of the Varlets remained in the house, no doubt afraid for their lives. One of their cows raised her head and released a long, mournful bawl. Pigs squealed, chickens squawked, and the family hound howled and barked in confusion.

The town gossips huddled together, twittering like small birds. "She deserves this. I knew this was to happen soon enough," one said.

"Silence!" the marshal demanded. "We have just reason to suspect these women on charges of witchery." He paused. "Not to mention the crimes of blasphemy, disorderly conduct and adultery."

Townspeople fell silent now, intent on hearing what the marshal had to say.

"We have those amongst us who have witnessed and seen the mischief these prisoners have wrought on our godly community. But we are a fair, just, and honest congregation. There will be an investigation and a trial. Until then, these two women will be cast into prison. We will diligently gather evidence, evidence that indeed the said individuals, Judith Varlet and Elizabeth Seager, may be in league with the Devil and may have familiarity with Satan himself." The marshal wiped sweat from his brow and off his nose. He pointed to Judith, who was panting and trying to break free.

"Place the prisoner in the cart alongside this other harlot. Now!"

Judith was hoisted into the wagon. Another guard carried her bundle of bed clothing and threw it over the wagon side.

"Make sure you tie the prisoner's hands together lest she tries to scratch someone's eyes out," Marshal Gilbert ordered the guard. "That's what she-demons do."

Reverend Stone managed to calm the crowd with a wave of his hand.

"Good people of Hartford gathered here today. Let us pray as we seek the truth from God in order to understand the Devil's snares. Bow your heads in silence and in gratitude."

I peeked across the road and saw that James Ensign had his hands folded, but one of his eyebrows arched up. He was glancing my way. Did he roll his eyes? What did he think?

Reverend Stone opened the Bible, and read aloud with fervor.

"I will say unto the Lord, He is my refuge and my fortress, my God in Him I will trust.

Surely, he shall deliver thee from the snare of the fowler and from the noisome pestilence."

Reverend Stone closed the Bible and commanded the people to pray.

Marshal Gilbert limped up to the stoop again. "That is all for today," he shouted. The three reverends nodded and bowed their heads. "The day is young," the marshal continued, "You have your chores, your preparations for the day and evening," he reminded the crowd. "The ministers and I have our work to do. Rest assured, we will be thorough in our undertakings."

The cart creaked and inched slowly off toward the jail. Stragglers on the side of the road pelted the two prisoners with rocks and clods of dirt. Both women held their heads down as the small group followed them, heckling and whistling.

"We need no witches nor strumpets in Hartford," shouted Mrs. Migat, who remained with the huddle of gossips. "They are nothing but Satan's whores, both of them. Imagine."

"Stop, Mrs. Migat." The words rushed from my mouth. "We know not what God has planned." Mrs. Migat turned and watched me with a stern, pinched look.

"What an impudent girl you are, Hester. How dare you speak to me this way?" Mrs. Migat could not and would not be silenced.

The gossips began to chant and point after the accused. "Satan's whores, you be nothing—but whores of the Devil."

"We shall meet you next on Gallows Hill," another said. "Ye shall be gone to the next life where Satan is awaiting you both."

"Divine Providence is indeed at work," a woman pronounced. "Our God is a just and righteous God."

"Well said that," replied Mrs. Migat. "Justice will be served, for it's all a part of God's great plan."

Then, I heard my mother shouting out my name. There was no time to tarry. I lifted up my skirt and started to rush down the road. Ann was still standing on her stoop, watching the crowd disperse.

"Hester, you mark my words. There will be justice after all. I am sure now," she hollered. "Justice for Betty!"

———

Dutch Judy was in jail but two days when her father Caspar had a heart seizure and died. I think he truly died of a "heart broken" as Judith warned months before. The Varlet family was allowed to bury Caspar's remains in the Old Dutch Cemetery near the fort, among a few graves marked with wooden crosses. He joined some of the Dutch families who had once resided in Hartford years ago.

The Varlet family, dressed in black, mourned their head of household, the colorful merchant and trader. His headstrong, beautiful, and outspoken daughter was not allowed to attend his funeral. For Judy was languishing with Goody Seager in the root cellar of Daniel Garret's home, awaiting her fate. He had been deemed their jailer, and they would remain there until a new, larger jail was complete. The old dugout of a prison held but a few people. I wondered if there would be more arrests.

Chapter 21

October 1662

Three weeks had passed since Dutch Judy and Goody Seager were hauled away and jailed on charges of witchcraft. I wondered if Judy even knew that her father was dead, lying in an unmarked grave, buried under a mound of fresh dirt.

A pall as heavy as the low, autumn clouds hung over Hartford. The harvest had begun in earnest. Corn still needed to be ground into meal, the flax separated, the ripe squash and pumpkins plucked from their thick vines. There was talk of Governor Winthrop's return with the Royal Charter in hand. He had been gone for over a year now.

Acting Governor Mason returned to Hartford from Saybrook. James told me he heard that Captain Mason came back to Hartford, in order to confer with Marshal Gilbert and the magistrates regarding the witchcraft arrests.

Everyone in Hartford knew Captain Mason's reputation. He had condemned women in Fairfield and Saybrook on witchcraft charges. Would he do the same here in Hartford? It seemed to me that the authorities were determined to rid Hartford of the scourge of witches, especially before Governor Winthrop returned home.

Inquiries into the behavior of Dutch Judy and Goody Seager had begun. Townsfolk were being called to testify against them. I was asked a few questions about what I had seen or heard, but I said naught. By speaking against them, I may be speaking against myself.

It was Thursday, our teaching day; the day of the week when the Reverend Stone, our teacher, helped us further understand the meaning of the Lord's Word. The meeting finally broke for the noonday meal. Most folks walked with heads down in prayer to the nooning house. A few stragglers huddled about the meetinghouse door or ambled to Jeremy Adams's Tavern. Many of them, like myself, tarried at the meetinghouse square. Although it was not market day, people enjoyed exchanging news and a bit of gossip.

I wondered if I should attend the noonday meal, usually some bread, cold meat, cheese, and a piece of fruit to tide us over until afternoon meeting. Should I instead bide my time watching the river flow while I read from my book of psalms? I decided that a walk along the Great River would suit my mood.

Leaving the square, I sauntered for a time and found my favorite tree stump near the cluster of oaks. Flocks of geese filled the sky with great V formations flying south for the winter. A slight breeze blew from the south bringing warmer air. The early autumn sun peeked out from the heavy fair-weather clouds.

I thought of Tom and wondered when he'd return. I glanced upriver, half expecting his raft heaped with goods to appear. It did not. Turning my head toward the south, I espied a white dot bobbing in the distance. It looked to be a small craft buffeting to and fro on the river. It seemed to have its bow pointed in the direction of the landing. I waited and watched to see what direction it would take.

The white ketch sailed closer, and I now recognized the orange, white, and blue flags billowing at both bow and stern. So, it was a Dutch ketch. Would it sail past Hartford to continue north?

The ketch traversed around the landing a few times, turned, and started sailing south. Where was it going? It reminded me of the graceful swans that traversed the Little River in search of plant foods.

At the merge of the Little River with the Great River, it bore a sharp right. A small dock jutted out near the Dutch Point. I could see but the stern of the ship, for trees and bushes blocked a full view.

Someone else had also seen the sail craft because the landing bell began clanging, loud and persistent. "Ship in, ship in," I heard the day watchman shout. "Docking south by the Little River near the Point. Dutch flags waving. Dutch flags a-waving!"

The bell continued to ring and ring until it made my head pulse. I looked up toward the square and watched the commotion. Townspeople emptied from the tavern and the nooning house; they began to congregate at meetinghouse square. Many of them had a pint of beer in hand, as well as a crust of bread to eat whilst awaiting the news.

I brushed a fallen oak leaf from my cap, smoothed my skirt wrinkles out and then pressed down on my neckerchief. Perspiration dripped around my neck. Dabbing it away, I made my way to the square.

I soon espied James in the crowd and settled in next to him. "What is happening?" I asked.

"I know not. Mayhap we await a message," he replied.

Soon most townspeople gathered on the square. It seemed no one knew why the bell was ringing.

I nudged James. "I espied a ketch with Dutch flags flying," I whispered. "It docked close to the Little River near the Dutch Point."

"Ay," he nodded. "Mayhap this is the reason we wait."

What had gone awry now? I could not help but feel anxious. I was starting to feel very alone in this circle of townspeople, all wondering what would happen next.

I did not have to wait long. I glanced sidelong to the right and espied someone coming out of the path leading from the Dutch Point. A short, pale man appeared and marched right into the circle. All eyes were on him. He wore a blue velvet cap that matched his blue hose and blue jerkin. His coat was orange. His black, buckled shoes shone with a bright polish. He carried under his arm a small brass horn.

The herald lifted his thin horn to the air and blew it with his might. A slender Dutch flag unraveled and hung off the trumpet.

"Hear ye, hear ye! A letter to be given to the Acting Governor of Connecticut Colony, the Honorable Captain John Mason, from the Governor of New Netherlands, the Honorable Peter Stuyvesant."

The crowd gasped. "What of this letter?" "What does Peter Stuyvesant want from us now?" I heard several people shout. I thought back to the stories I had heard of old "Peg Leg" Peter. Years ago, Peter Stuyvesant lost one of his legs in battle. He had a wooden leg now, covered with silver. He was said to be a mean and stubborn man; only his kindhearted sister Anna could calm his rages.

The herald blew his horn again with force. He proceeded to repeat his announcement and demanded an audience with the authorities.

"But, this is our teaching day. How dare this stranger intrude on our nooning meal," said Mrs. Migat. She was huddled nearby accompanied by her daughter-in-law Mary and Mary's children.

"Ay," said one man, holding up a tankard of ale. "Tell your governor to leave our governor be," and proceeded to drink up to his own words.

"An Acting Governor at that," I heard my brother Stephen remark. He was standing behind me with a catlike grin on his face. I smiled at him and beckoned him to the circle. He shook his head.

"Ay, and if our Governor Winthrop were back to Hartford, none of this would be happening," I heard someone whisper.

"'Tis true, 'tis true," the tanner George Givens muttered. "If he were here, none of this would ever be so."

The day watchman entered the circle, spoke briefly with the herald, and shouted that someone fetch Captain Mason and Marshal Gilbert. Trouble was astir.

——

"What have we here?" Captain Mason had finally arrived to the square. He flashed an angry glance at the herald. His musket was slung over his shoulder and his saber glinted from a side belt. He wore his steeple hat and although he was short in stature, his temper and booming voice made up for his diminished height.

More sounds could now be heard along the side path from the Dutch Point. I heard the noise of hard boots cracking down on leaves and the coughing and clearing of throats. The voices grew louder. Then two men approached, observed the crowd, and entered the meetinghouse square. They stood close to the herald speaking in Dutch.

"Captain Varlet, to what pleasure do we owe such a visit?" Captain Mason inquired, his stocky legs planted apart.

My eyes went wide. Captain Nicolas Varlet? Tall and fit, unlike his father Caspar, Captain Varlet wore a black beaver cap with a white feather plume jutting from it. Dressed in a black jerkin, black breeches, and boots, his black half cape swung as he paced about the cobblestones. His long wavy hair hung in black and gray ringlets to his shoulders. He had a wide forehead, long straight nose, and deep-set blue eyes that bore a resemblance to his sister Judy's. He carried a brown leather satchel slung round his shoulder. I caught my breath; I had nary seen such a handsome and dashing man in my life.

Caspar had often boasted of his son Nicholas to anyone who might listen—how Nicholas had married Governor Stuyvesant's widowed sister Anna, taken in her two young sons, and convinced Peg Leg to allow the remainder of the family to remove to Hartford. Peg Leg didn't have much of a choice, for Caspar had drunk away the family money. He created problems for Governor Stuyvesant; the same way he created problems for Hartford; always in court, always suing folks. But Caspar was dead now.

Captain Varlet was a distinguished envoy, and I could see why the governor's sister would find him so attractive.

Captain Mason and Captain Varlet faced each other like two dogs readying for a fight. Captain Mason seemed unfamiliar with whatever protocol the situation might demand. 'Twas a known fact that Captain John Mason, Indian killer and fighter, did not like Hartford, or relish being our Acting Governor. Also, 'twas a known fact that the townspeople cared naught for Captain Mason; but he was here, and there was naught we could do about it.

I nudged James. "Where is Marshal Gilbert?" I asked. "You would think he'd be present."

James glanced about before he spoke. "I heard he's off on a wolf hunt." James also mentioned that the marshal was sure to be angry about missing this meeting. I was relieved the marshal was nowhere in sight, though Captain Mason seemed to seek him in the crowd.

"Captain Varlet," said Captain Mason again. "What brings you to Hartford?"

Before Captain Varlet could reply, his remaining family had ventured from the homestead. Sarah, kerchief on her head could not contain her joy at seeing her beloved brother again. She ran to him with arms stretched and hugged him mightily. The older sister Maria with her babe and Mrs. Varlet, tall and pale, stood back and watched from a knoll close by.

Captain Varlet bent and kissed the top of his sister's head, spoke to her in Dutch, and then she returned to the family. I wiped a tear that sprung from my eye after witnessing such a tender exchange.

Captain Varlet took a step back. He unwound the thin cord from the satchel as if it was a sail and removed a long scroll sealed with red wax. He held it up for all to see.

"I bring with me tidings and a letter from our Director General, the Honorable Governor Peter Stuyvesant," he announced in a clear Dutch accent. "I carry this letter with great urgency."

I noticed the young man accompanying the Dutch captain. He took a small black ledger from his pocket and began writing down words with a lead nub. He had bright black beads for eyes that darted about like a squirrel. After he wrote a few words, he lifted his dark head to glance around, taking in the whole circle of townspeople.

"And who might this young greenhorn be?" Captain Mason demanded, pointing to the young man who had resumed scribbling in his ledger book.

Captain Varlet cleared his throat. "This is my stepson, Nicholas Bayard. He is also nephew to Governor Stuyvesant. He apprentices for clerk and secretary for the governor. He will continue to record this meeting."

Nicholas Bayard was a distinguished young man only a few years older than Tom. He kept his eye on his stepfather and continued every so often with his writing.

Captain Varlet strode around the square as if he were stomping on grapes in a barrel. "My sole purpose, Captain Mason, is to deliver this letter to you with great urgency," he stated.

People now huddled close together, bending forward in a sea of white caps, black hats, shawls, skirts, and black boots. They reminded me of the black and white cows in the ox pasture—mouths hanging open with wide, silent eyes.

Captain Varlet offered the parchment scroll to Captain Mason with a flick of his wrist. He then bowed low, lifted his hat, and retreated to stand with the herald and his stepson.

Gasps and soft chitchat could be heard round the square. I noticed many women's eyelashes fluttering at the captain. He seemed to have cast a spell over the women of Hartford, with his flair for the drama!

Captain Mason wiped his brow and shook his head. "In my haste I have forgotten my specs." He motioned to Clerk Bayard to come forth. "You, boy, read what your Uncle Stuyvesant wants from me, from us. Now!"

Clerk Bayard unsealed the parchment. He began to read the contents of the letter in a clear, crisp voice. His command of English was much stronger than his stepfather's.

Most Honored and Worthy Sirs,
By this occasion of my brother-in-law, Nicholas Varlet, being necessary to make this voyage for his distressed sister Judith Varlet imprisoned as we are informed upon the pretend accusation of witchery, we believe from her knowledge, education, lyrical conversation, and profession of faith, you must assure that she is innocent of such a horrible crime, and therefore doubt not you will formally find your Honors, the favor and aid for the innocent.

Your loving friend and neighbor,
The Honorable Peter Stuyvesant of Amsterdam in New Netherlands
Dated 13 October 1662

The crowd was silent. Then Mrs. Migat shouted, "Pooh! Pretend witchery? Lyrical conversation and education? Bah! All lies."

"Who is this man to tell us what to do?" an older man cried out. "Send the Dutchman back to New Netherlands. To Holland, for all we care!"

Captain Mason looked down, and shook his head.

"I must confer with Marshal Gilbert and the magistrates about this."

Captain Varlet pivoted smartly toward the Varlet homestead.

"You have but twenty-four hours for a decision. I, along with my stepson and our other companion, will remove to my family's homestead for the night. During this time I will continue to take inventory regarding my deceased father's estate."

He glared at Captain Mason. "I will return to the square at noon tomorrow. We will expect a reply."

"And if you don't get a reply by the morrow?" asked Captain Mason.

"We shall return with your decision and will report to Governor Stuyvesant," he said. "Rest assured," he added. "I think you want not to anger the man."

Chapter 22

The next morning following the Dutchman's arrival was bright with autumn sunshine. A crisp, westerly breeze rustled the curtains and filled the house with fresh air. After finishing my chores: dusting the keeping room, stirring the fire, churning the butter, and collecting fresh laid hen eggs, the sundial out back in the yard shadowed close to half eleven.

Mother sat spinning and humming a hymn near the fire, her eyes downcast as if in prayer. It seemed she inhabited a world all her own. I wished I could sit, spin, and hum like my mother but the sitting still was always a problem for me. "You've got the roving spirit in you," my father would say, shaking his head. "How to tame that roving spirit only God knows, for I know not."

"Mother, mayhap I'll go to the landing for some air," I said. "I'll seek out wild grapes to pick along the path. The bushes are still full of them." I waited for her answer. Mother glanced up from her spinning, nodded, and smiled a faint smile. The breeze blew little wisps of her yellow and gray hair around her face. Her cheeks flushed rosy from the fire's heat.

"Ay, Hester. Make sure you are home for afternoon chores." The orb of the spinning wheel seemed to thrum faster and louder. I dizzied watching the whir of the wheel. Truly, my mother could accomplish many tasks at once. When she was spinning and singing she seemed to find her peace from life's toils.

Perhaps she had forgotten about the meeting with Captain John Mason and Captain Varlet at the hour of noon today. I forgot naught. I wanted to make certain I would be down to the square by noon.

I recalled the bitter exchange between the two men the day before. And how I overheard people say that the only things Captain Varlet would sail home with were a few of Caspar's possessions, but not his sister Judy. Captain Mason and the marshal would make certain of that.

I knew not what would happen to Dutch Judy. I had a feeling Marshal Gilbert would be present with Captain Mason today. Captain Mason was still Acting Governor, but Marshal Gilbert was the law.

I wrapped a light blue shawl around my shoulders and found a small tin pail for the grapes. I decided to walk behind the Varlet homestead, through the orchards, and then down to the landing.

All seemed unusually quiet at the Varlet place. What were they thinking and saying amongst themselves? I watched the red, gold, and orange leaves from the surrounding oak trees quiver and spin down like whirligigs. Some spiraled straight to the ground while others floated for a time upon the breeze.

I found some wild grape vines and elderberry bushes along the path. Before I realized it, my pail was half full. I couldn't help but eat a few of the ripe fruits.

I made my way toward the square. A few people had gathered, including Ann and Sybil Whiting. Watching them from across the square was a sight plentiful enough. I had no desire to make small talk with Ann.

But she had seen me. Ann and the young girl crossed the square and greeted me with bright, eager eyes.

"Hester, I reckoned you'd be here for the announcement. What thinks you?" Ann's round eyes stared at me; she awaited my reply.

"I know not, Ann. Dutch Judy is my neighbor and yours." I tried to conceal the disgust I felt toward my friend. But I kept my tone calm.

"Yes, but *you* know about Dutch Judy. *We* know about Dutch Judy."

"*We* know about Dutch Judy?" I repeated.

"We know she's a witch," chimed Sybil. "My father thinks so too."

"The justice of the Lord will be served," said Ann. "Mark my words." And then under her breath she whispered to me, "She'll be hanged yet."

"The Lord's justice is good," I replied. I met her eyes. "Yet *we* know not who is good and who is evil."

Sybil stared down at the pail filled with grapes.

"Yes, you can have some grapes. Mind you but a few," I told her. In that moment, Sybil reminded me so much of Betty that it pained my heart.

———

A trumpet blared and the bell finally rang for noon. The herald, Captain Varlet, and his stepson, Nicholas Bayard stepped off the path and into the crowded square. People congregated whispering about the proceedings and waiting for the authorities' decision. Would Judy be freed or would Marshal Gilbert take a stand against the incorrigible Governor Stuyvesant? How I wished our real governor returned to Hartford.

The Varlet family followed behind Captain Varlet. They looked scared, as if they might be accused next: Sarah with her kerchief, Maria with her baby, and Mrs. Varlet, who looked as pale as ice. She had suffered so many losses this last month.

Captain Mason and Marshal Gilbert strode to the square and halted to confer with one another. Alongside Captain Mason was his top lieutenant, Thomas Barnes. He had received many acres of land in Farmington. Thomas was often seen with Captain Mason and did his bidding. Mary, the wife of Thomas, waited by his side. She was a small, graying mouse of a woman who said very little.

All three men seemed to be arguing; their heads and hands moved every which way. Marshal Gilbert's face was plum red. I wondered if he and Captain Mason had a disagreement.

Captain Mason cleared his throat and began. "Good people of Hartford, those whom we serve tirelessly and with honor. We are here at this hour of noon to announce the fate of Judith Varlet, hereby accused of witchery and mischief in our godly town."

"And godly we shall even remain, praise God," one woman said.

A chorus of huzzahs echoed in the square.

"Quiet down," shouted the marshal. "We shall conduct this proceeding with dignity."

I could see Marshal Gilbert was unable to keep still. He paced at the entrance of the square. Drops of sweat poured from his bulging forehead. He kept using the palm of his hand to swipe it clean.

Captain Varlet stepped forward to face the authorities. "Your Honors, I as well as our Honorable Governor Stuyvesant eagerly await your reply. I assume you have reviewed his letter and all the evidence he writes of my beloved sister. Now is the allotted time and hour. What say you?"

A hush came across the crowd.

"Guards, bring out the prisoner—now!" shouted Captain Mason. His brow wrinkled and the two appointed guards hurried toward the jail.

Minutes passed as we all awaited the arrival of the prisoner.

Finally, the guards returned and pushed the prying crowds to the side. "Move back," one of them commanded. "Get back!"

Dutch Judy, held by each arm, stumbled to the center of the square. Her violet skirt, slashed and begrimed, displayed her dirty and faded undergarments. Her black hair dripped over her face like spilled ink. Her boots were mud caked, and bits of straw clung to her from head to toe. She wore iron shackles with chains around her legs and hands. She looked defeated, confused, and distraught.

"Behold the prisoner," said Captain Mason.

The gossips began squawking, remarking how poor Judith looked, how dreadful was her character, and that of course she was guilty.

"Why, I've heard her curse our good marshal," one said.

I nodded to myself, thinking I had heard that curse as well.

"Look at her dress; she is naught but a harlot and witch," yelled Mrs. Migat. "Hang her in Hartford! Hang her!"

Someone began to beat a drum to silence the crowd.

Judith stood in the center of the square, eyes downcast, silent and subdued, unlike the fiery Dutch woman we all knew. Her spirit seemed broken.

"What say you to my sister in such condition as this?" Captain Varlet gestured to the pathetic figure that was Judy. Secretary Bayard shook his head and looked stricken as well.

"She's no witch," Captain Varlet continued. "Governor Stuyvesant has further explained this in his letter."

At the sound of her brother's voice, Judy lifted her head and raised her manacled hands into the air.

"Nicholas, brother, help me!" She crumpled to the ground and lay there motionless and limp. Captain Varlet tried to run to her, but a guard stopped him with a pike laid across his chest.

"No further, Captain Varlet. These are the orders," said the guard. "We must await the decision from the authorities."

The two guards hoisted Judy up and stood on either side of her. All was quiet, for the fate of Dutch Judy was nigh.

Captain Mason cleared his throat again. "We have reviewed the letter from Governor Stuyvesant in full. This letter claims that Judith Varlet…" He pointed to Judy. "The prisoner we see before us, is a woman of fascination, a woman of intelligence and fine upbringing." He paused, his eyes scouring the crowd. "But this same woman is accused of the heinous crime of witchcraft in Hartford, a crime punishable by death."

"To the gallows she belongs, to the gallows she must go," Mrs. Migat shouted. She shook a knobby finger at Judy. "'Tis the punishment for entertaining Satan."

No one dared silence Mrs. Migat. I had tried. She was accustomed to speaking at will.

"To the gallows, to the gallows," people began to chant in low tones.

"Enough. I will finish now," replied Captain Mason. "As Acting Governor, I command you to refrain from comments, lest any of you desire a few hours next market day in the stocks. We will not abide disorderly behavior."

The crowd grew silent again, but I still could hear the hum of whispers all over the square.

Captain Mason continued. "Marshal Gilbert and I, along with Magistrate Wyllys have reviewed the evidence in painstaking detail." He stepped forward and removed a scroll from his vest. He unraveled the paper, pushed his specs further down his nose, and began reading.

"Upon this day of our Lord, anno 1662 in the month of October, we, the authorities of Hartford, have reached a decision regarding the fate of said prisoner, Judith Varlet. According to the laws of Hartford, the above mentioned was and is accused of mischief and the crime of witchcraft. Magistrate Wyllys has found sufficient evidence to hang this woman on the gallows." A gasp went up in the crowd and Nicholas Varlet lunged forward before being once again barred by a guard's pike.

Captain Mason held up a hand for silence. "Be that as it may," he went on, "we have reached a decision, and it was not unanimous. Due to our utmost respect and affection for the Honorable Peter Stuyvesant, our neighbor and friend, and after reviewing his letter with careful consideration, we have concluded that we will release the prisoner into the care of her brother, Captain Nicholas Varlet.

Signed this 15th day of October in the year of our Lord, 1662
Captain John Mason, Acting Governor of Connecticut
Marshal Jonathan Gilbert, Constable
Magistrate Samuel Wyllys"

No one spoke a word, for all were too shocked.

"Guards, bring forth the prisoner. Remove her shackles at once," ordered Captain Mason.

Both guards dragged Dutch Judy toward her brother. With a swift blow of his pike, one guard lanced off her hand chains. Then he bent down to slash her leg chains, and Judy was free.

Judy lifted her head and collapsed in the arms of her brother. I was glad for her freedom, for she and her family were never made welcome to Hartford. Maybe now she would have a chance to meet a man who would become her husband, far from Hartford's river shores.

Captain Varlet embraced his sister. His black cloak stretched out like bat wings that folded up around her. He held her close and whispered in her ear, words no one could hear.

"You are free to leave now," grumbled Captain Mason. "Take your sister, and your whole family, for that matter. The sooner the better. Give my regards to the Honorable Stuyvesant."

Marshal Gilbert hobbled around the square, his black eyes flashing and his musket lifted high in the air. Titus, leashed to a post began barking and snarling at the Dutchman and his sister. The dog always seemed to know when his master was angry, and to whom his master was angry at. Townspeople buzzed like wasps, questioning the decision to free Judy. But it was too late.

Ann was seething as well, wringing her hands, clenching her fists, and crying out about the unfairness of this decision. I remembered Ann in the Ox Pasture claiming she had won. But Judy was free. She would not be hanged on Gallows Hill after all. I bit my tongue and swallowed these thoughts like medicine. I was relieved and perhaps a bit envious of Judith's new freedom.

But suddenly I was no longer focused on Dutch Judy, her brother, or Ann. For trudging up the path from the landing came the peddler, Sam Flagg, followed closely by Tom—at long last!

Chapter 23

No one noticed—for all eyes watched Judy—as I dashed across the square and then greeted Tom with a warm welcome. I nodded to his father and shared with them all that had passed since they were in Hartford last: the hanging of Mary Sanford, her husband's removal, the arrest of Goody Seager and Judy, and now the release of Judy into the hands of her brother.

I knew not how I felt over Judy's release. Perhaps it *was* envy and relief all at the same time. Her words from that fateful night sounded in my head: "Curse this town. What I would do to be free from this Puritan town." She was free now, free from Hartford for good. Mayhap her dreams would come to pass for her back in New Netherlands.

My heart wished it so, for I knew that Dutch Judy was no witch. She was a worldly woman, too worldly for Hartford. She was bored with our pious, dull lives. Even Ann's fits and her mocking rants in Dutch tones would not send Judy to the gallows. She was one of the lucky ones who managed to escape the noose, the noose that swung on the great elm overlooking the rocky ridge on Gallows Hill.

But with Goody Seager still in jail, the specter of witchcraft hovered near.

Tom's father left us and headed up to the tavern for a "pint, some victuals, and more news." I had some time before I must return home, so Tom and I strolled along the Great River's banks as we had many times before. Only this time, Tom gently grasped my hand. I grasped it back. I needed my own comfort.

He appeared hearty and hale, bronzed and filled with sun. We found shade under a drooping willow tree and sat for a time. "I am glad you've returned at last," I said. "Before autumn muster as you promised." I paused. "Life has been hard. I've felt much alone here in Hartford these past months."

Tom turned to me. "Hester, you know my feelings for you. Although we have been friends many a year, it's different now. My feelings have grown stronger. What think you?"

I nodded. "I've thought of you often. I feel the same."

He stood up and gestured toward the landing, "What say you, that I sweep you up now and take you away? Like Judy's brother?" He smiled. "Am I, a lowly peddler's son, as dashing as Captain Varlet?"

"Ay," I said, laughing. "More dashing than any young man in this town."

Tom became serious now. "No one is safe in Hartford, I'm afraid. For I am certain Marshal Gilbert and Captain Mason are angry to release Judith to her brother. It's clear it was nary the choice they wanted. They may demand someone in her stead." He shook his head. "That foolish friend of yours, Ann. She is the cause of all this."

That full moon night last January came pounding into my memory again: the fire on the green, the chants, the brew, the figures cloaked in darkness, the creature with the stag horns atop his head. I had *tried* to help my friend. But truly, I had finally realized there was no helping Ann.

"I must tell you something Tom. Something that's been a burden to me all these long months." He stared at me with concern in his eyes. And could it be a flash of jealousy? Tom knew that James Ensign had taken an interest in me.

I let out a long sigh. "No," I quickly told him. "I have no other suitors in Hartford. Why, I may think the same of you in Boston where women wear lace, silk, and satins. Not this dreary homespun." I looked down at my brown skirt and plain brown bodice. At least the blue of my shawl gave me some color.

Tom looked somewhat eased. "I care not about clothes, Hester. I care for your heart, your soul, and your mind. But speak on and tell me what troubles you."

"Remember we spoke briefly of Robin Goodfellow? The one from the ballads you gifted me. Can you tell me again what you know?"

Tom watched the river rafts floating down the Great River's currents. He took off his hat and scratched his head. "I know only the stories Granny Flagg told me of Robin Goodfellow and his mischievous pranks. How he'd pinch young girls if they hadn't done their chores. You would not dare be out late, for you might meet Robin at the crossroads. He may appear as a stag, a hound, or maybe a horse. One never could be sure…but he could help the lasses as well. He would grant them a kiss and spin all their flax during the long evening. He could lead them to a future husband as well." He took a long breath in. "But Robin Goodfellow is naught but an old folk legend from England."

He frowned as if frustrated with our talk. "What of the *Sonnets* I gifted you, Hester? Why so much concern over the ballad of Robin?"

"Is Robin Goodfellow another name for the Devil?" I persisted. "Does Satan work through this Robin?"

"Ay, Hester, the Devil may work through us all, given the means. Perhaps the Devil works through your friend Ann. There's nothing godly about her rants and fits."

He watched me with a serious look. "What has happened to cause this concern?"

I took a deep breath in and began: "Many months ago in January, when the full moon was out, I saw Ann leave her house," I told him. "In the middle of that cold night, mind you. I bundled up and found her distraught, gazing at the moon. She noticed smoke from the South Green and wanted to see what transpired. I attempted to dissuade her but then Dutch Judy came upon us, for she was walking to the green herself."

"What is this?" Tom's eyes grew wide. "Why would Judith be walking to the green at such an hour?"

"She told us it was the Feast of St. Agnes, when single women can see the face of their future husbands in the fire. And they were to have a full moon Merry Meet."

Tom chuckled. "I hope you saw my face in the fire."

"There is little humor in my telling."

I could see he struggled to speak gravely. "So, what happened next? What did thou see?"

"Ann was intrigued. She acted as though she were under a spell. She wanted to know if they be witches!"

"Papists perhaps. Or heathens. Mayhap they are believers in the Old Ways. Tell me the rest."

"Judith left us and cursed Hartford. She seemed determined to find a man to help her escape this town."

"She got her wish in the end, now didn't she?" Tom said.

"Ay, and that night we followed her to the green and hid behind trees and rocks. There around a fire and kettle stood Rebecca Greensmith, her husband, the Ayreses, Judy, Goody Seager, James Wakely, Mary Sanford and her husband Andrew amongst others. They were stirring up a brew that looked and smelled like a sack posset. Rebecca Greensmith led the merry meet. Being scared, cold, and worried, I wanted to flee. But Ann wished to stay and watch. Could I but leave her there amongst the likes of these people? No, I could not." I took a deep breath. "Then I heard a strange chant that ended in ho, ho, ho. Later, as I read the book you gifted to me, I recognized the chant as part of the same ballad, "The Mad, Merry Pranks of Robin Goodfellow."

Tom's eyebrows lifted. "They were reciting the folk tale of Robin? Doest thou know Hester, that this Robin Goodfellow is similar to Puck?

"Puck?" I shook my head. "I know naught a figure named Puck."

"Why, Puck is an impish creature from Shakespeare's play, 'A Midsummer Night's Dream.' Many people have him and Robin as devils. They are filled with mischief in the play."

"I know naught of such a play," I said.

"Of course you know naught of this play. Plays and masques are not allowed in Hartford," he reminded me.

"But the author of the play is the same who wrote *The Sonnets* I gifted you."

"I did not know that Shakespeare wrote such a play. What of this Puck—and Robin?"

"Robin and Puck are hobgoblins. They are fairies and filled with gleeful pranks."

"But why would these people care for Robin Goodfellow and Puck? Are these the devils that they call up and make a merry meet for?"

"Perhaps they seek merriment with folktales from the Old Country," said Tom. "They seem to celebrate some Catholic or even the old Pagan holidays, so they revel in their beliefs in creatures like Robin." Tom became quiet. "But continue on, I must know what else transpired." He slid closer and watched me.

I told Tom of the antlered figure. Then I said, "Somehow, they knew Ann was amongst them. Perhaps Judy warned them. They invited Ann to join them. I remained hidden behind the rock. Ann came forth, gazed into the fire, and screamed out for her mother. Then she ran back to the rock. Goodman Ayres and the others laughed and jested how 'She runs to her rock.' I know not what it all means, but Ann in her fits at the fast mentioned how they ruined her chances of marriage because 'she runs to her rock.'"

Tom grabbed for my arm. "Did they see you, Hester?"

"Mayhap some did," I said, unable to meet his eyes. "We ran back home through the woods. God had His hand upon us that evening, making certain we arrived back to our houses safely."

"And soon after, Ann's fits started?" Tom asked.

"Ay, soon after Betty's death. Betty's claim of Goody Ayres pinching her and the story of the dark man upset Ann. It upset us all."

"So Goody Ayres filled the little girl's head with tales of Robin Goodfellow? Betty was impressionable and scared of course." He paused. "Remember, Hester, that scores and scores of parents have told their children of the merry pranks of Robin Goodfellow, colorful tales that would scare them into obedience and to tidy their rooms." He shook his head as if he could not believe what he was hearing.

"But this Robin Goodfellow," I pressed on. "He is a creature of mischief and darkness, so he must be a devil,"

Tom frowned and sighed. "'Tis but a fanciful tale that is hundreds of years old. The authorities in Hartford will find the Devil wherever they may." He took my hands and looked into my eyes. "There is danger lurking here, Hester. I like it naught. I pray you have told not a jot of this to any soul?"

"None but you. I trust very few people in Hartford now."

"Ay, you are a wise girl, and that's what I love about you."

We had spoken long enough on this matter. I knew I had to return home. I could not take the risk of being late. Tom and I said our goodbyes, planning to meet again soon.

I ran home, my neckerchief flapping like a bird's wings, hoping my father was not angry with me.

Chapter 24

---

*F*inally, Autumn Muster day was here. The last of the red, gold, and brown leaves, veined, cracked and dead, whirled down in small circles to lie like a patchwork quilt on the ground. A hint of winter hastened on the breezes.

Tom and I planned to meet up on the South Green. After the drills, the games, and the amusements, we would walk to the Dutch fort behind the Varlet's orchard. Tom had something important to share with me.

Mother's linens, fruit pies, and her autumn muster cake were all prepared. I was to carry them to the women's tent, the same tent where the annual autumn quilting bee was held. A taste of cake, the firing of musket shots, the drills, and watching children laugh and scamper about was all I cared for; it was one of the few times the townspeople of Hartford could frolic and enjoy the harvests of the season.

"Will you be meeting Ann on the green today?" my mother asked. She fussed with a new bonnet, carefully tying the strings under her chin.

I shook my head. "I care naught for what Ann does these days. Her fits and strange talk frighten me."

"Hester, God spoke through her. 'Tis her way," my mother replied. "I will watch for you on the green."

Distracted, I wrapped my thick blue shawl about me, checked my hair and cap, and smoothed out my skirt, apron, and neckerchief. Then I set forth.

The green was already filled with townspeople milling about, curious as to what goods they could find today. Tents were marked with ribbons streaming like thin flags. Livestock pens erected along the sides of the green held bleating sheep and lowing cows. Chickens roamed freely, bobbing their heads and pecking the ground for a stray grain or two.

Upon finding the women's tent, I left my mother's basket of goods. I made certain her muster cake was placed in front on the baked goods table. Her cakes usually won the blue ribbon.

I discovered Tom, along with his father, stacking open boxes and small chests to display their wares. Then I noticed Ann bent over a box of pins and buttons. She lifted something from the box and spoke with Tom.

"Good morrow," I greeted them. Tom's face brightened when he saw me. He raised his hat and rolled his eyes toward Ann.

"I wondered when you'd be here today, Hester," said Ann sounding agitated. Her lips were pinched and she stared hard into my eyes, as if I had done something wrong. Perhaps she was still angry that Captain Mason and Marshal Gilbert had released Dutch Judy. There was naught Ann could do; the fate of Judy was out of her hands. I could not understand her strange moods.

"Ay, I've left my mother's homespun and muster cake by the women's tent." I said. "Now I'm free to roam for a time."

Tom laughed lightly. "Don't forget to save me some time later for a walk and a roam." I wished he hadn't expressed this in front of Ann.

Ann watched the two of us. "A walk and a roam? Can I join you?" she asked.

Tom fumbled with the silverware chest that made a tinkling sound like bells. "Hester and I have some business to discuss," he said, winking an eye at me. "Serious business."

"Ay, so I thought," grumbled Ann before lumbering off in the opposite direction.

—

We finally found time for our walk. Tom's father told us he'd gladly stay and look after their wares.

The South Green was abuzz with activity. The quilting bee had begun in earnest. A musket fire signaled the beginning of the drills. No one would miss us except for nose-in-everyone's-business Ann.

We ambled through my father's flax fields, our orchards, and then down to the Varlet orchard. Most of the apples had been picked by townspeople in search of extras. Winter was coming, and barrels of cider were always in demand.

Finally, we arrived near the Dutch fort. Settling under a sturdy oak tree, I pulled out some corn cakes Mother baked the day before. Tom had a small flask of cider that we shared.

"So?" I asked. "'Tis a pleasant enough day for an outing. But what have you to say to me?"

"Ay, but you know. I mean to speak with your father tomorrow. I'll ask him for his permission to formally court you." He watched the boats sail by the fort heading south and sipped from the flask.

"But you know enough of my father," I said. "His temper is quick to rouse. He can be unpleasant."

"I am brave and you are worth the fuss. I've proven myself over the last years. Here, I am nothing but a peddler's son. But in Boston, I am making a name for myself." He let out a sigh and shook his head.

"You are more to me that that," I said. I fumbled in my apron picket. "Perhaps it is time for some wisdom from the psalms." Pulling out the book, I closed my eyes, prayed for guidance and opened to a page. It was Psalm 119, verse 45. I read aloud, "And I walk in freedom for I see thy precepts."

Tom grinned. "There you have it. God's words. You follow His laws and you—we—walk in freedom."

"How I wish it were true. I have little freedom in this town." I glanced up the river and imagined traveling on a ship or even a small craft. I felt stifled, trapped. Hartford, my home, now felt strange to me. I liked naught the idea of witches, hangings and punishment. Was our God, the God of the Puritans, truly a just God?

"What say you? Can I pay a visit tomorrow?" he asked.

Eating my corn cake, I nodded. "What will you say to my father?"

"I'll tell him the truth and I'll tell him of my intentions. You and I have been friends for years. Our friendship has grown to something more. Something stronger."

I prayed silently to myself. So tomorrow would be the day.

Tom took my hand in his and kissed my cheek. We embraced. The strength of his arms around me truly made me feel protected, loved, and accepted for who I was becoming, a grown woman who could think for herself.

Tom told me he wanted to visit the warehouses at the landing to discuss some business with the workers. He reminded me again about the next day. "Don't forget, I'll be there. Answer the door."

I ambled along the path toward my house. As I passed the abandoned Dutch fort, I heard voices inside the brick ruins.

"Governor Winthrop will be back by-the-by. He'll save us from this madness," a woman said.

"Witchcraft? Bah!" spat a man.

"Ay, he'll save us sure enough. But who's to say when he'll return?" said another man. "We know not. He is traveling about the Continent visiting the Crowned Heads of Europe."

"So, what say you?"

I then recognized the voice. It was Rebecca Greensmith. I crept up to one of the old chimneystacks and peered into the hull of the fort.

There was Rebecca, her husband Nathaniel, James Wakely, and a couple from Wethersfield, the Blackleaches. "We could naught have our May or June merry meet," spoke Rebecca. "But Christmas will soon be upon us. Let us plan for a Christmas merry meet."

Christmas was a holiday no Puritan was ever allowed to celebrate. Christmas in Hartford was strictly forbidden. Reverend Stone admonished us that this was a time the Devil was afoot. Christmas in Hartford was a solemn day, marked by a Fast and Day of Thanksgiving.

"Tell the others who might care to join us. You know of whom I speak," said Rebecca.

"What of Elizabeth?" someone asked.

"Governor Winthrop will save her, or as she says, the Devil will save her." Rebecca cackled. "Remember, Judy is free now."

Why had I the need to tarry and listen to this talk? I shook my head and looked to make certain no one had espied me about the fort. But then I saw that curl and the round figure trying to hide behind a maple tree. Had she heard what I'd just heard about the Christmas merry meet?

It was too late for my escape home. She espied me and came running, out of breath.

"Hester, did you hear this, what they said?" she asked.

"I know not of what you speak." I lied. Then I knit my brows and spoke sternly. "Did you follow me and Tom here?"

"No, I mean yes. But it makes naught a bit of difference. What matters is that Rebecca Greensmith, the Devil's minion, is planning a Christmas merry meet. I heard it all! It will be just like the one you and I witnessed that full moon night!"

"Oh, Ann," I said sighing. "I will never speak of it—nor must you—lest they accuse you of witchery yourself."

Ann's eyes widened, but I knew she understood. I felt certain she would never tell a soul.

Chapter 25

It was late afternoon the next day, when the knock sounded at the door. My heart flew to my throat. Father's mood had been foul all day—as foul as the weather—dark, rainy, and cold. Something seemed amiss. What was upsetting him so?

I thought back to my own actions of yesterday. Did he know I had been to the Dutch fort? Had Ann spoken with him? Did he know Tom planned a visit today? Whatever the reason, he fussed about the house. I tried to stay out of his way.

"Answer the door, Hester." Mother sat spinning whilst a kettle of fresh vegetable soup bubbled over the hearth. I had baked apple oatcakes earlier in the day, father's favorite. Even the smell of his favorite cakes helped his mood naught.

I scurried to the door and opened it. There was Tom, standing on the stoop like a drenched cat. He carried a small wrapped box in his hands.

"Why Tom, you are soaked. Come in quickly before you catch a chill." I showed him to the keeping room.

"How do, Tom? Sit by the fire and warm thyself," father said. "Strange how I was thinking of thee. Yes, I'm glad you've paid us a visit."

It had been months since Tom visited last. Was father truly happy to see Tom? Perhaps his mood would take a turn for the better.

Tom dropped the package in front of mother by the settle. "For you, Goodwife Hosmer. I hope you find the gift useful." Then he sat on a stool by the hearth. I found a place on the settle across from him.

Mother thanked him and smiled. It was a kind smile. She continued pumping the treadle that spun her wheel around and around in a fury.

"Will you be in Hartford long?" father asked.

Tom rubbed his hands together. "Just over a fortnight. We'd like to raft upriver before a hard frost strikes. Farmers are predicting a cold snowy winter."

"Ay, the signs point to a cold winter. The squirrels and turkeys are eating every acorn on the ground. The woolly caterpillar has a thick coat this fall. Flocks of geese left early this year. Looks like it is going to be a tough winter ahead indeed." Like all farmers, father enjoyed discussing the weather. "But God gives us naught we cannot handle. He gives us strength to endure," father added.

"Ay, the strength to endure," Tom repeated.

Father sat next to me on the settle. "So, what brings you round the Hosmer home today, Tom? We have naught to fix. Neither are we in need of any nails, buttons, or other wares. What say you?"

Father fixed me with an eagle's glare. "Hester, busy yourself. Perhaps Tom would like some soup with an apple oat cake." He flung a finger towards the kettle. I obediently ladled a bowl out for both of them.

"Mother, would you care for soup?"

Mother shook her head. "Not now child. You see I'm spinning."

We removed to the table board, with father sitting at the head. He recited a lengthy prayer of thanksgiving over our food, and we began to eat. "So Tom, what be your intentions this day?" he asked.

Tom took a bite of the oatcake, coughed and drank a sip of soup. He cleared his throat. "My intentions are that I would like your permission to officially court your daughter."

Poor Tom, I thought. He had gotten the words out at last.

"Court my daughter?" My father looked stunned. "Court my daughter? Lad, I have yet to see that fine head of yours at meeting on Sabbath Day. Or even on a teaching day. Are thee a Christian or a heathen? I know not your comings and goings." He squinted at Tom. "How do I know how you lead your life when I see you naught at meeting? How can my daughter. a pious maid, be court-ed by a common peddler's son? One who travels to Boston? What dost thou have that a good Christian lad in Hartford does not? What be your intentions, lad? Speak!" Father banged a fist against the table board that made me jump.

"Father, there is no need for such harsh talk," I said.

"Enough, daughter. Let the lad speak for himself."

"Goodman Hosmer," Tom began. "You've known me for many a year now. As a young boy, I visited my Granny Flagg many a time in Hartford. Hester and I have been friends for many a year. We have much in common, and my love for her deepens every day."

Red-faced, Father stood up, wiped his mouth, and towered over Tom.

"Common? How can thou have common bonds with my daughter when I see you not in church? Are you too busy trading and selling on Sabbath Day?"

"I trade and sell not on the Sabbath."

"What dost thou do on the Sabbath then? Dost thou read the Bible? What say you?" My father jabbed a finger toward Tom as if he were under arrest.

Before Tom could speak another word, Father breathed out a long sigh and addressed my mother now. "Frances, fetch me what thee found yesterday."

My mother rose from her spinning stool and stared blankly into the fire. She looked not at me or at Tom. Then I saw her wipe her eyes with her apron.

A feeling of terror spread through me, and my stomach lurched. What now? What had I done? I knew not. Whatever it was, I had made my mother cry.

"I'm sorry Hester." Mother said. She shuffled to the cupboard and reached into the back of a drawer. As she lifted out the bundle, her hands were shaking. "I found this tucked under your bed yesterday. I changed your quilt for a warmer one. With winter soon upon us...."

She began to weep in earnest. She handed the packet tied with cord to my father.

"What says thee to this?" He shook the bundle as if to throttle it, then slammed it down onto the table. "I address this question to both of you." He ripped the cord asunder. Out spilled the *Sonnets of Shakespeare*, the Ballads, and the Almanac.

"Dost thou know that books, poems and plays of Shakespeare and the likes of these love poems and fairy ballad songs are strictly banned in Hartford? What art thou filling my daughter's head with? Naught, but folly and fanciful notions. Bah!"

Father began storming about the keeping room glowering at Tom. My father had once again taken on the role of constable, quick to anger and quick to accuse.

"Both of you," he shouted. "Both of you could be arrested or thrown into the stocks for a day. What would the townspeople of Hartford think? We'd be removed from the church or worse. We have a godly image to maintain. Never forget this."

Father continued to pace and fret, combing his fingers through his hair. "But I have a better idea. I will take care of this *now*."

With that, he snatched the books and letters, marched to the fire, and flung them into the roaring flames. We sat watching the papers furl up and blacken over the great log. Whispers of smoke rose as though the fire was breathing, and red and blue sparks snapped from the flames.

I felt embarrassed and humiliated by my father's rude behavior and grieved to lose my books and letters. Neither Tom nor I deserved his wrath. I sat like a stone and did not move.

My father was not finished. "Daughter, what of the sermons and tracts of Increase Mather, Thomas Hooker, and Joseph Cotton I have given thee? This is what thee should be reading. Rest assured thou must continue to read your psalm book and God's Word. We shall have no other heathen writing in this house. To think my daughter is reading fairy stories and love poems. From the Devil they are and back to the Devil they have gone." His face was white with rage.

Tom sighed a great breath. "But Goodman Hosmer, what of the witch panic in this town? I worry for Hester. Folks from Boston and Springfield are talking. 'Tis a dangerous time. Thou know I travel about these parts and I hear the rumors."

"Talking? My daughter has naught to fear. She's a godly maid. She's done no wrong with the exception of reading fairy stories and fanciful love poems from you. She fainted at the Fast due to her worrying over Ann. We have raised her well."

Father turned and gazed back at the fire. "We are in the palm of the Lord here in Hartford. And for those in Hartford who practice the Dark Arts—God, the Marshal, and Captain Mason will exact their vengeance. Mark my word. These people will meet their justice soon enough."

Tom stood up, took his hat from the peg, and started to make for the door. "I'm sorry I took up your time this afternoon, Goodman Hosmer," he said.

"And I have nary an answer for you yet, lad," my father answered. "Mayhap I will see you at the next Sabbath for meeting. Then mayhap I'll let you court my daughter."

Chapter 26

"*B*ut for the cowardly and unbelieving and abominable and murderers and immoral persons, sorcerers and idolaters and all liars, their part will be in the lake that burns with fire and brimstone, which is the second death."

Thus began the Reverend Stone's sermon on this teaching day. It seemed everyone was at meeting today. There sat Ann, prim and proper, next to her father and brothers in the Cole family pew. My own family's pew was full today as well. My sister, now heavy with her first child, sat beside her husband. They seemed happy and content with their life together.

And there sat Tom, alone in the first row of the men's gallery, his curly dark hair smoothed back with grease. He wore a blue jacket that puffed out at the shoulders with shiny, copper buttons. *He's trying*, I thought, *trying to please my father*.

He made a handsome figure among the dour and melancholy folk settled in the meetinghouse. I could not help but swivel my gaze his way. Only after the tithing man tapped me firmly on the shoulder with the blunt end of his tickle stick, did I look afore me. I could feel my father's stern eyes on me as well.

It seemed the only folks missing were the Greensmiths and the others I had overheard down by the Fort. They dared not show themselves at meeting, for today Marshal Gilbert and Captain Mason sat in front, listening to the Reverend Stone preach his words based on the Book of Revelation verse.

"How many here amongst us, our brethren, know of the liars, those sorcerers, witches, and heathen? Ay, they are amongst us here in Hartford. Look upon one another now."

I looked to Tom who was rolling his eyes up and yawning.

"Know that the abominable, the liars, the sorcerers, know that God in His power and glory shall see that those sinners shall find their place in the lake of fire and brimstone! Amen."

A chorus of amens echoed through the cold meetinghouse.

"And I have been given word from the Lord, that the abominable will be exposed and the stains removed from our godly town for good. Amen!"

Another thunderous round of amens resounded from the congregation.

The gathered sang a hymn of praise to the Lord, and meeting was finally over. After four hours sitting in the frosty meetinghouse and listening to sundry admonitions, I was ready for the service to be done.

People rushed out of the meetinghouse doors and congregated outside, making small talk. The day was gray and chilly, typical of late November. Tom was watching and waiting for me. I slipped by my parents, who spoke with the Reverend Whiting and his family.

"Can we find time for a walk *now*, Hester?" He smiled, winked, and put a hand on my shoulder.

"Father said we could walk as long as you showed yourself at meeting." I observed the townspeople scurrying about for crumbs of gossip like mice scampering for a bit of cheese. "And thee hast certainly made a fine showing at meeting today, Tom. There's naught father can say about that."

"Mayhap you could ask him if we may walk now?" Tom asked.

"Mayhap you could ask my father yourself, Tom?"

He stiffened up his shoulders and boldly proceeded to join father and the Reverend Whiting. Most likely they spoke of the crops, the harvest, and the weather, father's favorite topics. But perhaps they spoke of witches as well.

I glanced sideways at Tom speaking with my father. Father briefly exchanged words with him, nodded, and dismissed him with a fling of his hand. He seemed preoccupied with other matters.

"Yes, he said we could walk today. But you need to be home for prayers after noon. We have but a brief time."

We ambled arm and arm along the Great River Path. We walked under the willows, oaks, and black locust trees that spread over the riverbank. Canoes and rafts dotted the river, making gentle waves and currents. Finding a quiet stand of willows, we sat watching the light cast silver threads atop the water.

"Pa and I will take leave soon," Tom told me. We plan to winter in Springfield. Mayhap I'll travel to Boston once before the winter truly sets in." He stared down at his black leather boots. Then he watched me with a pained look upon his face.

"Know that I will be back soon. Nat has decided to stay on in Hartford for a time. He's gone funny for the Greensmith daughter, Elsbeth."

"Nat is now courting Elsbeth?" I asked.

Tom nodded. "I believe so. He's keen on her all right." He chuckled out loud. "Seems fate would have it that both Nat and I would fall in love with maids from Hartford." He shook his head in disbelief. "I'm going to tell Nat to keep a close eye out for thee. With all this talk of witchcraft, we know not who is safe. With a mother such as Rebecca, I fear Elsbeth may be in danger as well."

"Rest assured, I am safe." I smiled, thinking how good it felt that someone cared enough to worry about my safety.

We continued north along the path of the Great River. There was not a soul about, it being teaching day. The wind blew from the north and Tom wrapped his cloak around my shivering shoulders.

The few trees on the riverbanks opened to a copse of woods. A thin path held a wooden marker pointing north with the words etched on it, "To Windsor and Springfield."

"Pa and I have passed this way many a time. Now you know how to find me in Springfield." Tom laughed, trying to lighten our mood.

"Oh, but you will find me in Hartford time and again," I reminded him.

Tom's lips tightened as we quieted. "Ay, but if I could take you away from here, by my powers I would."

We continued into the woods, chatting and nibbling on nuts I carried in my apron pocket. The trees, mostly bare now, seemed to wrap us in their twisted branches.

I heard a twig snap and a rustling, and then a low growl sounded from behind a tree. Tom began to load his musket with powder and shot.

"What is it?" I heard the growl again. This time it was louder.

A muzzle appeared from around the tree and a yellow eye peered out at us. I saw the glint of teeth now bared. We had come upon a wolf, one that would bring a great reward if dead. Its head would be another hung upon the meetinghouse door. By the look of its slavering teeth, it was ready to attack.

"Stand back, Hester. I'll take care of this beast. Once I kill it, we'll drag it back for reward to the meetinghouse," Tom whispered.

Then I saw them. "No, Tom, wait." I pointed. Behind the wolf, two cubs perhaps but a few months old, blinked up at us. "She's got young."

Tom lowered his gun. "You are right, Hester. I could naught kill a she-wolf with cubs. 'Twould be cruel to leave them orphaned." He wiped sweat from his forehead and backed us away, never taking his eyes from the wolf.

The mother wolf turned around and loped off with her cubs. I knew then that Tom was truly a kind man. He would never kill an innocent animal or a living thing unless he had to.

—

"Late again, Hester?" my father asked, as I burst through the door, panting and out of breath.

"I was but walking with Tom. He and his Pa will be leaving any day. He was at meeting today."

Father looked long and hard at me. "You know, Hester, I like the boy. I remember the two of you playing when his granny lived by the Little River." He brushed his hand across his forehead.

"But forget naught that you are my youngest daughter. I want the best for thee and a godly husband I desire for thee."

"Thank you, Father," I replied. His anger was gone now, like an ember that burns itself out. I started up my afternoon chores sad to think Tom would be gone again.

"By-the- by, Hester. There will be news tomorrow. News that I heard from Reverend Whiting."

"What news, Father?" I asked.

"I am not privy to speak of it. Rest up after chores and then we shall pray, for the morrow may prove taxing for some."

Chapter 27

The next day a cold wind whipped down from the north. I gazed out my loft window. I knew Tom and his father would be leaving soon. My heart sank as I contemplated the long, lonely winter ahead without his company.

What would today bring? I had but little time to think for my chores included sweeping out the barn, milking the cows, and collecting eggs from the chicken coop. I thought upon the news my father had spoken of so passionately. What would it be?

While sprinkling corn for the chickens to eat, I heard noises coming from near the South Green. Loud shouts and cries echoed up the road. A man's voice rose above the others, sounding impatient and angry.

People started coming out of their houses, including Ann, who ran down the street, her white apron billowing in the wind.

"Ann, stop a moment. Pray tell me, what is happening?" I asked her as I hurried toward the road.

She stopped and faced me. "There's word of arrests. That's right. Arrests." She was out of breath and had a slight smile on her face.

She pushed her blonde curl to the side. "I will meet you there." She puffed out her chest and started to make haste toward the green.

Why not? I have a right to know. Quickly, I stepped back to the barn and shut the door tight. My chores could wait.

—

A small crowd had gathered on the South Green. I pushed my way between townspeople who stood on their toes, trying to get a glimpse of what was happening. I espied Tom standing with Nat on the side near the Greensmith house. They spoke between themselves. Nat's brow furrowed up with worry lines. There was Ann across from me. She stood alone, waiting.

"Good morrow," I said, approaching Tom and Nat. Both nodded to me in silence. "What is happening to create such a stir on the green this morning?"

"We know not exactly what transpires, but we know it cannot be for the good," said Nat.

Tom clasped my hand so no one could see. "I'm glad you are here," he whispered.

The door to the Greensmith house was open. A barking dog guarded the entrance with little success.

Suddenly, a great wail sounded, "No!"

Elsbeth flung herself out the door, scoured the crowd for faces, and found Nat. She ran to him and fell into his arms. He held her close, murmuring something in her ear.

Marshal Gilbert appeared at the door and stood on the Greensmith stoop.

"Stand back all of you and keep your distance," he ordered.

The crowd fell silent as first, Rebecca Greensmith and then her husband Nathaniel, removed from the house. Both of them bowed their heads low, their hands and feet bound and shackled. Prodded by guards, they trudged down the stoop stairs.

"What doth this mean, Marshal?" Nat shouted, clutching Elsbeth tight against him.

"What it means, young man is that these people are under arrest for the crime of suspected witchery." The marshal studied all the faces in the crowd. "There be chores to do; now get ye all home." He slammed the butt of his musket down hard. Titus, by his side, proceeded to bark and howl in agreement with his master's orders.

I was not surprised at the arrest of Rebecca and her husband. They caused trouble for the authorities, and with Ann's accusations, I knew in my heart it was a matter of time. A wagon awaited them alongside the house. The prisoners were forced to climb into the cart, like Judy and Elizabeth Seager. I could see Rebecca shaking, her body shivering with cold. Nathaniel raised his face and glowered at the marshal.

"Carter, take the prisoners to the house of Daniel Garrett," said Marshal Gilbert. "He will jail them in the cellar of his home— for a price. There, they will join Goodwife Seager."

A guard appeared with two large white bundles and heaved them into the back of the cart, no doubt the Greensmiths' bedding. Like Dutch Judy and Goody Seager, they were required to bring what they had to sleep on.

"Be off now," ordered the Marshal. "Now, I say!"

The carter snapped a whip onto the back of the draft horse. The wagon tilted, then straightened and made its way toward the Garret home. I watched the wagon sway as it hit ruts and rocks, almost tumbling over. But the carter sent the whip against the horse's back again. The wagon steadied and was soon lost to sight.

"No worries, they shall soon be freed," Nat reassured Elsbeth. She shuddered and clearly was in fear for her mother and stepfather. I offered some words of solace. She buried her head against Nat's shoulders, inconsolable.

Tom grabbed me by the arms. "This is why I worry so. What with the Greensmiths officially arrested and Goodwife Seager in jail, who will be next? He shook his head and spat on the ground. "I understand naught what Marshal Gilbert has in mind. Or mad Ann. I do not feel comfortable thinking of thee here, amongst such travail."

We watched the tender exchange between Nat and Elsbeth.

"Nat will look out for thee whilst I'm gone. Isn't that right, Nat?"

"Of course," Nat assured him. Elsbeth lifted her cloak and cuddled up to his shoulders. She blinked away tears and looked up at him. Nat quickly kissed the top of her head. "I'll let naught happen to you, Elsbeth or you, Hester. This I solemnly promise."

I did not consider Elsbeth a close friend like I had considered Ann. But I thought what it must be like to have your parents dragged out in manacles and carted off like beasts. My heart warmed to her plight.

"Where is your sister?" I asked, concerned. "Where is Sarah?"

"Mayhap she is still in the house hiding? I don't know." Elsbeth clutched onto Nat even tighter.

"Where will you stay, Elsbeth?" I asked.

She sniffed and wiped her face. "We are to be indentured to the Ensign family. For seven years unless my parents are found innocent. But what be the chances? 'Tis a dreadful fate." She burst into a fresh torrent of tears, soaking Nat's jacket. "But my mother is naught a witch. No matter what they say, I know she is no witch."

"Hush now, Elsbeth," said Nat.

I stiffened up and drew myself close to the distraught girl. "I will pray for you and your family," I said grasping one of her hands.

Tom and I returned up the road to my house. The spectacle of the arrests had wearied me.

"I shall be in touch with you through Nat. He'll let me know how things fare down here," Tom said.

"How?" I asked.

He chuckled. "Have no fear. We have our ways."

I could do no more but trust him, as I trusted God.

We stopped in front of my house. Tom took both my hands and watched me with a tenderness that seemed absent from the rest of Hartford. "I will be back as soon as I can," he promised. He pushed his hat back and we embraced.

"You always do come back." Choking on my words, I burst into my own frenzy of tears.

"Now stay strong, Hester. You must. I will write as soon as I can." Then he whispered, "Your father may have destroyed the books, but no one can destroy what is between us."

"Please, must you go now?" I pleaded.

"Ay, you know business calls me up north. I'll be back come late winter, early spring." He tried to smile and took his hands and placed them on my waist.

While we stood near the house, Ann waddled by, with Sybil Whiting following her. Ann called over to us, a big smile filling her pale, round face.

"What say you, Hester? The marshal has finally arrested these witches. Huzzah, at last!" She clapped her hands in triumph.

Sybil clapped in imitation of Ann. "Ay, huzzah at last!" Then they both exclaimed in unison, as if they had practiced, "Who knows, but perhaps to the gallows they must go, must go, must go!"

"To the gallows they go? What know you, Ann? Take the little girl home," I cried.

"I know just as much, Hester. *We* know, and now it's all coming to pass." Ann beamed. She grabbed Sybil's hand as they skipped, singing their terrible ditty, all the way to the Whiting house. "To the gallows they must go, go, go!"

Chapter 28

―――――――――

December 1662

*T*he day after the Greensmith arrests, my father announced at breakfast that the authorities had released Nathaniel Greensmith.

"Why?" I asked him, but he had no good answer. I remembered months before, when the authorities hanged poor Mary Sanford. And for some reason, they acquitted her husband, Andrew. Perhaps Marshal Gilbert and Captain Mason thought witches only to be women?

True enough, my father's news was correct. For when I glanced out the window, there was thin, wiry Nathaniel, trundling down the road with a sack slung over his shoulders.

What a relief for Elsbeth and Sarah; now they would no longer be indentured out to the Ensigns. Although Nathaniel was not their true father—Rebecca had been married three times—they could remain with him at home. Perhaps Marshal Gilbert's heart had softened thinking about the two girls alone in a strange home, orphaned.

The trial was set for a week's time. Both Rebecca Greensmith and Elizabeth Seager would be accused of "familiarity with the Devil" and "entertaining Satan." My father told me that Jeremy Adams's Tavern was decided upon as the perfect place for the trial. He told me Captain Mason made the decision. For the meetinghouse in December was cold and dank, thoroughly unsuited for a witchcraft trial.

With the tavern's roaring hearth-fires, beer, victuals, and with gossip spreading, the trial was certain to attract attention. A witchcraft trial meant business and most likely would attract visitors from up and down the Great River.

Tom left with his father soon after we spoke. They piled their goods onto their raft and crossed the Great River, planning to trade with the Podunk Indians before heading up north. "We're leaving another raft for Nat," Tom had told me. "The two of us will be partners in a year's time. I trust him. And he may need it to get Elsbeth away if the verdict goes against her mother—or something happens to her stepfather. They plan a life together now." He paused and waited for my response. I could do nothing but blink back tears. "I hope the same is true for us, Hester." His kind eyes smiled down at me, eyes filled with hope and understanding. When Tom was near, I felt hopeful and strong.

Father said naught else about the afternoon of Tom's visit. After he dashed the books into the fire, his anger seemed to have burnt up in the flames. I knew he would like me to settle down with a more God-fearing man or one studying for the ministry. But my father could think on but a few matters at once. For now, he seemed taken with the arrests and the imminent trials of Elizabeth Seager and Rebecca Greensmith.

—

On the first day of the trial, a biting wind from the north brought chilly air and light snow flurries. Frost covered the ground. The brown grasses and bare tree branches stood stiff with iced crystals.

I had just finished baking gingerbread, one of father's favorites. The smell of cinnamon, nutmeg, molasses, and ginger filled the house with warmth and a feeling of comfort. Fresh-dipped bayberry and pine scented candles flickered in their sconces. Early that morning, father gave me permission to attend the trial. I was old enough. As long as my chores were finished, he reminded me.

Before leaving to the tavern, I retrieved my psalm book and opened it to a page for guidance. Psalm 59, verse 1 was afore me and I read, "Deliver me from thine enemies, O My God, defend me against those that rise up against me." *What did this mean?*

I wrapped my woolen cloak about me and braced myself against the wind and cold. Mother decided she would stay home to spin; she would pray and enjoy her quiet communion with the Lord.

As far as Ann, I knew she would be in attendance, most certainly arriving early to await the trial's commencement. She, after all, was the chief accuser of Rebecca, Nathaniel, and Elizabeth Seager.

Townspeople walked to the tavern dressed in their best Sabbath Day clothes. Women chattered and gossiped with one another along the road, their heads bowed down like crows pecking at a dead squirrel.

"That Elizabeth Seager is a true harlot and witch. By- the- by, she will be found guilty of witchery," exclaimed a gossip. "'Tis all true what they say about her."

"Ay," said another, "And that Rebecca Greensmith will be swinging on Gallows Hill, I wager."

I brushed by the gossips and fell into the long line leading to the tavern. The line ran from both ends of the tavern porch. Finally, I entered and breathed in the heady smell of the pine candles that filled each corner of the great hall. They dripped and sputtered, sending plumes of smoke up to the ceiling.

In front of the blazing hearth-fire, two long trestle tables had been set up. Behind one table stood a carved and ornate chair. Several other chairs placed alongside the other table provided seats, I surmised, for the jury members. A Bible the size of an ice block lay on the center table. Benches and numerous small stools and tables were arrayed in front of the makeshift courtroom, providing ample space for townspeople to witness the proceedings.

Both keeping rooms on the right of the Great Hall were purposed for travelers and those in need of a meal. People began lining the staircases up to the second-floor balcony for better viewing, many carrying a tankard with them.

The Great Room's hearth-fire cast shadows that further blackened the soot-filled walls. Logs popped and cracked, sending little whiffs of smoke up the vast chimney. The fire's backlog, a beech timber, looked as if it could burn for several hours. A haunch of venison churned on a spit over the flames. Jeremy Adams himself had trained his little terrier dog to turn the spit when he gave the order. This was often entertaining for guests, but today was all about the business of witchcraft.

I studied some of the faces I had known for years. The marshal's hawk eyes and beaked nose, the scar that ran across Captain Mason's cheek. Ann's round moon face. All of them, so familiar to me, appeared as if they were now strangers. And I too, felt like a stranger in the town I had always lived in. I knew nothing else, no other life but what I'd heard from Tom. I wondered how much I really did know of these people; how much I really knew of myself.

There was Nat, sitting all alone, so I joined him. For the trial we could sit wherever there was a seat. Elsbeth was nowhere about. Who could bear to witness one's own mother on trial for witchcraft? I could not imagine my own dear mother in jail or on trial. 'Twas too dreadful a thought.

Marshal Gilbert stood up and shuffled folks to their seats. Samuel Wyllys was clearly the head magistrate. He appeared in a long black gown, a black cap securely round his head. He found his appointed chair, the ornate one, and sat ready for the proceedings to begin.

Twelve men also dressed in black filed in and sat in the chairs behind the table to make up the jury. Their faces looked white with worry, as if they had not slept this last week. The Reverend Stone, Reverend Whiting, and Reverend Haynes walked solemnly along the side, carrying bundles of papers and books. Captain John Mason was present to watch over the proceedings. Everyone knew he had years of experience with those accused of witchcraft. He sat up front in his soldier's stance, legs apart with his hand on his saber, surveying the crowd. His eyes darted back and forth. He seemed restless as a caged beast.

The Reverend Stone began. "Good people of Hartford let us bow our heads and ask the Lord for truth and justice. Let us pray." All was quiet as townspeople bowed their heads.

"Dear Lord, bless this trial as we gather together in Your Name. We ask that justice be served. Guide us and provide us the knowledge whether those accused have danced and supped with Satan and have made merry with the Lord of Darkness and whether they have caused mischief to the lives of innocents in our town. Amen." The trial had officially begun.

—

Rebecca Greensmith and Elizabeth Seager were dragged before the court. They looked like a heap of rags with string for hair. They sat side by side on stools, each awaiting their turns.

Goody Seager's trial began first since she had been in prison the longest. Judge Samuel Wyllys now donned a wig indicating his importance. He initiated the proceedings by swearing her in and reading the indictment aloud:

"Elizabeth Seager, thou standest here indicted as being guilty of witchcraft for that thou, not having the fear of God before thine eyes, has had familiarity with Satan, the Grand Enemy of God and mankind, and by his help hath acted in a preternatural manner." The magistrate leaned against the table. "How doth thou plead?"

"Innocent, your honor," she plainly stated. "Innocent on all charges." She pursed her lips and stared dully out at the crowd.

The first person to be called to the witness stool was old Mrs. Migat the town gossip.

"She'll have plenty to say," I whispered to Nat. He nodded for although he hadn't been in Hartford long, he had heard Mrs. Migat's sharp tongue many a-time.

Mrs. Migat, hunched over, tapped her cane loudly on the plank floor as she hobbled up to the table. She placed her bony hand on the Bible and was thus sworn in.

Magistrate Wyllys continued. "Please proceed Mrs. Migat, to share with the court evidence against the accused."

"In the springtime a little before the flooding, Goodwife Seager came toward me. Down by the Little River." She paused.

"Ay," said Magistrate Wyllys. "And what did she remark to thee?"

"Why," said Mrs. Migat narrowing her eyes, "she told me that God was naught. That's right. God was naught and that 'tis good to be a witch."

Several gasps could be heard in the tavern.

Goody Seager's eyes widened. She stood up and shouted, "'Tis not true!"

"Continue, Mrs. Migat. What else did she tell thee of God and witchery?"

The old woman continued. "She told me that I need not fear the burning in the fires of hell."

"And what did you tell her after this, Mrs. Migat?" asked Magistrate Wyllys.

"I told her I loved her naught, and then Goodwife Seager, she shook my hand, bid me farewell, and desired me to tell naught a soul."

"Liar," screamed Goody Seager. "I told her that God was naught *in this town*. For the love of God, I am innocent." She started to pull at her hair.

Magistrate Wyllys ignored this outburst. "Is there more you can share with the court, Mrs. Migat?"

"Indeed there is, your Honor." A slight grin appeared across her weathered face. "Another night last spring, with a moon full and shining, Goody Seager appeared like a ghost and struck me full across the face. Ay, when I was in bed with my husband, I awakened him, but then she went away. I dared not look out the door after her." The old woman shuddered and cried out, her veined hands covering her face.

"'Tis true what she speaks of," shouted old Mr. Migat.

"So you believe the accused has powers to fly?" asked the Magistrate.

"Of course," replied Mrs. Migat. She pointed a skeletal finger at Goody Seager. "How else could she have powers to come between me and my husband? In the bed?"

Loud murmurings filled the courtroom. Many thought witches could fly at night, with Satan's help and guidance.

"So, like a succubus of the night, she would try to come between you and your husband in the bed?"

Goody Seager's face was red with anger. She stood up. "Why I would want to visit your old husband in the midst of night and then smack you is beyond my understanding. This is naught but the ravings of an old, madwoman!"

But the damage to Goody Seager's reputation and name had begun. The Migats were well respected in Hartford and were considered honest and trustworthy.

"Is there more you would like to say, Mrs. Migat?" the magistrate asked.

"That is all." The old woman bowed and returned to her seat.

The court took a recess and would reconvene in the late afternoon.

Chapter 29

*A*fter the court recess, the next witness to be called up and sworn in was Robert Stern. I remembered that Marshal Gilbert told father that the man had witnessed a band of witches at a merry meeting on the South Green. Although the marshal's visit to my house was almost a year ago, the memory was still fresh in my mind.

"How doth thou testify?" asked the magistrate.

Robert Stern's hands shook and his mouth trembled.

"Speak up loud," demanded Marshal Gilbert, who sat by the side of the jury.

Robert Stern thus began. "I saw this woman, Goodwife Seager," and he pointed to her. "I saw her in the woods with three more women, and with them I saw two black creatures like two Indians but taller."

"Taller than Indians?" Nat shook his head and chuckled under his breath. But this was no time for laughter. Ann glared over at us and then flicked her head toward the proceedings.

"Likewise, I saw a kettle there over a fire," Robert Stern continued. "I saw the women dance round these black creatures whilst I looked upon them. One of the women Goody Greensmith, I believe said, 'Look, who is yonder?' and then they ran away up the hill."

"Goodman Stern, what time of year did this take place, and pray tell the court why you were out yourself that evening?"

"It was January and a full moon night. I could not sleep and ambled around the green."

I gasped aloud. Then all eyes were on me. Had Goodman Stern seen us running through the trees that night? Ann gave me a mean, hard stare and shook her head. Was she trying to tell me to remain silent?

"What happened next? Please continue, Goodman Stern."

"As the women ran away, I stood still, and the black things came toward me. I turned to come away."

"How did thou know it was Goody Seager and Goody Greensmith? How know you?" the magistrate demanded.

"Why, I knew these persons by their habits or clothes, having observed such clothes on them not long before," he answered.

The men of the jury eyed on another, as if in disbelief. What were they thinking? Perhaps they doubted this account. I could not tell.

The next witness to testify against Goody Seager was Daniel Garett, her jail keeper. His wife, Margaret, stood aside him, fumbling with her hands. She kept her eyes cast downward. Perhaps she had something to add because they were both sworn in.

"What say you, Goodman Garrett, you who have been jail keeper for this woman on trial? State your evidence," demanded the Magistrate.

"We—my wife and I do testify that this prisoner under our care, Elizabeth Seager, stated the following to us. Ay, she told us that she sent Satan to us, to Hartford, just because she was no witch."

A torrent of whispers rushed about the Great Hall.

"Why would Goodwife Seager send Satan to tell these folks that she is no witch?" questioned the magistrate. "Know you, Goodwife Seager, that you conjure the Father of all Lies?"

Goody Seager flipped her head around and stared at the judge. "It is because Satan knows I am no witch!" She screamed the words so loudly that they echoed through the smoky chambers. "You distort the whole of what I say." She stood up and shook a shackled fist at the crowd. "I brought into my argument the Book of Acts, right from God's Word. I remembered the story of the seven sons who spoke to the evil spirits in the name of Jesus, whom Paul preaches of. Alas, I forget the names of the seven sons."

She collapsed back onto her stool and drank from a cup next to her. The crowd was silent. Never had one been so bold and clever as to recite scripture in a witchery defense.

"Is this all, Goodman Garrett?"

"Ay," he said. "With the exception that the prisoner told me that all of Ann Cole's ravings at the Fast were naught but hodgepodge."

The next witness was my father. I had not seen him enter the tavern; he strode to the table, erect like a soldier, and was sworn in.

"What's your father up there for?" asked Nat.

"I know not," I replied, shaking my head and wondering what he had to say.

"Please tell the court, Goodman Hosmer, what happened at your home during the second fast that was held at my home, on account of Ann Cole's fits?" asked the magistrate. Marshal Gilbert now appeared to take control of the proceedings, providing a respite for the weary magistrate. He shuffled through several bundles of paper.

"On that day, my wife was attending the fast on account of Ann's fits. I remained at home tending to chores. My daughter Hester was ailing, so she stayed with me. During the course of the afternoon, in the midst of the fast, a knock sounded upon the door." My father dabbed at his brow. "I asked my daughter to kindly answer the door."

"Ay, and who was at the door?"

"It was Eliza, Goody Seager's daughter."

"And what business was she about on that afternoon?" the marshal continued.

"She carried with her a mess of parsnips in a large bowl. Claimed it was a gift from her mother."

"And what did thou say to such a gift?"

"I told the girl to carry the parsnips back home. My wife was attending the fast on account of the mischief wrought in this town. Mischief her mother, Elizabeth Seager helped wrought. I would never receive the parsnips into my house."

"Please tell the court what happened next?"

"Shortly thereafter, Goodman Seager appeared at my door. With the mess of parsnips—again."

"And what did you say to him?" asked the marshal.

"I told Goodman Seager that I could not accept the mess of vegetables because Ann Cole, at the first fast, right after Betty Kelly's death, had cried out against his wife as being a witch. Thus, I could not and would not receive her gift of the parsnips."

"What did Goodman Seager say next?" the marshal asked.

"He told me what his wife had proclaimed at the first fast that everything Ann Cole ranted about was naught but hodgepodge." My father, all eyes on him, seemed shaken up. Sweat trickled from his brow, and he wrung his hands together. Smiling, Ann nodded her head in agreement.

"Is there anything else, Goodman Hosmer?"

"That is all Marshal," my father said.

The next witness sworn in was George Givens, the tanner. Magistrate Wyllys, rested now, began the questioning again.

"What say you, Goodman Givens, to what you overheard Goody Seager say to Goody Ayres at meeting, months ago before the Ayreses escaped Hartford?"

"I heard Goody Seager tell Goody Ayres to 'hold your tongue, even if thee must grind your teeth.'"

"Why think you that Goody Seager would say this?"

George Givens seemed confused and dumbfounded for a moment. "Methinks it is because they are friends, and Goodwife Seager cared for the safety of her friend."

"So recall," the magistrate intoned, "what Goodwife Seager told you weeks before?"

The witness stared straight ahead and refused to look at Goody Seager. "She told me she hated Goody Ayres."

"Doth her action at meeting that day indicate she hated Goody Ayres?"

"Quite the opposite," George Givens said. "She appeared that she bore Goody Ayres more than ordinary good will by trying to relieve her in her troubles."

Goody Seager's eyes darted around the room like little gnats. "'Tis but lies and proves naught I am a witch. I try to be neighborly in all I do." She found her elderly husband in the crowd and cried out to him, "Richard, tell them I am no witch! I have suffered enough."

But her husband had no power to help her. Goody Seager's fate was to be decided by the jury and the magistrate.

Chapter 30

*R*ebecca Greensmith's trial began the next day. The jury consisted of the same twelve men, and Magistrate Wyllys once again presided over the hearing.

I was relieved I had not been called to testify against Goody Seager, or the others. My father was witness to the parsnip stew, and I told him what a fine job he did telling the truth.

"The truth will set you free, Hester," he said. "It's in God's holy book. We Hosmers always do right in times of turmoil."

The weather remained cloudy and cold, and business at the tavern was brisk. A slab of pork turned on the great spit and bayberry candles burning from their scones winked like little stars. Ale, rum toddies, and cider were available. Jeremy Adams, with his bright red bulblike nose, made certain all the spectators were well satisfied with comforting winter victuals and drink.

The tavern was packed with townspeople fussing, gossiping, and churning their opinions of guilt or innocence. Not finding a seat, I stood in the back. Ann motioned to me to come sit with her. She had saved me a seat. I shook my head, preferring to stand.

The Reverend Haynes and Reverend Whiting looked prepared, bearing thick pages of notes. Reverend Stone sat in front awaiting the trial. His face was ashen and wrinkled with worry lines.

Marshal Gilbert and Captain Mason waited on the side as well. Magistrate Wyllys appeared in his black robe, wig, and cap. He banged his mallet. Rebecca's trial was set to begin.

I noticed my parents seated in the crowd. Even my mother had taken time from her spinning to attend the trial this afternoon. Everyone seemed to be there; all except Rebecca's daughters and her husband.

Nat was sitting by himself this afternoon. Most likely, he would report to Elsbeth what transpired today. Perhaps she remained with her stepfather. Now that I knew Elsbeth better and knew Nat courted her, I prayed all would go well. For reassurance and guidance from God, I quickly opened my psalm book. Psalm 56, verse 1 appeared. "Be merciful unto me, O God; for man would swallow me up, his fighting daily oppresseth me." Truly, I believed God was merciful and I prayed that mercy would prevail in the trial.

All was now quiet as the charges were read aloud to Rebecca.

"Rebecca Greensmith, wife of Nathaniel Greensmith, thou art indicted for not having the fear of God before thine eyes, for having entertained familiarity with Satan, the Grand Enemy of God and Mankind. You are further accused of formally practicing the art of witchcraft and thou deservest to die."

Rebecca appeared like a captured wildcat. Her eyes scanned the room feverishly and she snarled with her teeth bared. Rebecca's linens, like Goody Seager's, were tattered and torn. Her gray hair hung like cobwebs from her dirtied cap. Her feral look seemed to shock even the boldest of our townspeople. No one dared to make a comment lest they be spat upon.

The magistrate asked, "How doth thou plead to these charges?"

"Innocent, your Honor," Rebecca replied.

The first witnesses to be called and sworn in were the Reverend Haynes and Reverend Whiting. Rumor had it that they had interviewed Rebecca in jail. What had she told them under the duress of prison life?

Magistrate Wyllys began, "Is it true, Reverend Haynes, that you spoke with the said prisoner in jail?"

"Ay, 'tis true. I have my notes here with me."

"And can you read what you have written that this prisoner said to you during the interview?"

Reverend Haynes fumbled with his notes until he found the right page. His hands were shaking. The young minister's light blue eyes glanced around the room as if he searched for help. "Goodwife Greensmith freely confessed that she indeed had familiarity with the Devil."

Gasps could be heard about the tavern.

"What else did she confess to you in jail, Reverend Haynes?" asked the magistrate.

"I asked her if she had made a covenant with Satan. She answered she had not. But that the Devil told her at Christmas they would have a merry meeting, and then the covenant would be drawn up and subscribed."

Loud murmurs erupted from the crowd. To admit to freely drawing up a covenant with the Devil at Christmas? Was this what Ann and I overheard down by the fort? Why tell the Reverend Haynes this? I shook my head; this made no sense. Even the lead foreman of the jury, Walt Fyler, scratched his head and pulled at his ear. The rest of the jury had their mouths wide open, listening to these words.

The Reverend Stone stood up. He seemed so much older than last year. His gray beard seemed grayer, and his wrinkles looked deeper and etched into his face. "If I may, I'd like to address these statements in order to explain. A commentary is required, so sayeth the Lord." With his hands behind his back, he slowly paced the makeshift courtroom.

"As we know, the devil loves Christmas, a papist and pagan holiday that we do not celebrate. We celebrate it not, because the devil makes merry at Christmas. We Puritans denounce Christmas in its fullest expression. Yet this woman here," he pointed at Rebecca, "is claiming they would have a merry meet at Christmas. 'Tis another fact to consider." He glanced over at the jury. Then he took a deep breath in. "Mark my words, good people of Hartford. We as a Puritan people loathe Christmas. Remember that we left England to escape the papists—those who believe in Christmas. To celebrate Christmas in Hartford is forbidden."

Rebecca stood up and faced the crowd, clenching and kneading the folds of her tattered skirt with her manacled hands. "'Tis not true—my words are twisted."

Reverend Haynes and Magistrate Wyllys approached her.

"How say you such, when we have your own words written before us?" the magistrate proclaimed.

Rebecca glared hard at both the magistrate and the cleric. "That man, Reverend Haynes, has twisted my words about. Why, I could tear the man to pieces with my bare hands. My flesh feels as if it's been pulled from my bones. How you wrong me!"

"Your flesh will surely be pulled from your bones after you hang from the gallows," George Givens shouted.

"Now tell us, Goodwife Greensmith, is your husband, Nathaniel a witch as well?" the magistrate asked.

"If I be a witch, then he be a witch as well!" Rebecca hollered out to the crowd.

"Why do you proclaim your husband a witch, Goody Greensmith?" continued the magistrate calmer now. He paced in front of the table, his black robe swishing back and forth.

"My husband Friday last came to visit me in prison. He told me that now that I'd confessed, to say nothing of him and that he would be good unto my children."

"Why else would thee think your husband is a witch?"

Rebecca sat back down on her stool. "One time we drove our hogs into the woods. I went to the woods to call them. I looked back and saw two creatures, black like dogs. My husband was close to them and one did seem to touch him. I was sore afraid because I heard so much of him before I married him."

"But you married him regardless of what you heard? Is this correct?"

"Ay."

"Is Nathaniel your first husband?"

"Nay, he is my third husband, for I was made a widow twice." More murmurings could be heard from the crowd.

"Did you know your husband has a record of stealing and cheating in Hartford?" the magistrate asked.

"Ay, so I've heard."

"Is there anything else you would say regarding your husband, Nathaniel?"

"Well, my husband being a man of small body and weak of muscle, I know not how he finds strength to lift logs onto his cart alone."

"Why, he's got to lift you, doesn't he?" a man yelled out.

Marshal Gilbert and Captain Mason were on their feet now. The marshal gestured to his friend, Thomas Barnes of the militia.

"Escort this man out. We will have no more commotions during the trial." The unruly man was promptly removed from the tavern.

"Please continue, Goodwife Greensmith," demanded the magistrate.

"Another time we were in the woods, and a red creature began following my husband. He told me it was a fox, but I *knew* it was no fox!"

Rebecca had the full attention of the audience. Perhaps she thought by blaming Nathaniel, she would be acquitted herself? I knew not why she would say such things about her own husband.

"So, if you knew this was no fox, what think you that this red creature was, Goodwife Greensmith?"

Rebecca paused, as if for effect. "Why, of course I knew what the red creature was—he was a familiar of the Devil—perhaps a minion of Satan himself."

She held her head high and seemed proud of her statement. The tavern remained still.

"Is this all, Goodwife Greensmith?"

"I say all of this out of the love for my husband's soul, and it is much against my will that it is now necessary to speak against my husband. I desire that the Lord would open Nathaniel's heart to own and speak the truth."

"So your truth is that your husband, Nathaniel is familiar with Satan? That he has cavorted with dark creatures and that although he is but a small wiry man, he hath the strength of a devil?"

"Ay, I am afraid 'tis so," she said. She studied the lines on her hands then covered her face with them.

Chapter 31

———————

*P*oor Nathaniel! Although he was not in court, surely he would hear of Rebecca's accusations. Soon enough he would know. Why not leave him be so he could care for Elsbeth and Sarah, rather than tell fanciful tales about him?

I knew from hearing about past witch trials that many accused witches were spared the noose by admitting they did have familiarity with Satan. But the danger was, that if you admitted you were a witch, it could also be used against you.

—

The afternoon session began in earnest. Only this time Nathaniel was brought before the court to testify. He must make an accounting of Rebecca's accusations. He sat in the corner looking like a trapped animal, small and scared. His eyes looked strained and several times he covered his face with his hands. There was naught he could do but await his turn.

Rebecca was called up again once the jury was seated.

"Please continue with your testimony, Goodwife Greensmith," ordered the magistrate.

Rebecca glared over at Nathaniel, her eyes like two burning red embers.

"I also testify that I was in the woods at a meeting. My husband Nathaniel was with me. Also with me were Goody Seager, Goodwife Sanford, and Goodwife Ayres. And at another time, there was a meeting under a tree on the South Green by our house. There was James Wakely and Judith Varlet as well. There we danced and had a bottle of sack." She stopped and stared dully ahead, avoiding any looks from Nathaniel.

"Then another night we were in the Varlets' orchard. I was with Judith Varlet and something like a cat called me out of the meeting."

"So this was a signal, a sign for your meeting?" asked the magistrate.

"You could say that," Rebecca mumbled under her breath.

"What did Judith Varlet say to you that night?"

"She told me she was much troubled with Marshal Jonathan Gilbert."

The magistrate pursed his lips. "And what else did she say?"

"She said that if it lay in her power she would do him a great mischief—or what she could."

The crowd gasped. Even my mouth opened wide, for I also had heard Dutch Judy curse the marshal back on muster day.

"I have but a few more questions, Goodwife Greensmith, before we swear your husband to oath." Magistrate Wyllys fumbled with his notes, and with his specs perched on his nose, peered closely at the writings. "Did you in fact visit little Betty Kelly when she was ailing? Along with your friend, Goodwife Ayres?"

"Ay, so I did. Nothing could save her precious life." Rebecca wiped at her eyes.

"But you knew that Betty had accused your friend, Goodwife Ayres, of pinching and trying to harm her? Is that not so?"

"Ay, but I cannot help this. I had naught to do with the little girl's death."

Magistrate Wyllys continued. "What of the stories about the Dark Man? What know you about the stories Goody Ayres told the little girl?"

Rebecca bit down on her lower lip. "Goody Ayres did tell the little girl stories. Ay, she told Betty she had met a dark, handsome man in London and how they planned to meet at the church. But when she saw the man near the church she beheld he had hooves instead of feet."

"Are there any other stories Goodwife Ayres told the impressionable girl?"

"She might have told Betty if she did not do her chores or clean her room, the little man would pinch her. But if she cleaned her room the little man would help her."

"Help her?" the magistrate asked incredulously.

"Help her with her chores," said Rebecca wearily. "But these are mere stories from the Old Country. Folktales. I know not what it all means." She pressed her hands over her face and shook her head. Then she lifted her head and wailed, "Poor Betty. I had naught to do with her death. I loved the girl like my own." There was silence through the courtroom. "Some years ago, Goodwife Ayres lost a little girl—just like Betty," Rebecca went on. "She mourned for her dead daughter, so yes, she spent time entertaining the child." Rebecca started to cough and weep.

"Let's move on," called Captain Mason. "Clearly, the woman was embroiled with this circle of witches." He let out a long breath and began whispering to the marshal.

Magistrate Wyllys continued his questioning. "Please tell the court, Goodwife Greensmith, and know we have your written testimony from Reverend Haynes when he interviewed you in prison. When did the Devil first appear to you?"

Just the mention of the Devil silenced the whispers from the crowd. No one wanted to miss a word about Satan or how he had appeared to Rebecca.

"Why," Rebecca said, lifting her head and wiping away her tears, "The Devil first appeared to me as a fawn or deer skipping about me. At first I was not much affright. But then he began to talk with me and the meetings became frequent."

"Did this involve meetings of an intimate nature?"

"Ay," Rebecca continued with a faraway look in her eyes, "The Devil had frequent use of my body."

"Frequent use of your body?" the magistrate repeated. "What of your husband, Nathaniel? Did he know of this?"

"Ay, and he did not seem concerned," she replied.

Nathaniel stood up. "This is naught but a lie, and I will not have my own wife besmirch my name!" He glared at Rebecca and shook his fists at her.

"Sit down, Goodman Greensmith! You must a-wait your turn. Your shouts of display are uncalled for."

Like a child who had been chastised, Nathaniel returned to his stool. He slumped over and kept his eyes to the floor.

"Let us continue. Did the Devil appear to you in another guise?"

Rebecca seemed sullen and serious, but then a tiny smile fanned out on her fleshy face. "Often the devil would appear as a crow," she replied. "For our merry meet, many of the company came in many shapes. A crow was but one shape."

"Are we referring to familiars, Goodwife Greensmith?"

"You could call them that," Rebecca replied.

"Why do you think the Devil came to you as a crow?" the magistrate asked.

"Why? Crows be black as night. That's why."

"Ah, like the Devil himself, black as night?"

"Ay, you could say that."

The magistrate was sweating now. He wiped his brow and declared a brief recess.

———

After the recess, when everyone was seated again, Magistrate Wyllys read the accusation against Nathaniel: "Nathaniel Greensmith, thou art here indicted for not having the fear of God before thine eyes. Thou has entertained familiarity with Satan, the grand enemy of God and mankind, and by his help hast acted in a preternatural way beyond human abilities in a natural course, for which according to the law of God and established law of this commonwealth, thou deservest to die."

The magistrate proceeded to ask Nathaniel about what his wife had claimed on the stand that morning and if it were true. "Remember you are under oath for far more than petty thievery and lying. You are now charged with the crime of witchcraft!"

Marshal Gilbert now took his turn drilling the little man.

"I confess to nothing. I confess to none of the charges that the court and my wife accuse me of." Nathaniel turned his face, shook his head, and shuddered.

"So you will admit nothing regarding these charges?"

"Nay, I know nothing of what my wife raves about," he cried. "'Tis fanciful storytelling, so she can save herself!"

"So be it," said the marshal, turning back to Captain Mason.

The trials of Goody Greensmith, her husband, Nathaniel and Goody Seager were finished. Their fate now lay in the hands of the jury and in the hands of God.

Chapter 32

The day after the trial finished, snow began to fall. At first, fluffy white flakes wafted in the air like pieces of powder. The sky, heavy with clouds, hung low like a shroud. It seemed to wrap itself around every inch of Hartford.

Then the wind shifted and began to blow out and swirl. Our barn's weathervane spun wildly in all directions until it pointed to the northeast.

"Looks like we are in for a northeaster," my father decreed. He piled more wood near the hearth. "We may be inside for days, Hester. Check the root cellar for provisions."

We had plenty to tide us over, lest the snowfall turn into a raging snowstorm. The snow began to blow sideways, causing blinding conditions. The windowpanes rattled and bare tree branches scratched against the house. Even the candles' lights bent and flickered as drafts snuck in through the windows and hearth.

"What of the trial, Father?" I asked.

"The verdict will be postponed," he said. "No one can make way to the tavern in this weather. Perhaps it is God's way to allow the jury more time for a fair decision. Imagine the Devil coming to Rebecca Greensmith as a fawn. A crow! Hmph! Who knew the extent of what Satan has done to this town?"

He spoke as if he were reliving and reviewing every aspect of the trial in his mind. I had done the same. In this way, I was just like my father.

Mother sat spinning by the hearth. "Hester, help me with this yarn." A basket filled with stretches of yarn lay beside her. A steaming kettle hung over the hearth.

"If you could steam and then dry these skeins, you can set the twist for me. This would be of help."

I picked up the basket and prepared to do as she asked. Once steamed and twisted, the yarn would be clean and ready for the spinning wheel.

"After you finish with the yarn, sit with me for a time," Mother requested.

I pulled up my stool, waiting for the strands of yarn to dry.

"Did thee hear at the trial your father defending the family's good name? Why he refused the parsnips?" She smiled to herself, her leg thrumming on the treadle pump. "The Hosmer side of the family hath always been outspoken and forthright." Mother stopping her spinning. She turned to me. "I know you do not like spinning, weaving, and the like. I know, daughter, 'tis not your true nature to enjoy the domestic life of a woman here in Hartford. You have always been different, with your wanderlust, your need to roam and read."

She placed a free hand to mine. "I am sorry I found the books and told your father. We only want the best for you, Hester. We want you to be a godly woman who loves but also fears God." Her golden brown eyes brimmed with tears. "God's plan for you is stronger than anything else in this world. Remember that."

But I knew not what God's plans were for me.

—

An urgent knock thudded at the door. My father rushed to answer. The wind howled and blew snow inside. It was the tithing man making his rounds. All I could see was his red nose and red cheeks; the rest of him was covered with snow.

"What news?" my father yelled, the wind whistling round the house.

"The verdict of the trial is to be delayed. Once this weather clears, it will commence again." With the news now shared, he was gone, heading to Ann Cole's house across the way to pass the tidings along.

—

The northeaster lasted for three days. Finally, the snow stopped falling. Now a solid foot of heavy snow lay on the ground. Hills of snow piled up on the side of the road. Even the front and back doors had snow blocking the way.

I had some time to think and pray on what had transpired at the trials. Why had Rebecca said what she did? Why accuse her own husband of being a witch? Did she not care about Elsbeth and Sarah? What would the jury ultimately decide? Would Ann's rants and fits, taken so seriously by all, help send these people to the gallows?

—

That night I suffered a terrible dream. I awoke in a cool sweat that soaked my neck and nightshift. I sat upright, wiping moisture from my face. Everything was black; the morning bell had not even rung.

In the dream I walked in darkness. But I knew someone followed me. I could feel it as if someone's or something's breath was close. I recalled trees, their dark twisted branches reaching out to grab me.

Then Betty, pale and bruised, appeared from behind a gnarled tree. Her eyes held no expression. They looked like two pieces of spent coal, gray and lifeless.

"Hester, save me. She pinches me! He pinches me. They all pinch me. Hester, help me!" Her thin arms reached out for me. When I tried to embrace her, she vanished. Now in her stead stood a wolf, its red eyes piercing the dark.

"Tom, Tom!" I screamed. "Where are you?"

But in the dream, no one came.

Chapter 33

$\mathcal{A}$t last the sun appeared along with some blue patches of sky. The northeaster was done. I spent hours with my father helping him clear a path to the barn, and one to the road. My brother Stephen, trapped at the forge, was unable to help the family.

With the road cleared, Mother asked me to deliver some linen up to the Adams's Tavern. Almost a week had passed since Elizabeth Seager and the Greensmiths had taken to the stand. Several folks huddled about in anticipation of the verdict. They seemed restless, wondering when the trial would start up again.

Rumors swirled like the powdered snow that drifted off the wind-blown mounds. Would the accused be found guilty or innocent?

"Good morrow, Goody Adams. Have thee heard when the verdict is set to be read?" I asked the owner's wife upon handing her the basket.

"This afternoon some time, I've heard," she said. "So run yourself home. Our provisions are low because of the storm, but we always make do with what we have." She smiled, her plump cheeks raw from windburn. "Please thank your mother for me. She is a Godsend. God keep her and your family."

———

The meeting bell clanged and clanged. As I watched from my loft window, people began to traverse the road toward the tavern, pulling their woolen coats tightly around them. The sun had appeared but the cold lingered and the wind blew hard.

I saw Ann rush out of her house in a fury. Her hands grasped at her skirt ends as she ran up the hill toward the tavern. For certain, Ann was anxious about the verdict. But so was everyone else in town, including myself.

———

Most townspeople were present and seated when I arrived at the tavern. I found a place on a bench along the side of the Great Hall. The mood seemed somber and uneasy. Magistrate Wyllys spoke privately with Marshal Gilbert and Captain Mason. The Reverend Whiting, Reverend Stone, and Reverend Haynes stood next to the great table before the hearth. Their faces looked pale with dark lines under their eyes. They fumbled about with their stacks of paper and spoke amongst themselves in whispered tones.

Many of the militiamen were present today. It was due to their efforts we were here at all. For they had shoveled, swept, and pushed the snow into great piles, like little mountains all over town. A few stood stationed by the door and had scowls on their faces.

Next to Marshal Gilbert sat his friend and fellow militiaman, Thomas Barnes of Farmington. He was still a handsome man with dark hair that grayed on the sides. My parents arrived along with Ann's father and brothers. Even Elsbeth, accompanied by Nat, was in court today. People murmured among themselves, giving their opinions on the imminent verdict. Magistrate Wyllys found his mallet on the table and banged it several times.

"Order! We shall keep the order during the reading of the verdicts."

All was silent as the twelve members of the jury took their seats. Goody Seager was now escorted into the room. She looked cleaner than a week ago. Her auburn hair was tied in plaits around her head. Her cap, white and starched, looked new. At least the jailer had given her a chance, perhaps her last chance, for a wash-up.

I pulled out my psalm book and asking God for guidance, opened to a page, hoping this would help me to understand what God and the jury had in mind. I turned to Psalm 112, verse 7; "He shall not be afraid of evil tidings; his heart is fixed, trusting in the Lord."

"Do ye have a verdict?" the magistrate's voice boomed.

"Ay, so we do." The lead juryman, Walt Fyler, cleared his throat and turned to address the crowd. He was a short, stout man whose small eyes flashed across the onlookers and back to the accused.

"We have reached a verdict in the trial of Elizabeth Seager, accused of witchcraft and familiarity with Satan." He pulled a paper from his vest pocket.

"As regards the trial and fate of Elizabeth Seager, first it did appear by legal evidence that Goody Seager had intimate familiarity with other witches, such as Goody Ayres and Goody Sanford. Secondly, the accused Goody Seager admitted she knew these witches. Thirdly, she stated she did hate Goody Ayres but it did appear she bore her some great good, for when Goody Ayres stated at meeting months ago that the death of little Betty Kelly would take away her life, Goody Seager shoved her with her hand and told her to 'hold your tongue.' George Givens was witness to this, as he did doth testify. Fourth, when she was spoken to about the trial by swimming, the water test to discover a witch, the trial by swimming that both the Ayreses endured, Goodwife Seager told them to 'Have no fear. The devil that caused me to come here can keep me up and keep you up.'"

There were groans amongst the crowd. Where was this all leading? They wanted the verdict and became like impatient children listening to a lecture at meeting. No one wanted to be reminded of the Ayreses floating or sinking or the death of little Betty. The Ayreses were long gone and had escaped the hangman's noose.

"Now, about the business of flying," Walt Fyler continued. "Most of the jury thought it was not legally proved. Whether Elizabeth Seager truly flew as a witch we know not. Lastly, as regards to the witnesses Mrs. Migat and Robert Stern, only some of the jury believed the evidence. Stern's first words upon his oath were, 'I saw these women and Goody Seager was at the Merry Meet. I know God will require blood on my hands if I should testify falsely.' Also, Goodman Stern stated he saw Goody Seager's kettle, but being at so great a distance this but weakened his testimony. For as it stands, this evidence could take the life of Elizabeth Seager away. Further, the jury was confounded that Goodwife Seager would know what Bible verses to quote as regards her innocence."

He cleared his throat again and gazed with blank eyes upon the sea of faces.

"Therefore, by the decision of the jury being staggered, six in favor of guilt, six in favor of innocence, Elizabeth Seager is hereby acquitted of the crime of witchcraft."

Chapter 34

*A*cquitted? Cries of disbelief filled the tavern. I was shocked to hear the verdict as well. Goody Seager attended the Merry Meet that winter night a year ago; everyone knew she was best of friends with Goody Ayres. Everyone knew she spoke her mind and commingled with the likes of Dutch Judy and Rebecca Greensmith.

Was her acquittal due to the fact her father was a Founder of Hartford? Or her husband, Richard, older than her by twenty years, was a well-respected member of the community?

I thought Goody Seager's clever use of Biblical verses from the Book of Acts had helped free her. Being so quick of mind, she used God's word as a means of freeing herself.

———

The court adjourned for a nooning break. Richard Seager and the four Seager children rushed up to embrace the relieved woman, who had been sitting in jail for weeks now. Goody Seager might be free, but I knew her reputation was tarnished. In the minds of folks like Mrs. Migat, Robert Stern, Ann and others, she was a witch. Whether the jury deemed it so, it mattered not. Elizabeth Seager's life had been spared, but I knew she would be taunted and judged as long as she remained in Hartford.

People were as angry as wasps, buzzing about the tavern, questioning why Elizabeth's body would not swing on Gallows Hill after all. I heard a woman say that because Elizabeth could fly at night, she would destroy every good marriage in Hartford. She was a nightmare, a succubus, a witch! Shaking their heads in outrage, people could not fathom the jury's decision.

I spotted Nat comforting Elsbeth and made my way over to offer them some hope.

"Elsbeth, Goody Seager's acquittal may fare well for your mother and stepfather," I reassured her.

"I know not what will happen to me and my sister Sarah if the jury finds them both guilty. We will be orphans here in this hateful town!" She flung herself into Nat's arms. He held her close as if he were shielding her from the world's woes.

The verdict would soon be read. The fate of Elsbeth's parents lay in the jury's hands. I grasped her shoulder and told her God was with her and would never leave her side.

"Ay, and I'll not leave your side," Nat told her. "Be brave, my love. If the jury acquitted Elizabeth Seager, they are bound to free your parents."

———

The afternoon session was set to begin. Marshal Gilbert announced that the jury had reached a decision concerning the fate of the Greensmiths. Everyone was requested to return to their seats. Some folks gulped the last of their hot toddies, and in my case mulled cider and some warmed bread. The Adamses made certain everyone had some victuals to tide them over.

Once again the jury filed in. They looked weary with dark blooms under their eyes and flyaway, uncombed hair. Perhaps they had somehow worked through the storm, night after night, to ensure the right verdict was decided upon.

Again, Captain Mason sat alongside Marshal Gilbert and Lt. Thomas Barnes, with other militia members huddled nearby. The three reverends, like blackbirds sitting on a branch, stood erect, peering down at the crowd.

I noticed three chairs remained empty. Then I watched the guards escort Rebecca Greensmith, Nathaniel, and another woman I did not recognize—at first glance. Small and gray, she had a mouse-like, unassuming appearance. I then recognized her to be Mary Barnes, the wife of Thomas Barnes.

Some townspeople claimed that in the last few months, Thomas had often been seen with his children's nanny, a pretty young girl named Mary Andrus. She was but a few years older than myself. Her father was Constable of Farmington. But why was Mary Barnes sitting up front with the accused witches? What mischief was afoot now?

The Reverend Stone began a lengthy prayer extolling the virtues of God and how He loved us all, sinners and saints alike. I watched Ann breathing in his every word. She hated the Greensmiths and it was because of her words they awaited their fate.

The prayer was over. Walt Fyler, the jury foreman produced the paper the verdict was written upon. People began to fidget and whisper under their breath.

"Quiet!" shouted Magistrate Wyllys as he pounded his mallet against the table. "Head juryman, what say you? Hath the jury reached a verdict?"

"Ay," he said, and all the other jurors nodded in agreement.

Walt Fyler began. "As regards the case of said prisoner Rebecca Greensmith, accused of the heinous crime of witchcraft hereby accused of entertaining Satan and having familiarity with the Devil, the jury finds thus, that Rebecca Greensmith…." He paused to extract a cloth from his back pocket to wipe his brow.

"Firstly, that she forthwith freely confessed those things to be true, and that she and the others named by Ann Cole at the Fast, had familiarity with the Devil. Second, upon being asked by the Reverend Stone if she had made a covenant with the Devil she said, 'Not yet' but promised to go to the Devil when she was called. Third, the Devil but told Goodwife Greensmith that at Christmas they would have a Merry Meeting and the covenant be drawn up and signed, and most of the jury believed this. Jury members took note of Reverend Stone placing great weight on the Devil's loving Christmas and the heinousness of that dreadful sin. Fourth, the accused declared the Devil appeared as a fawn, skipping by her, then appeared in the shape of a crow. Amongst other things, she admitted the Devil had frequent use of her body."

The foreman stopped to drink from a tankard near his chair. In the silence, someone screamed forth, "She's a whore of the Devil!"

"I demand silence!" Marshal Gilbert shouted.

"Fifth, we the jury noted the prisoner's reactions in court. When Reverend Haynes read Rebecca's confessions from jail, we witnessed her frenzy and heard her scream that she would 'tear him to pieces.' Several of the jury felt this was a sign of demonic possession."

He took a moment to clear his throat. Not a sound was heard throughout the tavern. "Therefore, in an unanimous decision, we the members of the jury find the accused Rebecca Greensmith guilty of the crime of witchcraft, punishable by death."

Silence, then a loud burst of huzzahs rang out through the Great Hall. Ann held her arms aloft, yelling how our God was a just God. A few men patted themselves on the back as if they had wagered on the outcome.

From the small alcove near the door, I heard Elsbeth scream, "No!" Her body crumpled and her hands covered her face. Nat escorted her out to the porch with guards following them.

"Order!" Magistrate Wyllys reminded the unruly crowd. His mallet resounded with a heavy thud. "These proceedings are not finished. The court will come to order."

Rebecca sat as still as a stone. She had nary an expression on her face. What was she thinking?

It was Nathaniel's turn. The jury appeared to have a verdict. Had Rebecca, with her hasty words and loose tongue, convinced the jury he was a witch as well? I held my breath and waited.

All took their seats again while Nathaniel sat on his stool, face pale, his legs and arms in shackles. Mary Barnes sat beside him trembling. Perhaps she was being accused on a charge of blasphemy or adultery? I knew not.

"Pertaining to the case against Nathaniel Greensmith," read Walt Fyler, "accused of the crime of witchcraft, of entertaining Satan and having familiarity with the Devil, the jury finds thus, that Nathaniel Greensmith, first from the testimony given by his own wife Rebecca, that Nathaniel possessed superhuman feats such as lifting logs by himself. Being he is a man of slight stature, we the jury recognize the help he had from the Devil." Walt Fyler paused for a breath.

"Second, the accused's wife saw him with two black creatures whom he touched and spoke with. Third, Rebecca spoke with purity in her heart, expressing concern for her husband's soul. Last, the jury assumed and knows based on testimony of his accused wife, that Nathaniel attended all the Merry Meets and planned to sign the covenant with Satan at Christmas."

Walt Fyler's hand trembled as he held up the paper. "Therefore, in a unanimous decision, we the jury find the accused, Nathaniel Greensmith, guilty of the crime of witchcraft, having familiarity with the Devil and entertaining Satan, all punishable by death!"

Townspeople gasped, clapped, and many sighed with relief. Both Rebecca and Nathaniel had been found guilty of the crime of witchcraft. The punishment for their crime would be to hang on Gallows Hill.

What of Mary Barnes? She sat up front quivering and shaking. She seemed confused, wiping her eyes and casting glances about the room. Her husband Thomas ignored her. I watched him walk to the door where the nanny, Mary Andrus, waited with the Barnes children. He placed a hand on her shoulder and whispered something in her ear. Pretty Mary Andrus nodded and removed from the tavern, taking the children with her.

For the last time this day, the jury foreman stood up and produced another rumpled piece of paper. "We have here before us Mary Barnes of Farmington, accused of familiarity with the Devil and entertaining Satan."

Walt Fyler continued on. "Know ye that due to the severity of the northeaster we all suffered through this long week, we the jury reviewed the evidence against the accused Mary Barnes and we have reached a verdict."

I noticed Thomas Barnes leaving the tavern in a hurry. *No trial?* Why was his wife Mary accused of witchcraft *now?* Rarely had I seen Mary Barnes in Hartford. I saw her on the occasion at Market Day. Never once had I seen her with the other accused, with the likes of Goody Ayres, Goody Seager, Judith Varlet or Rebecca Greensmith.

No one else seemed to care or notice. Most people seemed satisfied to know that both Rebecca and Nathaniel would be swinging from the hanging tree soon enough.

"We the jury have found ample evidence that the accused Mary Barnes of Farmington, indeed had familiarity with the Devil, entertained Satan, and meddled in the dark arts of witchcraft. Therefore, we find the accused, Mary Barnes, guilty of the crime of witchcraft punishable by death." I grimaced and gooseflesh bristled alongside my neck.

Mary screamed out, "Where's my husband? Thomas, tell them I am no witch!" She twisted her fingers around in knots. But Thomas Barnes of the militia was nowhere in sight. He had connections with Marshal Gilbert and Captain Mason. Surely, they could save her life—if they so wanted.

Chapter 35

The three prisoners found guilty of witchcraft remained near the great table. Both Mary Barnes and Nathaniel looked distraught. Nathaniel cast angry glances at his wife. Rebecca stared ahead expressionless. I wondered what she was thinking. How she said what she did about her own husband confounded me. What of her daughters, Elsbeth and Sarah?

Hartford townspeople took little notice of Mary Barnes; they were relieved the Greensmiths were headed to Gallows Hill. Nothing else seemed to matter.

"Please remain in your seats. The sentencing will take place momentarily." Magistrate Wyllys shuffled through his papers and balanced his specs upon his nose. "The three prisoners before you have been found guilty of the heinous crime of witchcraft, punishable by death. Therefore, in three days hence, they shall be put to death by hanging on Gallows Hill."

Now Marshal Gilbert stood and addressed the crowd. "Before we end this proceeding, the Reverend Stone will lead the closing prayer. But before this, it seems fit to ask members of our congregation if they have comments, prayerful thoughts, or any other evidence regarding these proceedings."

Someone shouted forth, "Justice has been served. Praise God!"

I know not what came over me at that moment. My whole body became stiff and rigid. My breathing halted for a moment. Then, without a thought, I stood up, pointed to Mary Barnes, and declared aloud, "This woman is innocent. She is not a witch! How can this woman be found guilty but Goody Seager acquitted? Mary Barnes had no trial I was witness to!"

James Ensign stood up. "I agree as well. 'Tis an injustice." Eyes glared at James. He resumed his seat and said no more.

All eyes were on me now. What had I just said? In front of the whole congregation? In front of the marshal? But it was too late to take back the words I had just pronounced.

Marshal Gilbert fixed me with his sharp, slanted eyes. "And Hester Hosmer, please tell the court how dost thou know that Mary Barnes is not a witch? Answer the court!"

"Because," I faltered, "because she was not..." And I stopped.

"Ah, Hester, we see. Mary Barnes is not a witch because— she was not—there? Pray tell the court, of where you speak?" All was silent. It seemed every townsperson in Hartford awaited my response.

"Why, she was never with the likes of Rebecca Greensmith, Judith Varlet, or Goody Seager at the Merry Meets!" I shouted.

"And how might thou knowest all this?" the marshal asked.

"Because, I was...." I paused and could not continue.

"That's right, Hester. Because you, *yourself* were there. Is this not true?" The marshal grinned wickedly. "Were you in fact a part of these witches' Merry Meets?"

"No, I swear I was never part of their Merry Meets. I just so happened to...."

I took a deep breath in. I shot my arm out and pointed to Ann. "Why don't you ask her?"

"Ask who, Hester?" the marshal continued.

"Ann Cole. Why don't you ask her?"

Ann's face was like the moon, pale and unmoving. She shook her head. "I know not what Hester speaks of. I remember naught."

The marshal continued in haste. "Leave Ann out of this. Ann spoke during the fast. Ay, she spoke in Dutch tones at times, but let us make this clear. God spoke through Ann. We know she knows naught of what you speak."

Then the marshal opened his book of the *Connecticut Blue Laws, the Codes of 1650*. He pulled forth the ledger he carried with him to make note of people's transgressions. "Hester Hosmer, I have in my notes that you as well as Goody Ayres ministered to ailing Betty Kelly. You were with the little girl when she cried out and became ill. Is that correct?"

"Ay, I was with Betty and tried to help her," I answered.

"I also have written down that at the first fast, you screamed 'No' to Ann Cole's ravings and then fainted. Why would you scream out 'No' to the truth that Ann spoke?"

"I know not," I said.

"I have listed a host of other trespasses as well," said the marshal. "Now the whole town will hear. They include idling with the peddler's son on numerous occasions and missing the second fast at the Wyllys house. Further, you were seen at the Dutch fort and down at the Little River Banks on many occasions, including speaking with Judith Varlet when you should have been home."

Marshal Gilbert now approached Magistrate Wyllys and Captain Mason. "I've had my suspicions about this young maid for months. What say you?" he exclaimed to them.

"But she's from a God-fearing family," said the magistrate.

"It matters not," murmured Captain Mason.

The three of them continued their discourse in lowered tones. What had I done wrong but speak up for an innocent woman? Now the authorities spoke of my fate. Ann eyed me with a smirk of satisfaction.

Marshal Gilbert addressed the crowd again. "As marshal of the town of Hartford, I have held my suspicions concerning this maid, Hester Hosmer, close to my heart. We know she comes from a God-fearing family. But it appears that my suspicions are coming to pass." He stopped to take a long look around at the stunned faces.

"We have concurred that Hester Hosmer, under suspicion herself of witchery, shall hereby be put under house arrest until we can gather further evidence. But with this said, all those in our humble congregation, including she who will be under house arrest and Goodwife Seager, now acquitted, may and shall attend the execution scheduled three days hence. The hanging will commence at the hour of noon atop Gallows Hill." The marshal continued to scour the crowd with his eyes, making certain no other person would cause a spectacle or utter another word.

"Goodman Hosmer," he now addressed my father. "Take your brazen daughter home until we decide what to do with her!"

The makeshift courtroom was in a clamor. Everyone was speaking about the hanging three days from now. No one seemed to care a whit about my arrest. My father came upon me and yanked me by the elbow. My mother was there beside him weeping.

Trembling, I tried to keep from sobbing myself. I knew not how I could stand up and say what I did, but I spoke up in the name of God's truth. I had tried to save Mary Barnes. I had spoken when even her husband remained silent. If only I had spoken for the Greensmiths as well. But what could I say? Who would listen? Yes, they were on the green that fateful evening a year ago. But in my heart, I knew they merely practiced the old folkways of England. Now, all three would hang on Gallows Hill. And I must bear witness to the hangings, knowing I might be next.

Why hadn't I told anyone about Ann that night a year ago? Had I done so then, they might have believed me. But now, Ann was the golden girl in Hartford. She could do no wrong.

I wondered and worried; what stories might Ann tell about me now?

—

"Father, I don't want to witness the hangings, please!" I begged him.

"Daughter, you will do what the marshal orders. 'Tis a lesson and a reminder it might be your neck next."

He stomped across the keeping room floor, strewing the freshly laid rushes all over, making a mess. Then he approached me, his face close to mine.

"How could thee, Hester? How could thee say what you did? I understand this naught. Now I must plead with the marshal for your release." His eyes protruded from his face right into mine.

"As part of your house arrest, you will knit, spin, card wool, and everything else you must learn to become a God-fearing woman and wife to a Godly man. Not to a peddler's son either. That is…if you live!" He shook a finger to my face.

"But Father," I pleaded.

Then I decided I had to tell him the truth of that January night with Ann on the green. I told him everything. *Almost everything.* I told him how Ann was wandering outside, how she wanted to see what transpired on the green. "I tried to protect my friend, tried to prevent her from walking to the green. I tried. It was no use," I explained. "But Ann will admit to naught of this." I told him naught about the Horned Man or who was there or that Ann looked into the flames. "Ay, people were dancing around a fire but I know not what they were doing," I lied.

Father shook his head mumbling how Ann hadn't been right after she lost her mother and was disturbed by witches. "Now, I must seek out the marshal," he said.

I obeyed his command and sat with Mother, trying to learn the proper way to spin. She talked little to me, spinning and humming her hymns. All I could do was sit, spin, and wait.

Chapter 36

January 1663

The day of the hanging was cold. Low clouds, thick and gray, hung like dust over the town. The execution was scheduled for noon. We all must attend a meeting service beforehand to pray for the souls of those found guilty. Was anyone praying for me?

My heart broke for Elsbeth. Would she, Nat, and younger sister Sarah be forced to witness the hangings? I felt hatred in my heart for Marshal Gilbert and for Ann. On that full moon night a year ago, I had tried to help my friend. Now she seemed ready to accuse me.

Why did Ann not speak up for Mary Barnes? Ann did not care a whit about Mary Barnes or any of the others. She did not want a soul to know she was on the South Green espying on these people. Worse, she had entered their circle and gazed into their fire. She only cared to see the Greensmiths swinging by nooses tied to the Gallows Elm.

Why did I not tell on Ann? I could try, but who would believe me? It would be her word against mine. Everyone knew how highly the marshal thought of her. People wanted to believe Ann, wanted to believe these people were witches.

So I was alone—alone with my thoughts. Lonely, a-feared and filled with dread; dread of what I had done; dread of what my future held. I knew not. I clutched my psalm book for solace. It gave me hope and direction. I believed in the Word of God. For besides Tom, I had no one else who cared to believe my words.

I thought of Tom and the books he had given me to read, books that opened my mind and stretched my imagination. What had this knowledge brought me but heartache? But I felt a greater heartache when my father had flung my books into the flames. Why couldn't I read books other than the Bible, my psalm book and dull religious tracts? And why, when I had spoken my truth in court, had no one except for James spoken or come to my rescue? James had tried but had no power here in Hartford. After all, he was only a blacksmith's apprentice.

I walked the path to the meetinghouse huddled between my parents. They dared not let me out of their sight. I kept my eyes lowered and my hands firmly clasped together. My father held onto one elbow while my mother grasped the other. Her hand trembled with cold—and fear.

On the walk, I tried to ignore townspeople's cruel comments. "A friend of those witches? Ay, so she must be a witch herself!" It hurt to hear these words. It hurt even more to know that Thomas Barnes, Mary's husband, spoke not for his innocent wife. Did he conspire to be rid of her? I would take this reassurance to the grave if I must that I, in mine own eyes and perhaps God's, had done the right thing by speaking up for an innocent woman.

———

The service droned on for what seemed like hours. Babies squirmed and cried; people blew their noses, shuffled their feet and thumbed their hymnals. No one fell asleep during this service. Once Reverend Stone had finished his prayer, he proclaimed that the accused, if they so chose, could say some final words before the hangman slipped the noose round their necks.

Everyone knew who the hangman would be—Marshal Gilbert. I felt icy shudders down my back, thinking I might be next. But the thought today of these three people swinging on the Gallows Elm sickened my stomach and soul.

A hanging, like watching those shamed in the stocks or pillory, was a spectacle. People used the event as a reason to avoid chores and would, most likely, discuss the horrid details afterwards, over a pint at the tavern. Last June, Mary Sanford's hanging had occurred with few witnesses and little fanfare. Today would be different.

A sad, solemn drumbeat signaled the procession to begin. The noise pounded in my skull. The clergymen, along with Captain Mason, Marshal Gilbert, and Magistrate Wyllys, led the way toward Gallows Hill. They marched in a doleful and careful pace.

Next came the oxcart pulled by an old, gray workhorse. He whinnied, and puffs of white smoke snorted from his nostrils. He seemed none too happy to drag the cart up the rocky hill. Inside sat Rebecca, Nathaniel, and Mary Barnes, their faces pale and expressionless.

The rest of us followed the ox cart. I noticed Ann was dressed in one of her finest skirts, cap, and apron. She held Sybil Whiting's hand. The little child jumped up and down with glee.

"The witches will soon be gone, Ann. Maybe now they'll go to heaven to be with Betty and God!"

"Hush, Sybil, stay silent now. You are a big girl to attend the hangings," said Ann and patted the child's head. Then Ann turned to me and gave me a proud sneer that seemed to say, "So there, I told you so. I knew they were witches." Surely she realized it was because of her that these people were headed to an untimely death. Perhaps it made her seem important to be listened to and to get the attention she so desperately wanted.

We trudged the snow-covered path. Halfway up the hill, the wooden wagon became stuck in an icy rut. After several strong pushes from townsmen, it barreled over a sharp rock, almost overturned, then hung sideways on the path. Militiamen and guards surrounded the wagon. They made certain no prisoners would escape this time!

I turned around to look back at the long line. I noticed Nat in the procession. I saw no sign of Elsbeth or Sarah, mercifully spared the sight of their mother and stepfather swinging from the Great Elm. Elsbeth must have sent Nat as a witness, praying for a miracle. I prayed for a miracle as well.

"Keep thine eyes straight ahead, Hester," my father said. "People will talk. Mind to the business at hand."

The tattoo of the drum kept time to the somber march. Light snowflakes had started to fall. Finally, we reached the top of the rocky ridge, just west of Hartford. There stood the majestic elm, Hartford's hanging tree. Along a low thick branch of the tree, with boles the size of a hogshead barrel, hung three nooses.

The horse and cart ambled up the ridge and halted right under the tree. I noticed a ladder leaned up against its trunk.

"Gather round, gather round, ye townspeople," shouted the day watchman. The crowd gathered near the tree and the cart. Young children gazed openmouthed at the victims, uncertain of what was to happen next. I knew not why young children could attend such a gruesome spectacle. But part of my worry was for my own life. *Would it be days to the gallows for me?*

The Reverend Stone stepped up, along with Reverend Whiting and Reverend Haynes in their woolen black cloaks. Their steeple hats seemed to stretch far up to the heavens. Perhaps that's why they wore such pointed hats. Perhaps they thought they were closer to God.

Mary Barnes, quivering like a rabbit, could not stop the flow of tears. Her small dark eyes peered around the crowd. Her husband Thomas was not amongst the people I could see. No one could or would save Mary; I had tried.

Reverend Stone launched into a sermon. "Behold the guilty, before us accused of the heinous crime of witchcraft. I have ministered to the guilty parties with forgiveness and mercy in my soul. Our God is a forgiving and just God, and we carry out His Will. Now we will observe some minutes of silence as these three souls prepare for the next world."

All was silent. People stood deep in prayer and contemplation. Then a loud crash came from the edge of the woods bordering the rocky ridge. Startled, I jumped to attention. People spun in the direction of the clamor.

A great stag appeared with large pointed antlers. He stopped, sniffed the air, and then bounded past the tree. Everyone gasped. I overheard one woman exclaim this was a sign from God. Or perhaps it was a sign from the Devil, since Rebecca had admitted she frolicked with fawns and stags.

Before anyone could aim and take fire at the beast, he bounded back into the woods.

"That's Rebecca's familiar, come to bid her farewell," shouted Mrs. Migat.

"It's a sign, a sign from God," someone else hollered.

"The Devil in the form of her stag has appeared," said George Givens. "He'll have no more carnal knowledge with this witch. 'Tis further proof the hag truly has a familiar."

With the stag gone, the drumbeat began again. The hangman, hood over his face, began guiding Nathaniel in the cart. According to the Reverend Stone, a hangman's hood was used for centuries in England. In this manner, the hangman's face was covered so he would not bear the responsibility for the execution. Rather, the town would acknowledge it to be the Will of God and the people. Knowing that the hangman was Marshal Gilbert sent gooseflesh up my neck. And there was no mistaking his boots or his lurching gait.

The cart remained under the three nooses. Nathaniel stood beneath one now, his head almost touching the first noose.

"What say you, Nathaniel Greensmith, convicted of the crime of witchcraft? Speak or forever hold your peace," shouted the hangman.

"I am no witch! I go to my grave a poor but innocent man!"

Next, Rebecca was asked to stand. The hangman positioned her under the next noose. "What say you, Rebecca Greensmith, convicted of the crime of witchcraft? Speak or forever hold your peace."

Rebecca cast swift glances about the crowd. Mayhap she was looking for her daughters for a final goodbye. "I have naught to say, for I have said much. Only God may know what is true. I go to my death willingly." She bowed her head low. It was clear she had accepted her fate.

The hangman climbed the ladder to adjust the nooses so they hung directly above the prisoners' heads.

Mary Barnes was asked to stand. Small, timid, and trembling with fear, she arose to face the hangman.

"What say you, Mary Barnes, convicted of the crime of witchcraft? What say you? Speak or forever hold your peace!"

Mary kept her eyes lowered. "I know I am no witch. God knows I am no witch. I thank God for my travails, for they strengthen me. And I thank the young maid who spoke up for my innocence. Only one soul believed me to be innocent. That is enough for me and for God; I can ask for no more." Mary raised her face up to the sky. "But for the sake of my children, I go to be with God. Curse my husband, Thomas, for he knows the truth and says naught." She began to weep in earnest.

The drumbeat began again. *boom,boom,boom.* It resounded deep in my ears, a loud and doleful beat. I thanked God silently for Mary's brave words; she had acknowledged my effort to speak up for her. I prayed for all of their souls; that they might greet God rather than Satan upon their death.

The three prisoners stood in the cart, nooses around their necks. Suddenly, the hangman gave the order. "Now!" Someone near the horse had a whip. He screamed "Get!" and the horse bolted several paces forward.

Thus, Rebecca and Nathaniel Greensmith, along with Mary Barnes, hung by the noose for many minutes. I could barely watch the bodies swinging. After witnessing their pinched, red faces turn blue, their mouths squirming for breath, feet kicking, and their necks strangled by rope, it was over. Mary Barnes was the last to go.

They hung there, swaying like clothes drying on a line.

"It is finished. God's Will hath been done," concluded Reverend Stone.

"The witches' bodies shall remain on Gallows Hill for all to see," said Marshal Gilbert, removing his hood. "There's to be no Christian burial. They shall be disposed of, in an unhallowed grave, location unknown." His words sounded loud and furious to me.

Everyone seemed subdued. Everyone except Ann. She skipped with merriment about the tree. "I hope you are not next, Hester," she hissed under her breath as she ran past me. "You see—I can win."

Chapter 37

*A*fter the hangings, most people walked the road to the tavern for free ale, hot toddies, and flips. Reverend Stone declared this a day of Thanksgiving and no one need work at chores.

Except for me. After all, I was on house arrest. My fate would soon be decided. So I spent the afternoon by the hearth, carding wool and spinning. My mother also had a vat of tallow ready so we could dip candles from the long row of twined string I lined up. I swept, dusted, and stacked up wood for the fire. The root cellar was still full of parsnips, yams, potatoes, and onions. I decided to make a stew for the family. My mother seemed pleased with the idea.

We sat in silence. All I could think of was the three dead bodies swinging from the hanging elm's massive branch. I heard in my mind over and over Mary Barnes's last words. That *I* believed in her innocence and spoke up for her.

Now, Marshal Gilbert would take any evidence against me. Most likely from Ann. Then a date for a trial would be set. How I wanted to implicate Ann, to announce that it was she who had spied on the likes of our neighbors Rebecca, Dutch Judy, and the others. Why, Ann, why?

Why had I chosen to accompany her that fateful night one year ago? My life had changed so much in a year. I trusted and loved Tom. I realized Elsbeth, Rebecca's daughter, was more than a daughter of an accused witch. She, like me, had found someone to love. At least she had Nat nearby. She had a caring shoulder to cry on. I had no one, just a God I desperately wanted to trust and understand.

—

"Did you carefully attend to the little child, Hester?" my mother suddenly asked me.

"What child, Mother?"

"Why, little Betty Kelly, of course. Were you watching her when she cried out in her bed against Goody Ayres? Remember how I told you to watch that little girl?" The spinning wheel whirred round and round.

"I did watch Betty. The best I could."

"Did you see Goody Ayres give her the soup?"

"Ay, I did. I thought naught of such an innocent act. Why do you ask?" Suddenly, I realized her meaning. Did my own mother suspect me of witchery? My heart near to broke.

"You know I meant no harm to little Betty," I cried. "I loved her dearly." Tears started flowing down my face and would not stop. I threw down the distaff I was winding wool upon. "What have I done, Mother, but speak the truth? I have tried to be God-fearing. I tried to protect little Betty. I tried!" I lifted my apron and sobbed into the cloth.

"Hester, I say this because the authorities may twist your words around. They may accuse you of poisoning Betty. Putting a potion in her soup. Or mayhap they think you know more about witchcraft and Satan."

Mother now began to weep, her shoulders heaving. "My beautiful daughter, I know thee to be innocent. I could not bear to see you hanging from Gallows Hill. 'Tis a wretched thought, and 'twas a wretched sight this morning."

I stood and clasped my mother's shoulder. "We trust in the Lord, Mother. We Hosmers are from strong stock."

"Ay, we trust the Lord, Hester. But I no longer place my trust with the authorities."

She wiped her eyes and continued to spin, shaking her head. "But rest assured Hester, your father will speak to the marshal."

—

Father still had not returned home from the tavern. My chores were almost finished. I stirred the vegetable stew, now hot and bubbling. The smells of onions and potatoes filled the keeping room.

"Hester, collect some eggs from the coop. And see to the chicken bedding; it may be damp from the storm. Clean them, if need be," said my mother, calm once again.

The neighborhood seemed unusually quiet. Townspeople would linger at the tavern; *to discuss the gruesome details of the hanging*, I thought. I walked to the barn, basket in hand. Hopefully, one or two hens had laid some eggs. In winter, with little sunlight, our hens only managed one or two eggs a week.

The barn roof was still heavy with snow. The cows, milked earlier, seemed content and made not a fuss. Even Father's workhorse stayed quiet in his stall.

Before I could see to the eggs, I heard a slight knocking against one side of the barn. Mayhap it was a hungry bird banging against the walls. Often they'd find insects buried in the wood. Our barn was riddled with woodpecker holes.

The knocking became louder and more persistent. Then, a pause and I heard the noise coming from the back of the barn. I gathered myself quietly and scurried out. If someone espied me—I was doing my chores.

Peeking around the side, I saw Nat huddled close to the back door. He beckoned me with his hand.

"Nat?" I said, catching my breath. "What brings thee to the back of our barn? Remember, I am on house arrest."

Nat whispered, "We don't have much time." He thrust a piece of rolled-up bark that looked like a scroll into my hands. It was tied with cord. "Read this as soon as you can. Then burn it just as quick. Godspeed and God keep us all!"

"Nat," I asked. "What is this?"

"There is no time to talk, Hester. People watch, listen, and gossip in this town. Take care now."

With that he turned on his heels, and headed in the direction of the Little River.

———

"The marshal is gathering evidence against you Hester," my father said as he walked through the door. He pounded snow off his boots, placed his musket against the wall, and hung his coat on the drying peg near the fire.

"Evidence? Why, there is no evidence but what I told you," I said.

"He seems to think there *is* evidence." He mumbled something about the marshal never being satisfied. "There were three hanged today. Isn't this enough? Hester, I know not why you spoke out at the trial. You have brought shame to the family name. You were meddling where you ought to have stayed clear away." He brought his blue eyes right to my face. "Haven't I taught thee anything, daughter?" My father's face was red from drink; I could smell it on his breath.

"Shame? I merely spoke up for Mary Barnes. Everyone knows she had naught to do with witches."

"But why *you*, Hester? Why? What will the neighbors think and say? That my daughter is a witch or meddles with them? Do you not see where this might lead?"

"I know not nor care not what others think of me." I lowered my eyes and stared at the floor planks. I hoped my father would not consider my words a sign of disrespect. "I am sorry to bring shame upon my family," I said quietly.

But Father was no longer listening. Hungry, he helped himself to a bowl of the vegetable stew simmering over the fire, muttering to himself between mouthfuls. Mother and I knew best to ignore him when he was angry and eating.

After dinner I excused myself and climbed the stairs to my loft. The moon, almost full now, beamed through the paned windows. I lit a candle nub from one burning on a wall sconce and sat on the stool at my table. Anxious to read what Nat had given me, I unraveled the thin piece of birch bark. The writing was a scribble. I read—

Dear Hester,
The time is nigh. Three days hence come the full moon, Elsbeth and I will leave Hartford. Tom has been made aware of your plight. Listen for the call of the "wolf."

Meet us on the banks of the Little River—near the raft landing after midnight.

We must cross the Great River—to arrive in Podunk. The Indians may keep us the night or provide horses, if need be. We plan on taking the back trails to Springfield. Tom will be waiting for us, God willing. If you are not there, we will know you wish to stay and fight.

Godspeed, Nat and Elsbeth

I rolled up the thin bark and dipped it to the candle flame. The bark lit and the contents of the letter burned with puffs of smoke. Now, a great decision lay ahead for me. I trusted God that I would make the right one. My life depended upon it.

Chapter 38

$\mathcal{T}$he full moon was but two nights away. I had time to contemplate my decision. Hartford had been my home for eighteen years. All of my family was here. It was true my sister and brother had removed from the house. My sister was to have her baby soon. I would be an aunt. To have a new life amongst so much death and sorrow was something to look forward to. There was always hope; hope that I would see my niece or nephew, hope that Marshal Gilbert would drop the charges against me, and hope that my family could accept Tom as my husband and helpmeet. I could still hope.

But hope was never enough in Hartford. By speaking up for Mary Barnes, I had brought dishonor to my family and suspicion about me. The thought of my own trial and how much pain this would cause my family agonized me. They had suffered enough with my brazen and forthright comments during the sentencing. Perhaps I had found my voice, a new and different voice. Perhaps I spoke for many others, too afraid to speak. Maybe there were others who felt the injustice as strongly as I did. I thanked God for James Ensign standing up for Mary Barnes—and for me.

I prayed to God for answers but I received no answers. On house arrest, I had no one to talk with; no one who truly understood how alone I felt.

—

Sitting by my loft window, I gazed up at the night sky. The stars in the heavens trembled like cold, hard bits of ice. The moon cast blue-black shadows as it emerged from rushing clouds. Everything seemed to be moving by me as I remained quiet and still.

I decided to see if God would speak to me from my psalm book. I had vowed to refrain from using God's word as divination, but I needed guidance. I needed to know what I must do. I pulled the book out and held it in my palms. "Dear Lord," I prayed, "guide me and guard me. You know I am innocent of witchcraft. The only sin I have committed is speaking up for an innocent woman. I am guilty of trying to aid my friend Ann, who has turned against me. I know not what to think or do."

My hands started to shake. Tears streamed from my face. I cried for little Betty, now gone for months; for the Ayreses who escaped the noose; for Mary Sanford, who did not. I cried for Rebecca, Nathaniel, and poor Mary Barnes. Mostly, I cried for my own plight. My chest and shoulders heaved until I felt as if I had no breath left in me.

But I had to open my psalm book. Ending a prayer with thanks, I opened the book and began reading from Psalm 112, verses four to seven: "Unto the upright there ariseth light in the darkness: He is gracious, full of compassion and righteousness. A good man will guide his affairs with discretion. Surely, he shall not be moved forever; the righteous shall be in everlasting remembrance. He shall not be afraid of evil tidings; his heart is fixed, trusting in the Lord."

I closed the book and thanked God for this message.

The verses calmed me. A feeling of peace settled over me. My decision had been made. All I could do now was wait.

—

Still, I had much to do. Finding a dusty sack in the corner of the loft, I snuck down to the root cellar. I stuffed it with dried apples, a few potatoes, and some hunks of cheese. I folded a skirt, blouse, apron, underclothes, and an extra cap into the sack as well. The leather boots on my feet would have to do. The only other item I owned besides my clothing was my psalm book. The book was my guide, my compass and with me it would go.

—

The next day, almost a week after the hangings, and the day before I was set to depart, Hartford suffered a minor earthquake. Pewter dishes crashed down from the cupboard. The hearth broom and kettles toppled over. For several seconds the house rattled and shook. The tremors came up through the rocky ridge, my father told me, the same ridge the witches hung from. The quake was felt as far as Windsor.

I wondered if this was a sign of displeasure from God. *Is He angry about the hangings?*

—

The day after the earthquake, more cold air and wind blew in from the north. I waited by the window. Flocks of blackbirds hovered overhead and flew in the direction of Gallows Hill. They cawed and croaked—loud, frenzied noises. Had they discovered the bodies hanging from the Great Elm? I thought the unhallowed graves Marshal Gilbert spoke of must be right there on the ridge; the bodies would be discarded, thrown off the great hill, and left to rot. I tried to put the thought of blackbirds pecking at the flesh of the dead out of my mind. I did not want to know what happened to the bodies. I had to take care—for myself.

I prepared myself for whatever was to come. Trusting the Lord and mine own self was all I could do. My sack, filled with provisions and what few items I packed, stayed under my bed. Busying myself with chores, I dusted, swept, polished, and scrubbed the house with determination. Tonight was the night. I wanted to leave everything behind in perfect order.

Chapter 39

$\mathcal{I}$ retired to my room early. I needed rest to clear my mind. Before settling down, I found a small paper tucked into my psalm book. Placing the paper on my table, I pulled my inkwell and quill from a drawer. I sat for a time before the words came forth. I began to write,

Dear Father and Mother,
I regret the dishonor I have brought upon the family. I meant no harm; I only meant to speak the truth. By the time you read this, I shall be gone. My life is in peril, and my presence in Hartford may threaten you. There are still many things you know naught of. Maybe someday you will hear and understand the whole truth. I do not claim to know everything. I do know I am innocent. God goes with me and guides my every step. May God be with you.
Love,
Hester

—

The howling sounded not once, but three times. *Is it close to the hour of midnight?* Quietly, I retrieved the sack with my provisions for the journey. The house was silent. I smoothed out my bed and lay the note atop it. It looked as forlorn and alone as I felt.

But I had little time to feel sorry for myself. During my week on house arrest, I had already spent hours agonizing over my spectacle in court. Now was not the time for thinking about my regrets.

Carefully, I crept down the stairs, found my woolen coat, and prepared to take leave. I beheld my house, regarding everything that was familiar to me, with love: the great hearth still crackling, the pewter I lovingly cleaned each week, the table board where my family shared so many meals together, the spinning wheel sitting idle by the fire. As if by second nature, I stirred up some dying coals and placed kindle on them, for it was bad luck to let a fire go out.

My first care was that someone would hear me leave. Then my father's loud snores honked like a goose from the other room. I prayed to God silently that He would let me leave in peace.

I left out the back door and headed to the barn. I thought about using the outhouse before the journey. Then I heard footsteps and a torch illuminated the path.

"Hark, who goes there?" It was the nightwatchman on his rounds.

"It is me, Hester," I said meekly, trying to think of an excuse why I was out so late.

He came closer. The tall muscled figure, wrapped in a cloak, became outlined in the torch's light. It was James Ensign. Suddenly I remembered. I recognized the form, the shape from that night last winter.

"What brings thee out here this cold night, Hester?" he asked with concern in his voice. His eyes moved to the sack I held against my cloak.

"I am leaving, James. Pray tell naught a soul of my departure."

"But there be wolves prowling this evening. And worse, the marshal and his dog are in search of them. Take heed. 'Tis not safe to be abroad." I ignored his concern.

"James," I said quietly. "It was *you* wasn't it? All those months ago. At the merry meet."

His brow furrowed and he squinted down at me. "What mean you, Hester?"

"You were the horned man that night, James. I see it now. 'Tis true, isn't it?"

"Ay, so I was. And I knew you and that silly Ann cowered behind that rock."

"James, why?" I asked, but I knew I had naught but a few moments before I must make haste. He cast a glance up and down the road. Then he bent down close to my face.

"Because I believe in the Old Ways," he said. "The heathen ways that my own grandmother taught me. But there is but little time for talk. I'll do everything in my power to keep the marshal away—and off your trail."

"And I will keep your secret, our secret, close to my heart."

"Ay, and I will do the same for you. Fare-thee-well, Hester."

———

I remained but a few moments in the outhouse. It was cold, and I could naught afford a chill standing inside the smelly shed. Everything seemed quiet. I opened the outhouse door and slipped into the shadows. I walked toward our barn. Silently, I said goodbye to the animals I cared for every day.

Pulling my hood over my head, I crouched by the barn for a time. Then I began to walk through my father's flax fields and orchards. All lay barren and fallow. Dead stalks poked through the powdered snow left from the northeaster. They cracked under my boots. Finding myself near the Varlet orchard, I thought of Dutch Judy and how lucky she was to escape the hangman's noose. But she and her family had lost Caspar, whose remains now lay near the fort. I wondered if she found a new husband in New Netherlands? Maybe someday I would know.

Shrugging these thoughts off, I crossed the less traveled bridge directly leading to the Dutch Point. It made no sense to cross the plank-wood bridge tonight. I might be seen. Thick oaks and elms aided my passage. I hid behind them, pressing myself up against their trunks, trying to maintain evenness to my breath, and staying out of moonlight.

At last I espied the rafts left by Tom and his father near Granny Flagg's house. But I saw naught of Nat and Elsbeth. Perhaps those howls I heard were those of a real wolf? Either way it was too late to turn back. If the marshal discovered I was missing or worse, if he found me, he'd surely discover Elsbeth and Nat.

The merging of the Little River into the Great River churned with currents that twisted in great circles. The moon rays sprinkled silver light onto the expanse of the Great River.

I made my way to the steep bank, hid behind a willow tree, and waited.

Chapter 40

Fog rose up from the river casting a white blanket atop the water. Wet from the mist, I shivered waiting for my companions. *Where are they?* I heard a snap of twigs and a rustling sound coming from the woods. Through the fog, a pair of yellow eyes appeared and blinked. I heard a growling, a sniffing sound; it's mouth exposed sharp teeth. I covered my head, crouched low and remained as still as a rock behind the willow. The wolf approached me, sniffing close to my sack.

Peeking out from my cloak, I watched the creature pawing the sack in the moon lit shadows. Then I saw the tail wagging. "Titus," I whispered, "It's me Hester. Come." I crawled on all fours to the sack. "Here's a good dog. You know me." I reached into the sack and pulled out a dried apple and flung it with all my strength in the opposite direction of the landing. Off went Titus, the marshal's dog on a fetch. He barreled off in search of the treat. Surely, the marshal was close by. I reached for my psalm book. It was still there. Then I grabbed the mangled sack.

"Hester, here!" I heard loud whispers near the water.

Nat and Elsbeth crawled up from the fog.

"Oh, thank God. I heard the wolf howls. But now Marshal Gilbert is about hunting down the beast. His dog is sniffing about as well."

Elsbeth snickered and Nat commented on his talent as a mimic.

"Methinks he hunts in the wrong direction," he told me. "We have little time now. Let us make ready."

We all made haste down to the raft. "What will become of Sarah?" I asked Elsbeth.

"She's staying on with the Ensigns, being indentured to them now. She's sweet on James as well."

"I'm glad she's safe," I said, thinking of James standing up for me during the verdict. He was a fine young man, one of the best in Hartford. It mattered not to me whether his beliefs were of the Old Ways, or the Puritan way anymore.

While Nat prepared the raft, I stood in the shadows shivering near a stand of trees.

"Hester, how brave you were to speak up for Mary Barnes," Elsbeth said. "But why not speak for my mother and stepfather?"

"I know not why I did what I did that day," I said watching Nat struggle with the ropes from the raft. "I am truly sorry, Elsbeth. Truly I am."

Elsbeth came forth and hugged me tightly. "I think naught could have saved my mother and stepfather. Damn that Ann Cole to eternity! May we leave our grief behind us," she mumbled.

"God willing," I replied softly. My eyes filled with tears. But this was no time to become weepy. We must all remain strong.

We crouched low and watched the Great River, its currents swirling around the bend leading south.

By the time Nat was ready, the moon dipped in the southwest, its light still reflecting off the river. "Let's wait until the moon begins to set further. With less light and no sun up, we have a greater chance to cross unnoticed," he said.

And so we waited until the moon began to set. We had few provisions amongst the three of us. But we would manage with the sacks each had brought. Two paddles and a raft-pole lay nearby. I knew we could not use the makeshift sail for the raft. The furled sail was white. Nat removed it to the ground and removed the rudely carved mast as well. It might cause attention, he said, so now we must paddle.

Nat warned us of the currents that swirled round the confluence of the Little and Great Rivers. We could be swept south downriver; so we must paddle toward the Dutchman's Island and circle round the back of it. We would have less chance of being seen behind the island. "We must keep a balance of this raft," he warned.

Nat readied the pole for our push-off.

Then I heard a rustling noise. Something was moving atop the embankment; it sounded like a deer crashing through bushes and brambles.

But it was no deer. Titus now hovered on the knoll, looking down on us. He bared his teeth and snarled. His eyes flashed in a wild manner. Panting and growling, he began to scratch his way down the hill and lunged at the raft. His teeth found my cloak and he tore a piece off. Then his jowls clamped down on one of my boots.

"Halt! Who goes there?"

I heard the voice that left me colder than the night air. The uneven gait, so familiar, limped ever closer. Terror filled my heart. I heard the sound of a musket cocked.

The dog clung to my boot, trying to drag me off the raft. Nat began to jab at Titus with his raft-pole. Distracted, the dog let go of my boot, clamped down on the pole, and tried to wrench it away.

"Here," said Nat. "Both of you grab hold of this pole while I get something from up front." Nat sounded like he was panting louder than Titus. I swung my legs around and both Elsbeth and I held the pole with all our strength. *What is Nat doing now? Will the marshal use his musket—on us?*

Nat retrieved something from his bag at the front of the raft. He stood up. In each hand he held two large rocks. "These rocks were supposed to be used for ballast. To keep the raft balanced," he whispered.

"Nat, get down," cried Elsbeth.

The sound of musket fire whirred over our heads.

"Two chances. Here goes," said Nat.

Titus clung to the pole, trying to pull it from us.

Nat began to hurl the rocks in tandem at the snarling beast. The first missed; but the second rock hit its mark—right off the beast's head.

The dog whimpered, slunk back a few paces, and fell to the ground.

"We have but a minute before the marshal reloads his musket," Nat said. "Let us make haste—now!" He pushed the raft off and the three of us covered in our cloaks, crouched low again.

"Halt I say! I know who you are!" shouted Marshal Gilbert.

"Do not look back," Nat warned. "I don't think the marshal saw our faces. But we cannot be sure." Nat and Elsbeth began to paddle. I promised to relieve Elsbeth when she tired.

Jagged ice floes drifted past us, The three of us made gains as we paddled across the Great River; my cloak was torn but I thanked God for my leather boots. And Nat's rocks!

We followed the sandbank near the Dutchman's Island, making sure we did not get stranded. The trees along the island's banks helped conceal us further. As we rounded the island, I could see the shores of Podunk. At the same time, the alarm bell began to sound from the shores of Hartford. Three rings—one ring, over and over.

Did the marshal get a view of us? I remembered the marshal often carried his spyglass with him.

"What to do, what to do?" cried Elsbeth.

"We move forward. Do not turn around," ordered Nat again.

Smoke from the Podunk Indian tribe signaled we were close. I went to grab for my psalm book from my pocket. It was still there. I pulled it forth for a brief moment—perhaps for comfort—perhaps for reassurance. I raised the book to the moonlight.

And then I lost balance but a moment and almost overturned the raft. Leaning one way to straighten the raft, a brisk, cold wave came aboard and washed over us. And in that moment, I realized my psalm book had slipped from out my grasp. It had fallen into the currents of the Great River. Trembling, I reached my hand to grab for it. But my treasured book quickly began to float away from me.

"It's gone!" I cried. "My psalm book is gone."

Elsbeth spoke to me in a hushed tone. "Your psalm book is gone, Hester. Just like my parents are…gone." She placed her hand briefly on my shoulder. "Sometimes we have to let go of someone we love—or something we love." She paused. "But we carry the memory with us—in our hearts. Nothing can ever take that away. Sometimes that's all we have left."

Nat reminded us again not to turn around. We had more to worry about than my psalm book.

I disobeyed Nat's order. I did turn around.

The moon, almost gone, dipped low over Meetinghouse Square. I turned back to the east, the direction we were paddling. Then I noticed the tendrils of light beginning to stretch up from the horizon. Deep violets with orange and red colors surrounded the small bits of light. They reached out and each moment grew brighter and golden. The sun was starting to rise!

On the banks of Podunk, I saw another familiar shape that I recognized: the curls, the hat. It was Tom waiting for us!

Torches blinked from the receding shores of Hartford and the alarm bell still rang.

I turned back to look at Hartford. And then I turned forward to face my future.

Author's Note

$\mathcal{D}$*ays to the Gallows* is based on the true story of the Hartford Witch Panic of 1662. The majority of the characters in this novel are derived from the Colonial Records of Hartford and Connecticut, but in many instances, have been fictionalized. The exceptions to this are Tom, the peddler's son, his father, and Nat Osgood; all are creations of my imagination. I changed one of Rebecca Greensmith's daughters' names from Hannah to Elsbeth due to Hester's sister being named Hannah. As far as the outline of the story, I tried to keep to the facts.

During this early time in our country's history, superstitions about people who were different aroused the specter of witchcraft, time and again. Many of the witchcraft beliefs in New England were carried over from England. Elizabethan times—the strife between Catholics and Protestants—and the Puritan rebellion against the Stuart dynasty that began in 1603 all clearly influenced the early settlers in North America. They rebelled in their own manner against both the Catholic and Pagan beliefs they tried so desperately to leave behind.

Yet many of the colonists carried those beliefs with them upon coming to North America. You can witness this by their manner of speech, their beliefs in witchcraft and many of their superstitions from the Old Country. Note that throughout the story, I often used the archaic language the colonist spoke—similar to the Elizabethan style.

It's interesting to note that the Hartford Witch Panic took place soon after the Restoration of King Charles II in England. Charles II had papist leanings and was angry at the Puritans who beheaded his father Charles I in 1649, sending his son into a lengthy exile. But in 1662, times were a-changing; Charles II was restored to the throne and many of the colonists who had Catholic leanings were well aware of the changing and conflicting loyalties in England.

Oftentimes, witchcraft accusations were based on arguments amongst neighbors, boundary or land disputes, petty jealousies, or any strange and inexplicable occurrences. Betty Kelly's untimely death is an example of this.

Hester Hosmer and Ann Cole were indeed neighbors and lived across from one another at the time of the Witch Panic. They lived across from the South Green. Both were "maids", unmarried young women who most certainly desired to meet their future husbands.

According to the Colonial Records, Mary Sanford was indicted on June 6, 1662 and hanged on June 13th, 1662; a short time after, her husband Andrew removed to Milford. There is mystery shrouded in Mary's death because there is scant mention of her case.

Geoffe, the regicide in his diary dated January 20, 1662/63(the Puritans used the Julian Calendar that began in March; we use the Gregorian calendar that begins in January) wrote, "Three were condemned in Hartford. After one of the witches was hanged, the maid was well." It's clear from the Connecticut records that these three hanged were Rebecca Greensmith, her husband Nathaniel, and Mary Barnes of Farmington. The maid was Ann Cole.

In March 1662, eight-year-old Betty Kelly began to complain of stomach pains after a visit from Goodwife Ayres. Soon the young impressionable girl began accusing Goody Ayres of "pinching her" and "wanting to harm her." She demanded that her father take an ax and "chop off Goody Ayres's head." Soon after, Betty expired.

Betty Kelly's autopsy is authentic and considered the first in the country. The bruises on her arm after her death further increased the suspicions of the authorities and townspeople. We know now that her bruising was a sign of rigor mortis.

Most likely, since the Ayres were first accused and taken to jail after Betty's death, they were the couple that endured the water test. The story of what transpired in the water test is true and the Ayres did escape Hartford and the hangman's noose. (The water test was yet another example of an old superstition from England used on "witches" for many centuries.)

Soon after the death of Betty, Ann Cole began having fits and raves. Her first fit was at the Fast for Betty. She accused the likes of Judith Varlet, the Dutch neighbor, the Ayres, Goody Seager, Mary Sanford and the Greensmiths. According to the records, she spoke in Dutch tones, "claimed these people were ruining her chances of marriage and that they laughed when "she ran to her rock."

The Varlet family was an anomaly in Hartford. Banned from New Netherlands by Governor Peter Stuyvesant, they were a colorful and contentious lot. Thirty years before the Varlet's arrived in Hartford, many Dutch families resided there. They had established the Fort of Good Hope at the Dutch Point. Although Caspar, Judy's father was indeed in Hartford during the Panic, his name ceases to exist from the records shortly after Judy's arrest. The only mention of Caspar afterward is an inventory of his estate in Hartford.

After Judith's arrest, her brother, Captain Nicholas Varlet arrived with a letter from his brother-in-law, Governor Stuyvesant demanding Judith's release. Captain Varlet's stepson, Nicholas Bayard was clerk to his uncle.

Although there is no evidence Nicholas Bayard was present in Hartford, the irony is that three years later, he married Judith Varlet and became Mayor of New York for a short time after the English take over of New Netherland in 1664. From all accounts, they had a loving marriage and one son Samuel. Judith did get her wish of marriage and did escape Hartford and the noose!

Although the character of Tom Flagg, the peddler's son is fictitious, peddlers began making their way from Springfield to Hartford and up along the Bay Path to Boston around 1650. Many of the early peddlers became well-known and wealthy merchants.

Marshal Gilbert appeared to rule Hartford with an iron fist. He was Constable of Hartford during the Witch Panic. Captain John Mason was Acting Governor during this time period while Governor Winthrop was overseas. The Reverends in the story are all true figures. Although in most accounts, Mason was a Major by this point; for the sake of the story he is called Captain.

The sad plight of Mary Barnes is true. Her story is shrouded in mystery. Mary was never accused as a witch by Ann Cole. The records on Mary Barnes are scant; some claim they were purged and discarded. Her husband Thomas did marry the nanny, Mary Andrus within a few months after the hanging of his wife. Ironically, he donated land in Farmington for a burying ground.

Elizabeth Seager, although acquitted the first time on charges of witchcraft, was accused and jailed twice more. She languished in jail and was finally freed when Governor Winthrop returned home.

Eventually, she and her husband Richard removed near the border of Rhode Island where they pledged loyalty to King Charles II.

Jeremy Adams' Tavern was the center for food, gossip for townspeople, and a place to stay for visitors. If you visit Hartford, the location of the old Adams' Tavern is the exact spot where The Traveler's Insurance Company Tower now stands. Another irony!

Meetinghouse Square, a center of activity in the novel, was located near the present day Old State House, overlooking the Landing. There, the stocks, pillory, whipping post and, jail were located. Over the years, The Little River became the Hog River then the Park River. Unfortunately, due to flooding and hurricanes, the river was buried underground. You can still find traces of the "little river" that runs through Bushnell Park and in other areas around Hartford.

The South Green remains in Hartford and is now called Barnard Park. Ann and Hester's old street is now called Wyllys St., named after the Magistrate Samuel Wyllys. Samuel Wyllys lived right up the hill from Ann Cole in a mansion. (In the novel, he is somewhat older than the records indicate.) Later on, one of the great oaks on his property would become famous as "The Charter Oak." This was the oak that Joseph Wadsworth hid the charter in 1687. In 1856, the Charter Oak was struck by lightning. Several scions from the original oak were grown around Hartford and one can still find remnants around downtown Hartford.

Captain Mason did have experiences with "witches" in Saybrook. He was a formidable presence and knew Marshal Gilbert and Thomas Barnes from the Pequot War. You can find a small statue of him atop the Connecticut State Capitol Dome.

Ann Cole finally did get married to a man named Andrew Benton. Ironically, they bought and moved into the Greensmith house overlooking the South Green. Marshal Gilbert was involved in the sale of the house to Ann. Did he claim it once the Greensmiths were hanged? I wonder how Ann, the accuser, could move into her victims' home to start life anew?

In his book *The Colonial History of Hartford*, William DeLoss Love mentions that the original gallows was located on the Road to Albany (now Albany Ave) most likely on the corner of Albany and Vine St. However, John Taylor in *The Witchcraft Delusion in Colonial Connecticut* states, "In January 1662, they were hung on 'Gallows Hill', on a bluff a little north of where Trinity College now stands—'a logical location', one most learned in the traditions and history of Hartford calls it—as it afforded an excellent view of the execution to a large crowd on the Meadows to the west, a hanging being a spectacle and entertainment."

Love also writes about the vibrant daily life on the river around the Landing, including travel by raft and a ferry that transported cattle and other livestock across the river to "Podunk," now aptly called East Hartford.

Although there is no evidence any of these people worshipped Robin Goodfellow, it's clear they knew about him. The fact that Betty claimed to be pinched, that she was a bad girl is indicative that stories were told to the impressionable child. In fact, the records indicate Goody Ayres told Betty about the Dark Man whom she awaited at the church in London and that he appeared with hooves! Also, the mention of the sack posset by Rebecca and the description of the shape-shifting nature of the Devil and how he appeared to her, clearly indicated knowledge of some of the old folkways and folktales.

Many of the common folk in New England were well aware of the folk ballads and Pagan beliefs from the Old Country. An example of this is the short story "The Maypole of Merry Mount," included in Nathaniel Hawthorne's *Twice Told Tales* written in the 1800s. Like most of his stories and novels, the setting is the 1600s. Most likely, many people kept these traditions alive through song and ritual and had to practice these beliefs in secrecy.

"The Mad, Merry Pranks of Robin Goodfellow" is attributed to Ben Johnson in 1628. However, the legend of Robin Goodfellow is much older than this date. The name of Robin is featured in many of the old legends, including Robin of the Hood, Robin Hood and of course, Shakespeare. There are also many books and tales available about the different legends of Robin Goodfellow and his pranks.

In the 1800s, Rudyard Kipling used the character of Robin in "*Puck of Pook's Hill*." Clearly, many authors incorporated the figure of Robin in their works. In 1841, John Payne Collier compiled this ballad along with others printed in "The Roxburghe Ballads." I have included a copy of "The Mad Merry Pranks of Robin Goodfellow" at the end of this book in its entirety. Astute readers may notice I omitted a line of the ballad for the story's sake (due to it's crude nature), but you can find it in the ballad.

The legend of the stag that appeared during the hanging is a true legend, mentioned in Odell Shepard's book, *Connecticut, Past and Present*.

Although more people would be accused of witchcraft in Connecticut, once Governor Winthrop, Jr. returned home, no more "witches" would ever hang in the Connecticut Colony again.

Katherine Spada Basto

Selected Bibliography

I have done extensive reading and research on the subject matter pertaining to the Hartford Witch Panic. Below are some selected sources, including books that proved helpful and supported my imagination as to what happened that fateful year in Hartford. Many of the original papers are available at the Connecticut State Library Archives and the Connecticut Historical Society. I am particularly indebted to scholars R.G. Tomlinson, John Taylor, and John Demos whose works are listed below. I referred back to them again and again. Also, thanks to David Hall for his outstanding book listed below. I remember purchasing the book a few years ago, never knowing about the story of Ann Cole and the witch panic in my own hometown! It was and is an informative and insightful read that helped me want to pursue this story

Original Papers
Records of the Particular Court, 1633-1663

New York Genealogical and Biographical Record, Volumes 9-10: New York State. 1878

Wyllys Papers, Brown Library. Providence R.I. Available on microfilm.

Selected Sources

Black, Robert C. III. *The Younger John Winthrop*, New York: Columbia University Press. 1966

Booth, Sally Smith. *Hung, Strung, and Potted*, New York: Potter, Inc. 1939

Burr, George Lincoln. *Narratives of the Witchcraft Cases 1648-1706*, New York: Scribner and Son. 1914

Demos, John Putnam. *Entertaining Satan*, London: Oxford University Press. 1982

Dolan, J.R. *The Yankee Peddlers of Early America*, New York: Bramhall House. 1964

Drake, Frederick C. *Witchcraft in the American Colonies, 1647-62.* American Quarterly, Vol. XX. Philadelphia. Winter 1968.

Earle, Alice Morse. *Home Life in Colonial Days*, New York: Grosser and Dunlap, 1898

Earle, Alice Morse. *Sabbath in Puritan New England*, Williamstown, Mass: Corner House. 1969(reprint of original 1891 edition)

Field, Edward. *The Colonial Tavern*, Providence Rhode Island: Preston and Rounds. 1897

Fisher, Sydney, George. *Men, Women and Manners in Colonial Times.*(Originally published 1897) New Jersey: Scholar's Bookshelf, 2006

Hall, David D. *Witch Hunting in Seventeenth Century New England*, Boston: Northeastern University Press, 1991

Hoadley, Dr. Charles J. *A Case of Witchcraft in Hartford.* Connecticut Magazine, Nov. 1899

Love, William DeLoss. *The Colonial History of Hartford*, Hartford: The Case, Lockwood and Brainard Co. 1914 (the most comprehensive book available on the subject)

Mather, Increase. *Essay for Illustrious Providence.* London: Reeves and Turner. 1890(originally published by Green and Browning in 1684. This contains Reverend Whiting's letter to Increase Mather concerning Ann Cole.)

Murray, Margaret A. *The Witch Cult in Western Europe*, London: Oxford University Press, 1921

Scaeva.(Isaac W. Stuart) *Hartford in the Olden Time, The First Thirty Years*, Hartford: F.A. Brown. 1853 (An invaluable book that is hard to come by and chronicles the early years of Hartford's settlement including information about the Dutch and the Dutch Fort of Good Hope)

Schuyler, Van Rensselaer, Mariana. *History of the City of New York in the Seventeenth Century. Vol.1*, New York: Macmillan. 1909

Shepard, Odell. *Connecticut, Past and Present,* New York: Alfred Knoph, Inc. 1939

Taylor, John M. *The Witchcraft Delusion in Colonial Connecticut 1647-1697,* New York: Grafton Press, 1908

Tomlinson, R.G. *Witchcraft Trials of Connecticut,* Hartford: Bond Press, Inc. 1978

Acknowledgements

I would like to thank Bonnie from the Connecticut State Library who years ago helped me find Dutch Maps, information on the Dutch Fort and helped me locate the witch trial transcripts. A special thanks to Ruth Shapleigh Brown from the Connecticut State Library and the Connecticut Gravestone Network for leading me to invaluable information as well. Thanks to the librarians who assisted me at the Connecticut Historical Society.

Many thanks to my readers who helped make this manuscript better, including my husband Ronald, and my dear friend, Alvis. Thanks to Trish Truitt and Carissa Darcy Spada for enthusiastic support.

Special thanks to Corvid Design; Duncan Eagleson and Moira Ashleigh who created a beautiful book cover and map as well as providing very helpful advice. Thanks also to editor Carol Gaskin of Editorial Alchemy whose advice, suggestions, and support made a positive difference in the revisions of this manuscript.

Thanks to Mark Spencer of WDU for encouragement to press onward with the manuscript and providing helpful suggestions. Thanks to author Carolyn McCullough and the class from Gotham Writer's Workshop. I appreciate all the useful feedback from the group.

The Mad, Merry Pranks of Robin Goodfellow

Printed in the Roxburghe Ballads, Ben Johnson, 1628

From Oberon in fairyland,/the king of ghosts and shadows there,
Mad Robin, I, at his command,/I am sent to view the night sports here.
What revel rout/Is kept about.
In every corner where I go
I'll o'ver see/And merry be,
And make good sport with ho, ho, ho!

More swift than lightening can I fly/and round this airy heaven soon,
And, in a minute's space, espy/each thing that's done beneath the moon,
There's not a hag/Nor ghost shall wag,

Nor cry "goblin!" where I go,
But Robin, I/Their feats will spy,
And fear them home with ho, ho, ho!

If any wanderers I meet/that from their night-sports do trudge home,
With counterfeiting voice I greet/and cause them on with me to roam,
Through woods, through lakes/Through bogs, through brakes,
O'er bush and brier with them I go,
I call upon/Them to come on,
And went me, laughing ho, ho, ho!

Sometimes I meet them like a man/sometimes an ox, sometimes a house;
And to a horse I turn me can/to trip and trot about them round,
But if to ride/My back they stride,
More swift than wind away I go,
O're hedge and lands/Through pools and ponds,
I whirry, laughing, ho, ho, ho!

When lads and lasses merry be/With possets(mulled drink) and with banquetsfine,
Unseen of all the company/I eat their cakes and sip their wine;
And to make sport/I fart and snort,
And out the candles I do blow;
The maids I kiss/They shriek, "Who's this?"
I answer nought, but ho, ho, ho!

Yet now and then, the maids to please,/I card at midnight up their wool;

And while they sleep, snort, fart and fease (poop) /with wheel to
threads their flax I pull;
I grind at mill/Their malt up still,
I dress their hemp, I spin their tow;
If any wake/And would me take,
I wend me, laughing, ho, ho, ho!

When house or hearth doth dirty lie/I pinch the maids there black
and blue;
And from the bed, the bed-clothes I/pull off and lay them nak'd
to view;
Twixt sleep and wake/I do them take,
And on the key-cold floor them throw; If out they cry/Then forth
fly I,
And loudly laugh I, ho, ho, ho!

When any need to borrow ought/we lend them what they do
require;
And for the use demand we nought/our own is all we do desire;
If to repay/They do delay,
Abroad amongst them then I go,
And night by night/I them affright,
With pinching, dreams, and ho, ho, ho!

When lazy queens have nought to do/but study how to cogge
(cheat) and lie
To make debate, and mischief too/twixt one another secret-ly;
I mark their gloss(exaggerations)/And do disclose
To them that they had wronged so;
When I have done,/I get me gone,
And leave them scolding, ho, ho, ho!

When men do traps and engines set/in loop-holes, where the ver-
min creep,
That from their folds and houses steal/their ducks and geese, their
lambs and sheep:
I spy the 'gin/And enter in,
And seems a vermin taken so,
But when they there/Approach me near,
I leap out, laughing, ho, ho, ho!

By wells and gils(rivulets) in meadows green,/we nightly dance our
hedegies(rustic dance),
And to our fairy King and Queen/we chant our moon-light
harmonies.
When larks 'gain sing/Away we fling;
And babes new born steal as we go;
An elf in bed /We leave instead,
And wend us, laughing, ho, ho, ho!

From hag-bred Merlin's time have I/thus nightly revel'd to and fro;
And, for my pranks, men call by/the name of Robin Good-fellow:
Fiends, ghost and sprites/That haunt the night,
The hags and goblins do me know,
And beldames old/My feats have told,
So Vale, Vale, ho, ho, ho!

CPSIA information can be obtained
at www.ICGtesting.com
Printed in the USA
LVOW10s0929070517
533590LV00002B/479/P

9 781536 978049